The House in the Light

Beverley Farmer was born in Melbourne in 1941. A graduate of Melbourne University, she married a Greek migrant in 1965 and for some years lived in the village with his family. During this time she wrote her first book, *Alone* (1980). The short story collections *Milk* (1983) and *Home Time* (1985) draw upon her experience of Greece. Her more recent works are *A Body of Water* (1990), part fiction, part writer's notebook, and the novel *The Seal Woman* (1992).

Also by Beverley Farmer

Alone
Milk
Home Time
Place of Birth
A Body of Water
The Seal Woman

The House in the Light

Beverley Farmer

University of Queensland Press

First published 1995 by University of Queensland Press
Box 42, St Lucia, Queensland 4067 Australia
Reprinted 1995

© Beverley Farmer 1995

This book is copyright. Apart from any fair dealing
for the purposes of private study, research, criticism
or review, as permitted under the Copyright Act, no
part may be reproduced by any process without written
permission. Enquiries should be made to the publisher.

Typeset by University of Queensland Press
Printed in Australia by McPherson's Printing Group

Distributed in the USA and Canada by
International Specialized Book Services, Inc.,
5804 N.E. Hassalo Street, Portland, Oregon 97213–3640

Cataloguing in Publication Data
National Library of Australia

Farmer, Beverley, 1941– .
    The house in the light.

    I. Title. (Series: UQP fiction).

A823.3

ISBN 0 7022 2719 6

These are the two olive trees, and the two candlesticks standing before the God of the earth.

The Revelation of St John the Divine

"The mysteries remain,
I keep the same
cycle of seed time
and of sun and rain;
Demeter in the grass
I multiply,
renew and bless
Iacchus in the vine;
I hold the law,
I keep the mysteries true,
the first of these
to name the living, dead;
I am red wine and bread.

*I keep the law,
I hold the mysteries true,
I am the vine,
the branches, you
and you."*

H. D., "The Mysteries, VI"

The author is grateful for the assistance of a one year Writer's Fellowship from the Literature Board of the Australia Council.

Thanks also to UQP and the Women's College within the University of Queensland for a residency at the Olga Masters Place to write during the final stages of this book.

Passages from this book have appeared in slightly different form in the magazines *World Literature Today* (USA), *Kunapipi* and *Ulitarra*.

"The Mysteries, VI" from H.D., *Selected Poems* (copyright © 1982 the Estate of Hilda Doolittle) is reprinted by permission of New Directions Pub. Corp. The extract on pp. 130–32 from Lati Rinbochay and Jeffrey Hopkins, *Death, Intermediate State and Rebirth in Tibetan Buddhism* (Snow Lion Publications, Ithaca, 1980) is reprinted by permission.

CONTENTS

Palm Sunday
1

Monday
27

Tuesday
55

Wednesday
83

Thursday
113

Great Friday
143

Saturday
168

Easter Sunday
200

Easter Monday
226

PALM SUNDAY

The grey green turbulence of leaves is the first new thing Bell will see when the bus goes lumbering over the bridge, the stony river. Even before the roofs crammed with television aerials and glass frames for solar heating, the enamelled cars crammed in under the vine-arbours, she will take in a new thick looseness and flicker of olive leaves in front yards all over the village, slender and flimsy, sparse in the wind, like gum leaves. This, when everyone laughed when she first came here. *Kalé, nýfi*, the old man said who is dead now, who died last year: you come this far inland and you expect to find olive trees? How would they live through a winter here in the north? And once she had a winter here she understood why: the ringing frost, and the village snowbound; the stream frozen solid, and the trees, iron boughs hung with glass.

Two hours and nothing to see out the window in the smoky damp but a slick of wet, a white blur of plums and cherries in flower. Now and then the bus sways through a village of shops with blank windows framed in blue, houses, the hump of a dim church. Greek churches have domes, for the most part, never spires, blue domes of heaven, in the islands, or of green slate; but here most of them are brick, like ovens, like bells, and have cupolas with a braiding of brick around their owl eyes. Another town, another village, a graveyard of blue cots and cypresses, coils of black flame. Valley after valley full of mist and sodden land and houses not like island houses, white though they are, foursquare and squat under red roofs. Not here the flow of land and sea, dome and arm of wall, niches, arches, of whitewash and grey stone in the sun. It is *ánoixi*, spring, meaning opening: of buds, of wombs, and this is all around; and of the sky, the weather, but of that there is little sign. The further north she goes, the more it looks as if the snow has barely melted; the land still has that tamped, discoloured and draggled look, like a mended leg when the plaster is taken off.

People are stealing curious looks but Bell keeps her eyes on the juddering pane, aware for the first time in weeks of how travel-stained she is and how outlandish in her tight black pants and jumper. As well as the suitcase on the floor she has her two cotton bags, one a paisley print and the other with NUCLEAR POWER NO THANKS on it, and a red sun ringed with a flare of yellow: her cameras and a spare lens are in that bag, and her dozens of rolls of exposed film. Her jacket, also cotton, is padded and printed in navy blue on aquamarine, a mass of swirls, speckles, strands and vortices. Around her neck she has a silver snake over a moon disc, a present from the friend who made it, and her mother's opal, each on a silver chain. "*Xéni*," she hears a woman insist at her back. Foreigner, that can be, or simply stranger. "*Médium eínai aftí*," someone else says in an awed voice. She is a fortune-teller: and Bell hides a smile. Better that than a tourist any day; not that a tourist is likely around here. The plain is a backwater, farmland, a maze of villages off the highway to Yugoslavia and not near any of the ancient sites of Pella, Vergina, Edessa. The village itself is too small to be on maps unless, perhaps, army ones, since the plain is an age-old battle-ground and the border less than an hour away.

Cold threads of smoke are drifting from the driver's seat. "Go ahead, friend, and stink us out," a passenger calls, but with humorous resignation, and the driver salutes with his butt and turns the music up. "She will have come up here for Easter," the first woman is announcing to her friend: "she must have people here." In the Greek, she must have world here. Bell smiles, this is so true, whatever some may say; because now the other woman is emphatic. "No, no, how could she have, since no foreigners live here?" And the other: "How do you know, *kalé*, that no foreigners live here?"

Not Bell, anyway. This will only be her second Easter in the world of the village, the first alone. *Páscha*. The other one was over twenty years ago and Grigori was with her, on the very same blue bus, quite likely, with the same driver on the same afternoon run. The windscreen is still curtained and tasselled like a stage, with postcards down both sides and a faded ikon of the Panagia and Child at the top. A blue enamel eye swings on a chain over the driver's head. The music is the same as ever. The only new thing is a NO SMOKING sign next to the ikon. It was spring that time as well, not a grey spring like this, it was windy, bright with poppies, green and red, a bridal day, and rightly so, although they had been married for years, because this was a homecoming, and long awaited. The whole village greeted her as *nýfi*, meaning bride and daughter-in-law, niece-in-law, sister-in-law, cousin-in-law. *I Afstralésa i nýfi. Nýfi* is the archaïc *nymph*, domesticated. A good all-purpose title and what a shame she no longer qualifies. As a *nýfi*, that is. Or a nymph.

She may not live here, but once across the bridge — the new grand bridge over the Vardari, not the old single-lane one with a sentry at each end — she is in a known landscape, the difference not so much seen as felt. This river is her border. The shanty suburbs, the industrial wastelands of Thessaloniki, are alien. Over the Vardari — still known by that name in the village, though officially it is the Axios again, as in the *Iliad* — she is at home. The Vardar, the Vardari. And they call the ice wind that blasts down over those broad, slow, brown waters, through the crags and ravines of Yugoslavia, by the river's name: the *voreás*, the north wind, a clean, sheer wind in any season, is always the *vardári*.

The bus is lurching around to pull up at the *kafeneíon* and she springs up, caught out, though, because this is the second last village, not hers. She ought to know with her eyes shut by now, what with all the bus rides up and down this road. When was the last time? Eight years ago when she also came alone, a divorced woman, to face Grigori's family; and if she was apprehensive then and unsure of her welcome, she is even more so today. It could turn out to be a mistake, at best gratuitous, superfluous, as she herself is now, here, in the family. A visit of condolence is all very well, now that the old man is dead: a week-long stay is another matter. What is there to do here for a whole week? Holy Week. No going back now, of course, and this was her idea. Seven whole days have to be got through somehow, and two half-days. Well, seven days, so what? Bell tells herself, when you were going to live here for ever once upon a time.

They are trundling over a bridge and she knows where she is now, turning suddenly stiff, barely able to breathe. Think, that last time, when was it? It was autumn, it was All Souls' Day. And meanwhile so many fine new houses with balconies have sprung up. And there are olive trees here! This is what she can't get over. Is it the greenhouse effect, global warming? Not that it feels any less cold; no, colder, if anything. For all that it's April and the clocks went forward an hour today for summer time, she has been shivering all the way. The cold she thought she had thrown off is clogging every socket in her head. And now with a snort the bus is pulling up to let her and her suitcase and her bags off at the church. The road is shining in her eyes. Nothing sounds but her footsteps, as if this is a dream of the walk to the house on the corner.

Under the knots of the grapevine a woman in black is stooped scratching at the porch with a twig broom. She peers up as Bell stops. Then, throwing the broom down, she runs to the gate and calls, "*Amán!* Isn't that Bella?"

"Mamma," Bell gasps.

"You are here! I thought it was tomorrow!"

"Did I come too early?"

"No, no, you did very well to come!"

And she is caught up, the black woollen arms straining around her and white hair in her mouth.

"Welcome. *E*, Bella! And how long has it been?"

"Eight years."

"*Má*, eight years. Come in quickly to the warmth."

Bell smiles, swallowing, unable to speak.

"What are you standing there for?"

Eight years, and look at her now in her mourning. You will

hardly know Mamma, Grigori has said more than once. She says this a curse on her, or the Evil Eye, or the wrath of God. The boy, you see, and then the old man. It's the boy, Bell is sure, more than the old man, who was over eighty, after all. But two years ago there was this fine strong beautiful boy, a grandson and only sixteen, struck dead by lightning in the sea. No sooner had she put on black for him than the old man took to his bed. Cancer, a swollen heart, a last-ditch operation. Bella, is that you? came Mamma's voice on the phone. The grandfather gave up the ghost, you tell our Yanni. And Grigori: He die, Bella, my father die; the two voices wavering on — it was the payphone at the hospital — until they were cut off suddenly. *Xepsýchise* was the word she used: he gave up the soul. Now Bell can see with her own eyes what all the photos of the last two summers were telling her, if she could have believed it: Mamma, swathed in her black wool, has shrunk away like a candlestick. In the photos she was smiling as she is now, in the act of passing plates around a table of grandchildren out under the grapevine, or picking apricots off the branch with both hands, as Bell has often seen her do, proudly, with quick little tugs, as if at a teat: smiling, and wasted, withered, her eyes in red slits against the sun, and wet, as they are now as well. The red lids pout. They are the eyes of any of the old beggar women in Athens who limp from table to table in the sun, one bony claw thrust out, and trail horror and shame in their wake.

The metal and glass doors grate on the tiles of the *sála* and Bell is ushered in. There are new shelves on the back wall, and photos in frames and others stuck on to the whitewash: photos that she took and others of her at her wedding, of her in the village with all the family, Grigori still at her side and Yanni naked in her arms, who is eighteen now and at university; and any number sent from Australia. Stepping closer, she sees two that she has not seen for — how long? Twenty years or more. One is the deckled black and white one — thirty years! — of her wading in a creek patchy with rocks and sun, the first photo Grigori sent over, the first they knew of Anna Bella. In the other she and

Grigori are in the snow, huddled in the red and black striped rug his mother wove for him to take to Australia. It hides how gaunt he is, how weak. It was soon after this that he collapsed with double pneumonia and pleurisy, a brush with death, the first in Bell's life. This is a stab she was not braced for. After all these years, what are they doing on the wall? Looking aside, she comes face to face with new photos, Grigori at the table under the grapevine in the sun with his new young wife — *I love the sun, the summer* — and the two of them at the river with Mamma. Again Bell turns aside. How much more painful, though, if the old photos were not here. Pain, either way. New and old, they spread from the back for some way along the side walls, a triptych reaching to the kitchen door on the left, and the storeroom on the right, both shut. All the rooms open out of the *sála*. And her, their, old bedroom door at the front is shut.

The other front room is wide open and Mamma is calling her in. A woman warming her hands by the *sómba* welcomes her by name and kisses her. A fat little widow — who is it? "You have well received her, Sofia," she is saying now, as the custom is, and Bell can only hide her bafflement in smiles, glancing about. This is the room — the black *sómba* rattling full of flames, a saucepan steaming on the lid — where Grigori's mother and father have always slept. She knows the handwoven floor rugs spread for the winter, folded away in summer; the lumpy old double bed; the television in the corner, the same black and white one now that all the village has colour; the folding window between shutters and water-tarnished lace.

With the coffee Mamma offers not chocolates but a bowl of olives. Hiding her surprise, Bell puts one in her mouth. But it is chocolate after all. "I thought they were olives!" she says.

"They are left over from the *mnimósyno* we had three weeks ago." Mamma has a shrewd smile of reproach. "For the first six months of the forgiven one."

"I see." She swallows and looks down. Of course, there are the memorial services, the anniversaries to come. Coffee will have been offered here in the *sála*, and liqueur and pastries, and portions of the boiled wheat *kóllyva* garnished with silver cashews and these chocolate olives, brought back from church after the blessing. The evening before, the *papás*, naming the dead man in a loud prayer for his soul, will have flung a spoonful of the *kóllyva* on the grave and then a splash of red wine. This eat, this drink. The old customs, hallowed, pagan, time out of mind: she has always loved them, for all that her knowledge was patchy at best, and has gone hazy with time. The family are no longer speaking of the dead by name, perhaps in case the ghost comes when called. The old man is *o synhoriménos* now, he who is forgiven, and *o makarítis*, he who is blessed. She rolls the thick chocolate with her tongue, warm in its melting. Six months already?

A silence. The visitor breaks it, leaning forward, her breath as sweet as grass in Bell's face. "What a beautiful eye that is," she says. "Is it new?"

"This? It was my mother's." Bell twists it to show up the sparks of fire. "It's a black opal."

Instead the old woman grabs her wrists. "*Amán!* What happened? You have blood!"

"No, it's only antiseptic."

She spreads her palms with their blazes of mercurochrome and the two old women peer, the visitor stroking the little lips of the cuts with her rough finger tip until Bell laughs and curls her hands up.

"How did you do that?"

"Climbing rocks."

"You might have fallen and broken something!" cries the visitor.

"My camera! I know, don't worry."

"*Ade*, silly! What rocks, where?"

"On Paros, was it? I forget."

"*Má!* You forget."

"You must have known, though, Bella, at the time." Mamma has the same sour smile. "About the memorial service."

"No. I thought — when were the six months up?"

This is a feint, Bell having forgotten, if she ever knew, that a service would be held for the dead after six months.

"It had to be brought forward because of Easter."

Yes, today is Palm Sunday, Bell remembers, or it is here, and Easter Sunday in the outside world.

"I see. I wish I had known to come."

"Yes, well, you should have known. And in any case, since you were here already" — she shrugs — "on Paros or wherever, on your journey — "

"Time was so short." She feels her face reddening. "The money would only go so far and I had a lot of ground to cover."

"I don't know what business you had going to the islands in the first place. We have nobody of our own there."

"As I told you."

Bell opens her hands.

"To take photographs?"

"That *is* my business in the world and it takes work. It takes time. There's only so much I can get done in six weeks."

"All the same" — she shrugs — "you only had to ring to know."

No answer to that. She was in Greece. She has been for over a month, having arrived in Athens a week before the Gulf War ended — a fact she only gleaned when it was old news, from a tourist on a ferry. The Aegean was empty, and so were the grey green and blue islands over which she made her way to the ruins and deserted churches and holy stones, the relics of the goddess. There in the south it was spring, full sun and a flat sea on all but two days when a sirocco went scudding and scouring over the shallow bay, ruffling it like cat fur, moving out to sea around the standing rocks and filling the olive groves with a hot, damp hiss, and grey, and silver. The sirocco of summer is a fire out of the desert, like the north wind where Bell lives, and on the islands they call it the "dragon's breath". But this was early spring and, although it was still a blast of wind so heavy that it closed the airports and snapped the cables of ferries in the harbours to leave the islands stranded, it was a welcome rush of heat, a hearth fire, no more, and at night beyond the shutters the hoarse long breathing in her sleep became a spirit lamp, a torch on a cave wall.

On Paros. On an island, we always say, not in, or at, where the Greek makes no distinction: on, the same as we do of a ship.

She had photos to take and nowhere near enough time; and how was she to know there was a memorial service on up here, and early, what's more, before the date you might have expected, when she was in another world? *Ade* — a world without phones? All right, so she only had to ring to know. If she could have made herself heard, with Mamma so deaf. And what was there to say? That was not it, though. There was something else, a barrier, an impediment, an invisible membrane or caul she could not break out of. Not fear precisely, not dread. Whatever, it was, in no possible world, not to save her life, could Bell have lifted a finger to dial this number. As, yes, she should have done.

When her friend is gone the old woman lifts the lid of the *sómba*, drops a log into the smoke and jams it shut.

"Still the *sómba*," Bell remarks, since by this time of year it has been moved out, as a rule, to the barn, along with the metal flue, and all trace of the woodsmoke that has seeped out over the winter around the hole in the wall has been whitewashed away.

"The weather seems not to want to open this year."

"Who was that, Mamma?"

"It's a nuisance. *Má!* You mean Zoumbou? I thought you knew. My cousin Zoumboulia — Yorgo's mother. She spends her days here."

"Yorgo?"

"You knew that his wife died? The new one refuses to have his mother in the house."

"What!"

"She grudges her food and firewood."
"But what a crime! How can she do that?"
"What is to stop her, tell me?"
"Yorgo?"
"Yorgo, do you say? *Sigá!*" snorts Kyria Sofia.

When Bell goes to the *méros*, nothing has changed. The passage is still gloomy and dank, with gallon cans and demijohns in a row down one wall, and flour and rice bins. The basin and the lavatory are at the end, in the light filtering through a torn sheet of plastic over a high, barred window. The same dusty lightbulb hangs down, but the switch is back in the kitchen, over the sink. And something has changed, after all: there is a little square tub, here in the village! And a telephone nozzle, and a small hot water service, turned off, as usual in Greece unless someone wants a shower. So no one has to stand white and shivering in the old copper dish any more, with the saucepans of water all around, or struggle to tip a gallon of suds down the lavatory and not all over the floor. Unless — the shadow over the plughole is water. A scum, a webbing of dust.

She squats and pisses and quickly flushes the piss away, only not quickly enough to avoid the warm gush of smell out of the cesspit. At least she has her sense of smell in spite of her blocked nose. Her pockets are full of snotty tissues she is not allowed to flush away; or burn in the *sómba* either, in case it chokes up with ash. They have to go outside or into the plastic basket by the lavatory bowl with the other paper, all to be burnt on the first dry day, or blow away and be scattered by the hens.

Her case is still standing by the phone in the *sála*. There are things in it that she wants, but the matter of where she will sleep has not come up yet. She will just have to contain her unease until it does: she can hardly ask. Last time as a matter of course she was given the old room, the old bed. Oh, please! She will be on edge until she knows.

The yard is full of puddles. Grimacing, she drops her tissues in the ring of stones in front of the new barn, as the brick barn is still known, though it was built before Bell ever saw the house; the old barn is close against the house, and made of hairy mudbrick. The new barn is where the cows and calves used to be, and the grey horse that carted the loads of manure to the fields. Against the fence the henhouse hangs open, tall as a sentry-box. The plum tree that shelters the roof, thick with white flowers, has a wet skirt underneath like snow in a thaw. A hen skitters away in the mud with a glare at Bell.

"My broody hen." Mamma says at her back. "I have her sitting in a manger here in the new barn. The others are in the bottom henhouse."

"At the river?"

"Yes, well. You know your way around."

She knows her way to the river. She remembers more sharply than the old woman, or maybe not, how they all woke in the afternoons to trail in the powdery late heat to the bend in the river in the shade of the plane trees on gravel and sand, where Yanni and his cousins threw stones in, drenching each other with waterspouts.

"Will we go down and feed the hens?"

"I have already been. Tomorrow."

On the way home they would always stop at a blue cabinet just this side of the bridge, a shrine like a bee box with a glass door framing an ikon of the Panagia. They opened the glass door and Kyria Sofia lit a match and touched it to a wick in the little wheel afloat in dark oil. She made her cross, watching as the boys made theirs.

"Is it still there by the bridge, the shrine of the Panagia?"

"Why would it not be?"

The bridge is a metal span floored with planks, still referred to as the new bridge, the old one having been burnt in the Civil War. At the spot where Kyria Sofia stood for the photo all that time ago, women washed rugs and raw wool; and perhaps they still do, although for much of the year the river flow is taken up by the pumps now and spat out in long feathers around the fields.

There is a spring in the bank, only a trickle, but pure and cold. A tethered donkey in the grass, she remembers, and two women bent over with their hands in the river.

"What are you thinking?"

"Nothing. How happy I was yesterday," Bell says, "to see olive trees here."

"Yes, he planted them," Kyria Sofia says.

"Who?"

"The forgiven one. Before he went into the hospital."

"All of them?"

"What do you mean *all*? We have two."

"*We* have? Where?" By here Bell meant here in the village, and only now does she see the two scrawny trees by the wire fence in front of the wilderness of the kitchen garden, pale flowers in single file in between them. "Oh, yes! Oh, you will have olives!"

"Oil."

"Yes, wonderful! Oil from your own olives."

"He had his heart set on it."

"Will they bear fruit?"

She shrugs. "Much good it will do him." She props the gate open for Bell to go in.

"I always *thought* olives would grow here!"

"As if you would know."

"Like bananas in Australia" — Bell is determined to plough on — "not growing as far south as we live. But I know gardens with good sun and a warm wall out of the wind where bananas grow and bear fruit." She turns and turns the leaves, green, silver and green.

"See the *zoumboúlia*," says the old woman, and Bell looks over at the gate for the little widow. No one is there. Again she has been caught out. The stress is different, of course, and the *zoumboúlia* are these pale flowers. She squats dutifully and fingers them. The garden never used to have flowers, and they are still the only ones, these pastel hyacinths. No chamomile, no rosemary. But there are long wild arms that may be herbs out there in the long grass, borage or rosemary or thyme.

"You like them, do you!" Kyria Sofia cackles. "The smell would break your nose. Grigori got me the bulbs last year and I chopped most of them up in the winter, I took them for onions, of course, there in the dark. He meant them for the grave but he is far too trusting. They would only have got stolen."

"Can we go to the grave?"

"It's nearly time for church."

"I will come too."

"You are tired from the journey. Tomorrow."

Kyria Sofia is tired herself, too tired to talk as they wipe their feet and go inside to the *sómba*. When the trees make oil, she thinks, I can offer it to the Church alongside the bread I bake. The good green oil of my own olives, as the daughter-in-law says, out of my own earth.

It seems to Bell that she has always known the river. She was on her way there years before she ever saw it. In answer to the photo he had sent, Anna Bella in the river on the mountain, his mother sent Grigori a black and white photo of herself standing in this river under the bridge, shadowy trees in the distance, her skirts hoisted, her feet a flicker of white on smooth rock. She was laughing. Her hair was a ball of light and her eyebrows, like Grigori's, met on the bridge of her nose. I love my mother more than anything, he said in slow English. When she young she our life. When she old her boys look after her. I look after. I older son.

And the father?

Him too.

He promised to tell Bell one day when his English was better, or her Greek, a story his mother had told when he was a boy, the story of the mother heart.

The what?

Mother heart. You will like, Anna Bella.

I am not so sure.

He laughed and sketched a map of the village, pointing to where his mother was standing for the photo. Bell wanted to know what the trees were.

Platánia.

She had enough French left from school to guess that *platánia* were planes, the same sturdy pollarded trunks as in the street outside, there in Melbourne, in Murrumbeena, with their leaves like waving hands and seedballs that spilled out fox fur in the cobbles of the gutters.

Koíta, she said at the gate: *platánia.*

Aftá sto potámi eínai ágria, he said.

She looked it up. Those at the river are wild? she said aloud. He nodded: *Kai pampália*, and that took some finding: And age-old, she read out at last.

She folded his map and kept it, since one day she was going to the village, map in hand, to live there. It was not long before his mother wrote that the loom was set up to weave a striped woollen apron each for Anna Bella and her mother. It was taken for granted that they would marry once his sister had a husband. His mother wrote that, foreign or not, Anna Bella would be welcomed with open arms as her *nýfi*. When will you come home? all the letters ended now, with *you* in the plural. Now and then his father added a scatter of words. She must still have the map somewhere at home. A maze of red ink, it shows the village strung along its river, the family houses with pointed roofs and a name on each, and the school, and the church. She kept it folded around a photo of Grigori leading a white horse — if it was white, because it could be any pale colour, blue or dapple-grey, roan, a palomino dappled with shade — through a grassy field of flowers. It was like the slow magnanimous horses she had known as a child when the milk and bread, the firewood and the ice were still delivered from house to house by big, curt men who hurried back and forth while the horses stood swishing their long tails at flies in the shade of the plane trees. A white horse with a rider once walked past her on the beach where she was on holiday, at twilight, its hoofs lifting pale plumes of wind and sand until it faded out of sight. Salt on her lips, and sand. Grigori rode to the river on hot days, he said. His face is darkly creased, grinning into the sun. The photo itself is creased from being kept under her pillow.

And the house? she said. What is the house like? He drew her a red plan of the rooms, with the barn and the stable alongside. The walls were white, thick. The wall is like znow, he said. The house of her dreams had white walls hung and luminous with grapes, and children, and hens like brown lampshades in the summer light.

Bell has new photos of Yanni for the old woman, who grabs the packet, jamming her glasses on, and shuffles them with hands that are ruckled, yellow on the bone, still strong. "Ach, *pásham!*" she cries out, as she did with all the children. Vaïa, Lefteri and Grigori were the same, always hugging the children when they were little, tossing and catching them in the air and crying out the Turkish endearments of their childhood. *Ach, pashá mou, gavrí mou! Pásham*, Grigori was calling Yanni from the very beginning, in Australia, and Bell had picked it up in no time. My Pasha, my little sparrow. Ach, *pásham*! So much so that when she gave Yanni passionfruit for the first time — he was a year old, still in nappies that he filled up with the golden mush and black seeds — he thought she was saying *pásham* fruit, therefore it was his fruit, and no one else should get any.

The old woman has lost interest in the photos. Her face is sagging with weariness as Bell puts them back.

Asking first, Bell turns the television on for the evening news but it must be out of order. The sound more or less works, but the picture flickers and shifts among silvery outlines no matter what she does, and in the end she turns it off.

"No, I can't be bothered with it either," Kyria Sofia says. "The little one knows how to fix it — Sonya — but she's the only one. No, Yanni does." She taps the packet of photos. "Your Yanni. He does."

"She must be a clever girl."

Sonya is Bell's niece, or Grigori's at least, his sister Vaïa's third child.

"She crawls underneath and joins a wire — who knows? She is, she's a clever girl. A little devil. They had better keep an eye on that one, I tell you to know —"

"She was a darling when she was little."

"If you ask me, she's a little whore."

"At twelve!"

"Thirteen. She's had her periods for two years."

"Has she? I started at eleven."

"She's spoilt, that's her trouble."

"I long to see her. And Vaïa, after all this time. All of them."

"Vaïa rang before. She will keep ringing. She thinks I am fasting too hard. She wants me to eat."

"She does well. What do you say?"

"I will, I do. She sends regards."

"They will come for Easter?"

"Why not?"

"And Lefteri and Chloï?" Bell's voice falters, because the dead grandson was the child of Lefteri and Chloï.

"No."

"Not on Easter Sunday?"

"No." Her face averted, she pulls on her black coat: "You rest. I will not be long."

These four white walls are a world and while she is here Bell will not miss the television at all, although at home she could hardly have lived without it. In the last weeks before she left, especially, when the Gulf War broke out, she sat in front of the screen for hours on end as the reporters huddled in bare rooms and the thumps on the soundtrack were shells exploding, and the flames and the dust were everywhere, and the ragged bodies on the roads, and the tanks, and splashes of blood. Everyone she knew was watching CNN because it was there, always on tap: under some obscure obligation, they decided it was, not to fail — at least not to fail — in their duty of witness. Since coming to Greece she has seen next to nothing of the war, a glimpse here or there in a restaurant before the basketball came on; a gush of fire under black smoke, a cormorant coated in grease, faces wailing on a scree slope. She is so close to the Gulf now that all her friends warned her against flying here, and yet she knows far less. If you can even call it knowing.

If she dared, this would be a good time to unpack the case still standing out there in the dark of the *sála,* as if mysteriously abandoned on a railway platform. But until she is given her room, unpacking anywhere would be presumptuous, if not rude. So, what to do now? She is at a loose end, having expected to go to church. Mark time — it's all she can do. Read, write in her diary. She has her notebook out, but she is not in the mood. The only book she brought from home is in the case. There are the two paperbacks in her cloth bag, though, one that the nun lent her on Paros and one she picked up at the hotel in the Plaka, from the shelf where the guests left their unwanted books, just to pass the time on ferries if she was bored, and on the train: both barely begun. One is inscribed in long black letters on the blank page inside the front cover:

> *Anna & love, M —*
>
> *Abstinence sows sand all over*
> *The ruddy limbs & flaming hair*
> *But Desire Gratified*
> *Plants fruits of life & beauty there*
>   *(William Blake)*

Did M write the inscription in reproach, Bell wonders for the hundredth time, to a coy mistress, or in triumph? It depends. Was it Anna who left the book on the shelf for any passing stranger to pick up, and if so, why? It must have been, since the book must have belonged to her; unless, that is, she gave it back to M, who then discarded it in anger, scorn, pique? Could Anna, or M, simply have forgotten to pack it, and so the proprietor with a shrug left it on the shelf with the other tattered offerings? Now and then Bell would see a couple on the deck of a ferry or in a coffee shop eating pastries, a woman with red hair, or blonde — and once, two women in love — and be suddenly reminded of M and Anna. Were they still together? Not if the book was thrown away. But if it was only lost? Maybe, in that case, and maybe not. She yawns. This is the one she means to get started on now. She spreads it flat on her lap, but — the dimness, is it, or the smoky heat? — she still has it spread open at the inscription when Kyria Sofia bursts in.

"Ah. Sleep took you, did it?"

"It must have!"

"This is where I will make your bed, anyway. In here with me on the divan by the *sómba*."

"Oh, please, Mamma! Can I have the old bedroom?"

"No, it's cold out there."

"I don't mind!"

"Why be out there in the cold, when we have all this room?" Kyria Sofia's face is stiff with insult.

"But I can't *sleep* in the heat. I can't breathe!"

"Well."

"Oh please!"

This far inland the only sound in the air is a nightbird now and then, like a mewling kitten.

The fuel stove in the kitchen has made way now for a white electric one, but Kyria Sofia begrudges the cost too much ever to turn it on if she can help it. Instead she takes the lid off the *sómba* in the front room, jams a saucepan into the flames and spills spaghetti into the boiling water, fanning it out like straight hair until it sinks. She sets up the card table and brings in bread and olives, apples and a knife; and in no time, plates of the soft spaghetti, with feta on top of Bell's, and a gloss of oil.

"*Makarónia*," she says and mutters the grace Bell only half remembers. "Eat," she says, watching Bell mash the feta in and stuff her mouth with the salty strings. "Is it good?"

"Beautiful."

Kyria Sofia stirs hers with the fork and makes a face. "Lenten fare."

Bell hides a smile. For as long as she can remember, Kyria Sofia has pretended to find fault with her food. "And this oil, Mamma, how it shines! So heavy and rich and green."

"Sigá!" Scornfully, but the praise melts her. "Vaïa bought it straight from the press. *Amán!*" she says, "I nearly forgot the fish," and brings a plate of little brown *sardélles*.

"Does the fishmonger still bring his van? The gypsy?"

"That's the one."

He patrols all the villages with his loudspeaker and brass scales and a son to help him weigh out the carcasses, silver and red, while the women wait in line with their bags and baskets. Father and son, each had a loose grin, a gold tooth, and hands with a crust of fish scales, baggy, like sequinned gloves, so that they moved with a milky sheen in the sun. Mamma will have lit the fire in front of the new barn. She has always cooked her *sardélles* out of doors, clamped in the bars of the *skára* and held over the fire, singed and dripping so that it flared high and black all around them. Bell has it in her mind's eye, she can even smell the pungent herb in the summer night, *rígani*, and fish oil, olive oil, and wood smoke: she has a sensation, like floating, of having lost the place. All this could as well have been yesterday as a day many years ago, or ahead, any day at all, a slide taken at random, unlabelled, unnamed. The awkward pose must be making the old woman's back and thighs ache, but she looks up with a smile; the white sweep of hair across her cheek and throat stirs in the fire. She is all white hair and smoke and a tremor in the hot air.

"Eat, Bella, what's wrong with you? Take a fish."

"There's no room on my plate."

"Go on, while they are fresh. On Palm Sunday we eat fish."

"Did you grill them outside?"

"In the rain, are you stupid? I fried them in the pan today for lunch."

"Well, they smell beautiful."

"Only I burnt them on one side. See?"

"I like the crust."

Kyria Sofia is hunched over to eat. Her long lashes are white now as well. So are her eyebrows at last, but for one black thread. Her hair is pure white, as it has been for the last thirty years.

"What are you looking at?"

"You."

"*E?* Me. They are like the fish of the monk of Vyzantion, these fish. The half-fried fish? You don't know the story! Well, he was frying fish in a pan during the siege when they ran in to say the Turks had taken the City. Some say it was the King himself, Konstantino. The fools! As if the King would leave the battle to go and fry fish! The monk said, I will as soon believe that these half-fried fish can live, he said, as believe the Turks have taken the City. No sooner were the words out of his mouth than those fish were out of the pan and in the wellspring, alive again, half-fried, and there they will swim until the day we take the City back."

"Very fresh fish!"

"So are these. Not that you care."

"I will have one, if you have one."

"Me? I have no appetite."

"*Ela*, you still have to eat. You have to keep your strength up."

"What strength?" But she picks one up by the tail and nibbles it.

"This oil! We would give our souls for oil like this at home." Bell licks her lips and smiles up in time to see Kyria Sofia's face go as stiff as wax, but why?

When the water boils, no more than three finger-widths of water, Bell washes up in the saucepan the old way, running a sponge of hot suds over the dishes and rinsing them one by one in a trickle from the cold tap. Kyria Sofia, ready with a teatowel, arranges each one upside-down on the marble draining board; everything has its place, as she explains, and how is Bell to know where? Bell agrees. The teatowel is one of hers, white linen worn as fine as muslin, with a stencil of a black-plumed swan — a pale grey now, almost not there — and ripples and a splash of red beak. We only have one tap, cold water, she wrote home in the early days, but a new marble draining board, you should see! A slab of pure marble. Everyone has marble here. Mamma says she got the builders to make it higher than usual because the *nýfi* — that's me — is tall.

"You knew I was tall before I ever came," she says out loud.

"When? What do you mean?"

"Before you ever saw me."

"*E*. I had photos, didn't I? I had eyes. *Ela*."

She ushers Bell back into the thick heat by the *sómba* for the reading of the liturgy for Palm Sunday. She reads painstakingly in a monotone, almost a chant, a quavery treble, and all Bell picks up is a word here and there, about the Mount of Olives, and the fig that is cursed and withered, and the people who cut palm branches on the way of the son of David mounted on an ass. She folds her hands and unfolds them, stiff under their scabby mercurochrome. They seem to be relics of another life, a dream in which she sat in a room over the sea with her hands spread, painting the raw cracks and blisters scarlet with a cotton bud one by one, carefully, like putting lipstick on so many little open mouths.

This is where Grigori was born, this very room. Only that was in the old house that was burnt down. Ashes and dust, a memory, a dream. This is the new house they raised in its place, raised bodily: Grigori has scars on his shoulders where the stones broke the skin. First the old man took the axe and struck the head off a young cock, which he buried in its blood in the foundations to make the house strong. The walls were built of thick stone and earth on those foundations, on blood and bone and ashes. She knows that no one has been born, or has died, for that matter, here in the new house. Nevertheless, it is the same room, since the new house rests on the old foundations, after all, cradled, these five rooms, in the house of the past.

In the end he told her the story she was not sure she would like, about the mother heart. A man was in love with a woman who scorned him. If you love me so much, she told him, prove it, go on: cut out your mother's heart and give it to me. So wild was his passion for the woman that without another word he took a knife and slaughtered his mother, cut the heart out of the breast that had given him suck and wrapped it in her own headscarf. As he was running to claim his reward he tripped on a stone and fell. The heart rolled out of his hands and lay open and dripping in the sun. He picked it up and to his horror he heard a sob. My son, the heart said, my little one! Did you hurt yourself?

Grigori's voice went thick with tears. You understand? And this is the mother heart.

All very well, Bell thought at the time and thinks again now, still not sure if she likes it: but what if it had been a daughter?

A cock crows. Kyria Sofia, her voice faded to a mutter, is still slumped over the prayer book. Each of them rouses herself with a start from time to time — the dim room, the world, the inside world — until she takes off her grey glasses at last and squints up through her white lashes.

"Well. Time to make your bed."

"Let me make it, Mamma."

"*E?* All right."

They kiss goodnight in the icy *sála* and Bell picks up her case at last and treads on her long brown shadow at the threshold of the other front room, halting, her hand from old habit finding the light switch.

"You see how cold it is." The old woman leans in, fingering the bedclothes.

"No, no, Mamma. See, the bed is even made."

This is the bed that she and Grigori bought, and where he and his wife sleep in the summer. They may even be the same sheets.

The old woman blinks up into Bell's smile and a grim change has come over her face. She looks — hard, is it? Bitter, worn? All she is saying, though, is something about blankets, finding more.

"No, Mamma, no need."

"Goodnight, then."

"Goodnight, Mamma."

"Sleep well." And still she is faltering at the door.

"I will."

Then the door closes at last and Bell can open the window a crack and let the mist sidle in through the shutters. Shivering, she unlocks and unzips her case, pulls her pyjamas on over her underwear and slips into the bed where she lies with folded arms and stares into the dark, flooded with shame. You are here on sufferance, that face was saying, you are yet another cross to bear. Bell shudders. The cold room is unforgiving and she has only herself to thank. She was right to be unsure of her welcome. *You did very well to come.* No, too late she knows better. What led her to trap them both, rushing back here like this on a flood of high feeling? Now she is stranded, and no way out of it — a week has to be got through together, a whole week, Holy Week. And that face! Harrowed. Not hard: harrowed. Sorrowful. Is it just the grief? She looks so ill, mortally ill, *fagoméni*, eaten away. Those hands! And her face.

The other door creaks shut. Silence in the village and the cock crows, once, again.

Grigori felt the cold, hated the cold.

Hwat's you name? Anna? Hwat is? Bella? Ah, Anna Bella! My name Grigori. You hev brother, sister, no, you only? I hev one brother and one sister. This only place. Very only here. *E,* Anna Bella? Cold, this mountain. This country, Afstralia.

She had taken a summer job and stayed on until there was snow on the mountain and almost overnight the Chalet had two hundred guests. Not that she could mix with them, since anyone who did was sacked on the spot — was *sent down the hill.* A social was held on Fridays for the eighty people, migrants mostly, who worked there, and at one of these one night she met Grigori. He was dark, taut, eager. Although they worked together, she as a waitress, he as a cook, there was hardly ever time to exchange a look or a word in the turmoil of the kitchens. Now and then she was on scullery duty, loading and unloading the dishwasher, trundle and slosh, rack after rack to be hauled steaming and dripping, rungs on them like grey gristle that has been chewed and spat out and left on the plate for the pig bins; like the soggy piles of old jetties. As for him, all day he ran between the coolroom and the black stoves that bulged and trickled with fire, stealing out into the open for a smoke from time to time, and there if she could get away from the scullery she would find him standing, his face blank, shining with sweat, in the snow that was printed with possum trails and the feet of the shrill incandescent parrots, blue and scarlet, that came swooping down after bread scraps. Lowries, she said and he repeated, one lowry, two lowries, their voices jerking, and the hair and skin frozen on their skulls.

She had knitted herself a ski jumper and offered to make him one. He chose a plain pattern in a new wool alternately twisted tight and rubbed, matted into wads, chestnut brown. In the half dark he whistled her down from her room. He had a tune of seven notes for calling her — *Am I your dog?* — and when, shivering, she came downstairs into the snow with her length of knitting — *See how much!* — he would thrust a bundle into her hands, a roast potato in a cloth, a boiled egg. *Patáta,* he said, *avgó, s'agapáo,* I love you, and kissed her. He turned a face of wet brass to her, stumbling back in over his hollow footprints.

With one sleeve to go, in the late winter he collapsed. The men's quarters had no heating. He lay in bed shivering, contorted, his forehead wet, breathing mist in and out. My chest is pain, he said, my back pain, Anna Bella. I carn breathe. The nearest doctor was in the town at the foot of the mountain. Hwat, doctor? Nuh, I know hwat is, Grigori said. Is cold. Is *revmatismoí*. From army when we must zleep in znow.

Radiators were banned because of the high danger of fire, but his roommate smuggled one in and switched it on, all of them sighing with relief as the bars sang and filled out with red light. Grigori had a tube of liniment he wanted Bell to rub in. The room stank of it, and her hands. She had never seen him naked before.

Is not enough, the cold is too deep, Grigori said. *Vendoúzes* I want. Go on, put me *vendoúzes*, he pleaded. The roommate brought wine glasses and a bottle of blue spirit, and fled while Grigori showed her how to dip a taper in the spirit, light it and hold the flame in the glass, and then quickly clap the rim down on his back. The rim burned and he gasped aloud. As it cooled, the glass clung, swaying on a fat blister of his skin. *Vále*, he said, put more.

No, I can't, she said, this is horrible.

Come on. *Vále!*

What if it's more than a cold? More than rheumatism?

Doesun mutter. My mother put me *vendoúzes*. First she put big fire in *sómba,* very hot, like *hamámi* — like one Turkish bath. Then she put me *vendoúzes*.

But did it help?

Is help, always. *Vále*, he said into the pillow, Anna Bella. Please.

The glasses breathed fire in her face; the taper burned fast and low. One by one the rims clamped and sucked hard until his back was a mass of moving bubbles, half red flesh and half air and at last she could stamp on the taper. Each glass had a window of light, a round wall, a lightbulb, a face, hers, swaying, although he lay so still, chinking softly. Soap bubbles torn loose from a child's pipe sway like that, bulging and lolloping off, filmy with rainbows. When it was time to tug the glasses off, each pop drew a clench and a shuddering breath.

Better? she said.

Little bit, he said. You put tonight again.

Let me ring for a doctor.

Next time you better cut with knife first. Thet way they filling with blood.

Oh, and then what? We drink the blood?

Icicles fringed his window. Mist flooded the valley and rose softly. Snow, clotting and sifting, had covered all the dark slopes. The red balls burned on his back, deeply rimmed, lovebites, nipples, smooth and hot to lick, and shiny where her tongue had been, fat red swollen udders.

MONDAY

When she wakes she is warm at last, hugging the ache of her belly to her like a hot-water bottle. She has come out of a blank sleep with a sickly sweet smell — jasmine? — in her face and the conviction that the old man's grave is out there in the kitchen garden under the grass and hyacinths, flanked by the olive trees. *Zoumboúlia.* They are what she can smell, not jasmine. Hyacinths. Flowers that can sprout and grow in the space of a jar in a cupboard, needing no light, as figs flower within the darkness of their own skin; and no soil either, their fat whiskery bulbs fattening like fungi on nothing but the dark water. They are too rich, too cloying, like bottled scent. They might as well be funerary immortelles out there, the old man's hyacinths, squatting on their leaves with petals of tinted plastic in thick shavings, pink, blue and white, so solid. Fleshy to the touch — she shudders — with the clammy coldness of underwater flowers that are animals in disguise, sponges and soft corals and sea anemones, windflowers, sea windflowers with their clutch of tentacles.

The village is too far inland for any breath of salt to come on the wind, even a south wind. How could I have hoped to make a home here, she thinks, so far from the sea? I was not alone in that. Grigori, all of the family, expected no less. They welcomed me as a bride to the house. The old man bought two kids that a neighbour had been fattening for Easter, slaughtered and roasted them at Aunt Magdalini's, in her beehive oven, whitewashed, an igloo out in her yard, filled with embers and soot, while we ate and drank there under the moon. Without saying anything too definite to my parents, who would only worry, we had all our household goods shipped over here in crates. To think that some are here to this day, white cups with a silver rim, a wedding present, and the red enamel pot, and the blue and white striped milk jug, cracked now, all going strong and set to outlast us all. Even the old teatowels are here. The black swans on them Mamma took to be a negative, never having seen any but white swans. Black swans? *Ade!* You are teasing me. No, Mamma. In a negative, I said, the beaks would have to be green not red, and her face set in an incredulous smile, Grigori's smile, loftily amused, tinged with pity, or scorn.

Within a week of our coming Baba fell ill. He blamed the roast kid, Mamma the ouzo and tobacco, while the rest of the village said it was his excess of joy in having his son home after ten years in the foreign land. Poor Barba Yanni, the joy was too much for him: all the wise heads nodded and sighed. Whatever the truth of it, in Easter week his ulcer perforated and for most of the summer he lay in bed, in the hospital and then here: back from the dead to the glory of God, agreed the wise heads. It was the ulcer, turning cancerous, that was to bury him in the end, nowhere near the kitchen garden — how could she have thought so? — unless in spirit. He is in the cemetery, *to koimitíri*. The sleeping place. *Koimísou kalá,* the words of parting, at the threshold or turning over under the covers, last thing at night. Sleep well. Here the dead have a field to sleep in, not the churchyard or anywhere near the church, but a field out on the main road in the middle of other fields, of barley, wheat, tobacco. What has the old man got growing over him, if not his hyacinths? There was a time when the hyacinth was a flower of the dead. As was the windflower. The Greeks of those days buried the dead in earthenware pots underground, along with the pots of seed corn that lay waiting to be born again. They sowed grain on the graves then, to the glory of the goddess, the womb of earth and sea, the *mítra*, ample Dimitra.

At least Bell is warm now. In the middle of the night the cold woke her more than once and kept her awake and shivering, rubbing her feet against each other in their thick socks. Without opening her eyes she was sure for a good part of the night that she was home. Not in her own bed: back in Australia in a swag under the sky, camping in the desert, like last year, in a deep frost. Her bladder was keeping her awake, swelling until she was a bubble of golden fluid lying under the black and white frost of the desert moonlight, a giant white-legged honey ant. It was impossible to get up and piss without disturbing the whole camp. Not until sunrise, with the ice shining in strings all around, the panes of ice crackling under the sleeping bags, could she squat at a safe distance and let it go steaming out of her with the soft hiss which where she comes from means a snake in the sand of the dunes, in the tea-tree scrub, a snake or a lizard; but here there was no cover and nothing alive in sight. The piss was stained red, she remembers, a shocking red, half blood, the start of her period, days before she was due. It ran away in darkening seams of the sand which spread on every side full of shadow and honey light as far as the horizon.

Even her breasts are aching now. Holding her breath she presses her fingers into her belly to measure the watery roll and quiver of it. If she could only get out to the *méros* and back without disturbing the old woman! Her own grasp chills her and she shivers. The warmest part of me, she thinks, is this hoard of body heat, this piss, molten gold. So I might as well hang on to it.

Eight o'clock, and no sound in the house. Opening the door on to the grey *sála* she catches a mutter of prayer: candlelight runs along the edge of the kitchen door. Yawning, she shuts the door gently and lies down again. The air is hard to breathe. The window will creak if she opens it any more, and Mamma will hear. The covers are musty, and the mattress where she always slept, and where Grigori slept only last summer with his new wife who is carrying — Bell reminds herself — a child. Unless she has given birth by now. The whole room is musty from the lack of sun. In the summer they will have flung the shutters wide open and flat to the outside walls first thing every day to let the sun in, just as Bell used to; and when she latched them for the afternoon sleep the gold heat of the afterglow would last until they woke at around five for coffee. This summer they will put the baby down and then lie down themselves, naked in the clear heat, the light.

She is asleep when the handle grates and the door is flung open. She has to roll on her back, yawning to cover her shock.

"*Kaliméra*. So, are you warm?" Kyria Sofia comes and thrusts her hands in under the covers, in a rush, the way Bell has seen her do in the hay under a broody hen. At her touch a twitch of shock runs through Bell, so strong that it must have shown in her face, only Mamma can't see it, she is almost on her knees by the bed, with her head ducked down between her arms. "Ah, yes. You are."

The kitchen is dark, as it always was even in summer. The window, which has no shutters and needs none, is half the wall wide but it looks straight out on the mudbricks of the old barn, where the flounces of dried tobacco used to hang from the rafters out of reach of the rats, like so many fox pelts in the gloom.

There is honey, and bread to toast on the lid of the *sómba*, but Bell has remembered the *trahaná* porridge of the old days. Kyria Sofia switches the light on and rummages in the dresser until she finds some that she made last year or the year before, from her own eggs and flour, of course, hand-rubbed and sun-dried: only not the milk sort, these are the sour ones, made with yoghurt. These are better, Bell says, and Kyria Sofia agrees: only fried with onions and peppers, not with honey. Yes, yes, Mamma. Don't they serve yoghurt with honey all over Greece? Well, then!

So at last Bell is allowed to boil a handful of the little grits until they swell like rice and the yeasty sourness comes to life; with milk, honey, the taste of the first days, the past.

On the way to the *méros* again Bell hangs back among the photos on the wall. A new ikon among the others on the side wall has caught her eye, a figure coffined in a dark blue shroud, a Panagia in gold leaf and lapis lazuli: a postcard of a fresco half-soaked into some old wall. *At Mistra, Love from Grigori* is scrawled in Greek on the back, with the new wife's signature underneath. The Dormition of the Virgin, Bell thinks, but when she looks closely it turns out to be a Nativity, in a grotto in a mountain of golden rock, spiny, with the flared mouth of a whelk and a ragged summit like a sheaf of ripe corn. The Panagia's eyelids are brown and swollen and her lips tight. She lies back stiffly, one hand to her cheek, as if she is carved of wood. A goat and a tawny ass drop their heads into the manger. The Magi draw near on horseback, and in the rocks are saints and angels in robes, suns at their heads, and twisted bodies so light that they float in a gold wind.

No sooner has Zoumboulia settled herself by the *sómba* than Theia Kalliroï drops in with a granddaughter and kisses Bell in welcome. "Here you are again. Well I remember the day you first came and the forgiven one, he nearly died of joy. You have well received her," she tells Kyria Sofia, who nods, intent on her crochet hook. Bell makes coffee and conversation, watching the girl as she flicks through the book Bell took out of her case this morning and murmurs phrases aloud. Theia Kalliroï smiles. "Lyka is learning English now, you see, Bella."
"Are you, Lyka?"
"Yes, I am learning English."
"Good! Do you like it?"
"Yes, I like it very much. What book is this?"
"Tracks. *It is by a woman."* Lyka looks blank and Bell goes on in Greek: "Who walked across the desert alone with four camels and a dog."
"An Australian? No! You have no camels in Australia!"
"We have now. Afghans went there with their camels and let them loose a long time ago. They run wild in the desert. But she bought hers."
"English, English!" Theia Kalliroï pleads.
"Have you gone into the desert, Aunt Bella?"
"Yes, last year, but on a truck, not a camel. And not alone."

"Are there petrol wells like in Iraq and in Kuwait?"

"No, and that is a great blessing," Bell says. *"Our wells only have water."*

Lyka is frowning with the effort. *"Do they have sweet water?"*

"Some have sweet water and some have salt."

"What is this word 'treks'?"

"Tracks? Íchni." Although *íchni* is more like traces. Struggling in the blankness of her memory, Bell comes up with *monopátia*. Paths, is that it? And there are other meanings, out of reach. "Monopátia," she goes on carefully in English. *"And póroi. It means many things."*

Lyka rewards her with a sunny smile. *"I love best the books of Enid Blyton."*

"Do you? I used to love the books of Enid Blyton!"

"The Five?" Lyka shrugs, abandoning English.

"The Five, yes. And the Seven —"

"The Secret Seven! We are in a gang like that, some girlfriends and I —"

"Lyka," says Theia Kalliroï.

"— and we go to deserted houses and look for adventures!"

"Lyka, speak English!"

Lyka shrugs. "Ghosts and secrets, you know."

"And have you found any?"

"Never! Not once!"

Theia Kalliroï asks after Yanni and Bell brings out her packet of photos. They pass from hand to hand, Zoumbou and Kalliroï exclaiming at each one. Ach, what a handsome boy! Look, Lyka, don't you think he's handsome? What do you say? Look how she's laughing! She's blushing! He looks so stern in this one. He has the sun in his eyes. He is a piece of gold, that boy, I always said so. Any time now he will come looking for a bride.

When they are gone Bell washes the cups, delighted. "That Lyka, Mamma! Isn't she a darling?"

Kyria Sofia has sat scowling over her lace the whole time. "Why? What's so special about her?" she says now; and after a pause, "What would she want to do that for?"

"What?"

"Her. The one who rides the camels."

"Well, to see the desert. To be there."

"To see the desert!"

"The desert is wonderful, Mamma. I want to go back when I can. She went alone to see if she was brave enough, and clever enough. As a test, you understand. No woman had ever done it."

"And how old is she?"

"Oh — twenty-something. I think she saw it as a sort of —" Pilgrimage: but she has forgotten the Greek, and the only word that comes to mind is the Turkish *hadj*.

"Well?"

"A sort of — *hadj*? The desert was a holy land."

"You have a shrine in your desert worthy of a *hadj*?"

"The desert itself. The land."

"It sounds like blasphemy to me."

The desert, the word, *i érimos*, is feminine, Bell thinks. And the land? *I xirá, i steriá*. Yes, and the earth: *i gi*.

"From the deserts prophets come," she says.

"Not any more they don't. Is she married? No? What's wrong with her?"

They go back to the warmth, and Zoumboulia asleep in her black hood.

Sweet water and salt. The desert is all water in times of flood, the plain brimful, sheeted in yellow and white washes that shrink into a salt lake and into a gulf, leaving a mat of grass and a few trees, alive and dead, like the thaw in the far northern steppes. There you find little piles of bones like cold campfires; lashes and coils of tyre rubber by the road, and pink animals with ruffs of fur, like fig mash, with a frosting of mould; a car body like the hide of a red cow; a cattle station curtained in corrugated iron, the tank stand broken, and the fences and sheds, and the heap of brown bottles glittering like water. This is the inland sea, the imaginary sea, the glass and air of mirage, a sea of stone and sand for millions of years, and ancient rivers that still run in caves under stone and sand.

A well in the desert, a bore, is a gush of light in skeins out on the plain, and a dark line of shrubs that twists down from there, green pools, for a short way until the sand sucks it dry. Steam drifts loose with a whiff of sulphur, and as you come near you catch sight of a dark standing pipe at the core of a spout of water falling in white frills with a dome, the throb of a glass heart. The rocks are green with slime, and the water slips as smooth as a glove over your hand, blood-warm.

All day the fall and flurry of white flakes from the plum trees. The stork comes and goes on its nest above the electric light pole. A parade of stiff hens scratches in the row of hyacinths, a neighbour's hens, but now that there are no seedlings they scratch where they like and Kyria Sofia never bothers to shoo them out. The house is dim and sour from the trickle of smoke out of the *sómba*. Bell snuffles, wandering restlessly in and out. From time to time Kyria Sofia riddles the fire with the iron hook and tosses the lid back on. Once, grabbing her belly, she gives a loud whoop.

"Sorry!" she gasps in English.

"Sorry!"

"You see!"

"Bravo, yes, you remember."

It goes back to the early days, of thinking how rude they all were. Even Grigori, after ten years in Australia, thought so. Living here meant trying not to expect please and thank you, let alone sorry, or to say them either, within the family, because it gave offence. Politeness was only for strangers, outsiders: was that how she regarded them? Even so, they met her half-way when they remembered, even Mamma.

" I have my bit of English still. It would be more if you had kept your promise to teach me. It's your fault." She heaves and whoops again. "*Amán*, I'm turning into a rooster" — patting her mouth — "and the pain! I have such wind!"

"If you ate more it might help."

"In Lent?"

"Old people are let off the fast, and babies, and travellers, and those in poor —"

"I know. Do you think I need you to tell me?"

For the walk to the cemetery Bell puts on a cleaner pair of jeans in the pocket of which she comes on her keyring with the heavy little silver hand hung on it, the thumb and middle finger meeting in a Buddhist *mudra*. She takes it out — it could be anything really, a trinket or a lucky charm — and when Kyria Sofia asks what it is, Bell says a doorknocker and the old woman gives a sniff, satisfied. A right hand, if anything it looks like an *ex voto*. Although Bell doesn't need her keys in Greece she likes them in her pocket, having got into the habit lately of closing her hand for comfort on the silver hand, warm — much warmer than hers — and strong, and her hand has a smell of silver now that no amount of soap and water will wash off.

No one is about in the grey mist of the streets or in the cemetery with its blue cages like cots, spread with white marble among the green shoots of grass and the crocuses in the fox-red mud. On the hills on every side are the vineyards she remembers and the fields ploughed and sown with green barley. Here and there are cypresses and low bushes, rosemary. The graves thin out towards the back. There is only one in the dip at the far end, close to a stand of bare black oaks, the map of their roots spread out in shadow on the grass, which marks the boundary. He is here, under a marble cross.

The headstone is a shock, the sight of those names which are also her own son's, both the Christian name and surname, and those of the other dead Yanni as well. (And where is his grave?) The headstone has a glass cupboard set in it: but no photo yet, she remarks. Well, there are plenty at home, but Vaïa is always forgetting to bring a frame from the city. Kyria Sofia sighs, bending to the jars with oil and water, setting a floating wick alight, and then the wax candles in a wooden hutch alongside.

"Here is Magdalini," she says on the way back, smoothing the headstone with her hand. "And Barba Nikola is over there. The old *psáltis*, if you remember."

Yes, Bell does. His chanting was a roar from the deeps that outdid the *papás*; and Kyria Sofia at his back coming in shrill and quavery on every response just a second before he did, softly, a bird's twitter, no more, since a woman must not speak or sing in church. But the song was stronger than she was; and louder too, the deafer she became. There was nothing wrong with Barba Nikola's ears, apparently. They turned red at the provocation and his nape bulged, bristling. It would send Bell into solitary ecstasies of joy, this by-play with the *psáltis*, the more so since Grigori — away on the right with the men, and out of earshot — refused to believe her account of it. He frowned, offended. Barba Nikola knew how to turn the other cheek. He was always hobbling in for a coffee and a talk with the old woman on some matter of the spirit. But the ears and the bristling are a fond memory.

"Poor Barba Nikola."

"So you do? We have a new *psáltis*. You will meet him tonight."

Bell stares around the stone beds. "And our Yanni's grave?" It is an effort to say the name.

"Not here. He's in Thessaloniki."

"Oh."

"Until they dig him out, anyway."

"They what?"

"Dig out his bones. Next year or the year after. They do that in the city."

"Oh. Of course."

In the city they take the bones out of the grave once they are dry. Will they bring them here then, to his grandfather's grave? But something about Kyria Sofia, a grimness, some tautness or apprehension, forbids the question.

For lunch the bread comes out and the margarine — Elaïs, made out of olive oil — and feta, apples, olives, the cold *sardélles*, and *halvá* with a chocolate ripple. Wrinkling her nose, Kyria Sofia slams a brown jar down for good measure and says her grace.

"You eat the fish."

"All of them?"

"Are there so many?"

"What about you?"

"Not today."

There are a dozen of them left, brown with white eyes and a cold, rich smell. Bell takes one by the head and nibbles it. A crust of bread fried in oil, a sandwich of white flesh in ribs and flakes: today the taste is so intense it brings on a rush of tears. "How *good* they are!" she says with her mouth full of bones as fine as dog hairs, taking another one. So far from the coast and so good, these distillations of the sea.

With an ironic smile, Kyria Sofia is spreading the paste from the brown jar on her bread. "You see," she says. "Last night they were good too."

"I was full last night."

"You can eat them all now, go on."

"Thank you. Is there vinegar?"

The vinegar is home-made, a few spoonfuls at the bottom of a slim ouzo bottle, the same size as the one Bell remembers from the first wedding she saw here. A cheering mob of the bridegroom's friends besieged the bride's father's house and bore her and the dowry away. Afterwards, capering and sucking at bottles of ouzo, blind drunk, they led the slow procession home from the church to the bridegroom's house. There in the yard stood his mother holding up an ouzo bottle which she handed to the bride in her hooped white dress. The girl took a long swig and hurled the bottle over her shoulder. A roar of joy went up. Why do they give her ouzo? Bell asked Grigori. Not ouzo, was his answer, it was the mother-in-law's spit in the bottle.

What! What for?

It was a sign that she was free of disgust and fully accepted her place in the house.

Will I have to do that if we have a wedding here? Bell asked, but she must have made too much of a show of her own disgust. No, he said, we are Refugees. We come from the Middle East and this is a custom of Makedonia. But his face was stiff with offence.

"*Tahíni*, Mamma?" Bell sniffs at the brown jar.

"*Tahíni*, *amán*. Every day for six weeks I have eaten *tahíni* until I am sick to death of it."

"Why eat it then?"

"You know why."

She does: *tahíni* is a staple food of Lent. Kyria Sofia is after praise, however, and Bell dips her knife in and spreads the *tahíni* on her bread. "I love it," she says dreamily, "I could never get sick of it."

"You soon would if you had it every day."

"I do at home." And she does, she loves the earthy smokiness of the sesame. She has it every day for lunch with feta and a handful of cherry tomatoes from the garden, an olive or two and a pocket bread toasted until it puffs up like a toad fish.

Kyria Sofia snorts.

In the room with the *sómba*, having read the day's church service aloud, Kyria Sofia wipes her eyes. "Now I will tell you a history," she says.

"A history? Not a *paramýthi*?" Kyria Sofia is known to generations of children as a teller of fairy stories.

"This one is true. The life of a great saint. And no need for that face —"

"Not at all, I wasn't —"

"*Sout* — because you will like it. This is the story of the life and the martyrdom of the holy one, the glorified, the healer, Pandeleïmon. He was a brilliant young doctor who treated the poor for nothing. He was another of the breed of the Unsilvered Ones."

"Like Grigori Lambraki. *Zei*. The Communist MP who was run down and clubbed to death in Thessaloniki. He was a doctor who treated the poor for nothing. There was a film. The Junta banned it. *Zei* —"

"This Pandeleïmon was a man of God" — Kyria Sofia takes a deep breath — "who lived and worked in Nikomedia once upon a time where he was the apple of the king's eye. Pandoleon was his name then and he worshipped the old gods of the city, knowing no better, until one day he met Ermolao, a wise old Christian, who told him Jesus Christ could cure any disease by his grace alone, more than the old gods could do, if he would only believe. And by the grace of Christ one day Pandoleon found a child lying dead by the road with an echidna at his side —"

Bell laughs aloud. "A what?" she says. "Really?" It sounded like echidna.

"*Echidna. Ochiá*, a sort of snake. You must know it."

"*Ochiá*, I know it! Yes, I see — *échidna*. But in Australia that's a little hedgehog. It lives on ants."

"Then you are mistaken in Australia. Bella, will you listen?"

"*Sorry.*"

"— he found a dead child with a viper at his side and in the name of Jesus he raised that child from the dead. Then he ran to Ermolao eager to be baptised, and Ermolao was glad and baptised him.

"A young man heard of this and came in despair to Pandoleon because he was blind and had spent his fortune on doctors who had promised to restore the light to his eyes, all to no avail. Pandoleon exhorted him to believe and made the cross with his right hand over the young man's eyes. Immediately the scales fell from them and he saw the light and asked to be baptised. After that his own father and many others saw the light at Pandoleon's hands, and he healed the sick for no other fee but their profession of faith in Christ.

"Eaten up with envy and hatred, his rivals, the other doctors, schemed to poison the heart of the king against this young doctor who was the darling of his court. And although Pandoleon raised a cripple when the other doctors called on their idols and failed, the schemers succeeded and he was put to the torture. The executioners broke him on the wheel. They hung him on a post and scourged him and burnt the wounds with flaming torches, but God healed him. They sank him in a pot of molten lead, and God put the fire out. They tied him to a rock and threw him in the sea, but God made the rock float as light as a leaf and so he came safely to shore. They threw him to wild beasts who only licked his feet and for that they themselves were put to death. God would let nothing harm Pandoleon. Then the king beheaded Ermolao and the young warrior who had been blind, and for that God in turn struck blind the tyrannous king who still would not see the truth before his eyes. Next they tied Pandoleon to an olive tree to behead him, and when the executioner raised his sword it melted like wax and the voice of God said, 'You are not Pantoleon from this day but Pandeleïmon, and through you many shall have mercy and be saved.' And the soldiers believed and fell on their knees. But he would have none of it. He ordered them to cut off his head and let him have his martyr's crown, and they obeyed and pierced him with swords and then they cut off his head.

"Then a miracle came to pass. Milk, not blood, spouted out of the veins of Pandeleïmon's throat and at the moment of death the branches of the tree, which was withered, burst into leaf and ripe fruit. Now and forever and in the centuries of centuries. Amen." She made her cross and peered up. "So. And what are you smiling about?"

"Oh, the miracle. Just imagining."

Imagining them hanging, the olives in their hundreds, ink black and bland, in a smoky light, in a pool of milk. What was that story in the gospels again, about the withered tree? Jesus was so angry with a fig tree for having no fruit that he struck it dead. In Holy Week, this was, in spring when it would hardly even have its leaves, or maybe a few, the first few closed green hands of leaf. How could it have fruit? But he got into a pet, as her mother would have said, and cursed it, and the tree withered. He even boasted to the disciples. Why didn't he give it fruit, if he wanted fruit? Bell objected in Sunday School and got a scolding. But it would have been a good miracle then, like the loaves and fishes! Why kill it, when he said he was come that they might have life? And I still stand by that, she thinks. Figs are hardy. Left alone it might have lived and borne fruit in its season for who knows how many more years. Maybe Jesus didn't know any better. A carpenter, after all, he worked in dead wood. But Pandeleïmon has made amends.

Kyria Sofia has a pamphlet she is flipping this way and that. "Let me see. 'The soldiers, although they were unwilling, obeyed and pierced the Holy One with swords and then cut off his worshipful head on the 27th of July in the year 304,'" she reads out. "It was full summer."

"What good fortune it was to be alive then and see miracles."

"Indeed. But the relics of his blood that they keep in the City, in Konstandinoupoli, run fresh again every year on that day."

"As milk?"

"As milk, as blood, how should I know, Bella? Have I ever seen? I can only tell you what the pamphlet says."

"You've told me the important thing. What a wonderful story."

"I said you would like it."

"You were right."

"Why did I choose Pandeleïmon? You know why? Because Grigori was born on that day."

"Oh yes! So he was. Grigori's birthday."

"That's how I always remember his and none of the other birthdays. I have more of these." She taps the ikon on the cover. "They are what you should be reading, Bella, the lives of our holy ones."

Bell has picked up her book. She has it open at her place, though she has not yet stolen a glance. Now she shuts it, smiling: "English is easier for me than Greek, Mamma. And the way you tell them —"

"I wanted to go on a retreat in summer," Kyria Sofia has suddenly leaned forward to say.

"You what? A retreat?"

"Yes, at the monastery on the mountain." She clasps her hands. "I wanted to get away from the world. It is my dream to end my days as a nun."

"I can see you as a nun." Bell puts her book down. "A Mother Superior!"

"A pity my children can't." She permits herself a sour smile. "Grigori said if I tried he would set fire to the monastery."

"*Did* he?" Bell shrugs. "He would never go through with it. What did Vaïa say, and Lefteri?"

"She wants me to go to them if I go anywhere. She won't hear of the monastery either."

"Why not, if that's what you want?"

"Well, I have my duties here."

"How have you?"

"Well, my duties as a householder. And now as a widow."

"What!"

"Once a wife always a wife."

They are on dangerous ground. Bell narrows her eyes. "That would be up to you."

"The grave to take care of, the *papás* to pray for the soul —"

"Baba wouldn't have wanted you to feel bound."

"Ach, wouldn't he, Bella, wouldn't he just!"

The bottom henhouse is as far as the graveyard in the other direction. They set out by a short cut with the tin dish of scraps, scattering the hens in other yards and fields of seedlings before they strike the dirt road down to the river, which from her field, the river field, is only a tangle of bare branches strung like hair, the age-old planes and the poplars. Kyria Sofia's hens come running through the tall docks and thistles at her call of *klouk klouk klouk*.

Where is Zoumbou? Bell thought she would be here. Well, she

goes to bed after lunch, Kyria Sofia explains, blowing the fire up in the *sómba* and rubbing her hands: while she still has a bed to go to. Poor Zoumbou, she is not strong. Make us a coffee if you want. Half a coffee for me, since the doctor insists. So Bell goes out to the kitchen. While the coffee is coming to the boil on the red ring she picks a couple of photos off the wall in the *sála* and takes them over to the window, now that she has the chance of a close look, unwatched.

One of them she must have at home somewhere. It is one she took herself, of Yanni on his first birthday — the date is on the back in her own black ink — cross-legged on the sand over the road from the new shop. He has the dark hill at his back, and the white surf and mist. He sits smiling, his hair alight in a slant of the midwinter sun, bell-shaped, a Buddha.

Grigori took the other photo on Yanni's third birthday. Kyria Sofia is standing in the brutally hot sun outside the barn next to a borrowed donkey, probably Chrysoula's, but all that shows of it is the brown head, ears cocked, because it has a bale of hay roped, dry and green — so it is lucerne, from the river field — to each flank. She has just lifted Yanni on to its back and he is reaching with both hands for the mane. His face is grave, his back straight and proud. His hair is shiny with a grain in it like pine wood. He is just three and this is his second summer in the village, the first one without his mother, and the first time since he was born that they have ever been apart for as much as a day. Not that she and Grigori have separated: that is still a year away. She has stayed behind in Australia, that is all, keeping the shop open, because her father has died and now her mother needs someone with her.

Mamma, her face split in a laugh under the white fuzz of her hair, is wearing a loose blouse that Bell must have left behind; one she had cut out and sewn herself on her mother's treadle machine from a length of sea island cotton so fine that the body inside its blues and greens showed as a clear, firm shadow like a fish underwater, as it does in the photo too. It was one of the first things Bell made after they left the mountain; the material was far beyond her means but she loved it the first time she saw it in the shop when the colours were deep, and no less when it faded and wore thin. So many years of wear she got out of that blouse and it looks like new in the photo. It must still be folded in some trunk or cupboard. Mamma never throws anything out. But being in mourning now — a monochrome in black and white, never to be in colour again as long as she lives — she will have dyed it. She will have stirred it around in the boiling, inky salt water with her other clothes to make a blouse like black water, the patterns of depth and flow obscured.

Kyria Sofia makes a sour face, but she puts aside the lace she is making and sips the half cup of coffee. "Our health. *Amán!* Leave the reading for once." Because Bell has automatically reached for her book. "You will ruin your eyes, Vaïa."

"Vaïa!"

"Oh well, Vaïa, Bella — is it the camel book?"

"No, this one is *The Golden Ass*." She passes it over. "What about *your* eyes?"

"Golden asses and camels, what next? I don't know." Kyria Sofia peers at the picture on the cover, a mosaic of a dumpy, furtive woman with a head ballooning on each shoulder. "Where is he, then, this ass?"

"He tells the story."

"Ach, an ass who talks. An ass who writes. A *paper-ass*, is he?"

Hartogáidaros. Kyria Sofia has made a joke. She is pleased when Bell laughs, although not enough to be deflected. "A lifetime with your nose in one book or other," she scolds. "What good is that?"

"Since it's my nature. I'm a paper-ass myself. What good is making lace? You do it for the love of it."

"No, Bella, I was joking: you are a paper-*mouse*."

Hartogaïdoúra, hartopondikína. "What does it matter?" Bell says with a shrug.

Kyria Sofia purses her lips. "It matters. We never call a person an ass, it's rude. It's an insult."

Paper-mouse, *Hartopondikína*: Grigori used to call her that. He had a fondness for nicknames used as a caress or as a whip in a quarrel. *Vre, vlamméni*, he would shout, which meant damaged, flawed. *Vre, vlamméni*! He often called her an ass. *Vre, gaïdoúra*! Jenny-ass. Not being rude, just meaning that she was stubborn; *gaïdoúra*, he would say, and *xerokéfali*, dry-head. *Hartopóndikina* was much the same, only milder, an affectionate cuff over the head.

"Well," Bell sighs. "This one in the book is an ass who *was* a person but a witch has put a spell on him. And he is caught and worked half to death until one night out of the depths of his despair he prays —"

"You see!"

"— to the Holy Mother by all her names and she appears to him. She makes a man of him again."

Kyria Sofia has her glasses on and is peering at the cover. "Here is the witch."

"No, this is Psychi."

"What are those things on her back, wings? With eyes. Is she a fairy? A butterfly?"

"Psychi, yes, you could say that."

"The Soul, did you say? Then they are guardian angels."

"Most likely human faces, Psychi's sisters. She had two wicked sisters. It says this is a mosaic in Antiocheia," Bell puts in for good measure, that being one of the holy cities of the Patriarchs.

"*Amán*, you are confusing me. Now you say she is Stachtopoula?"

Cinderella.

"Well, she is, in a way, only she is a princess in her own right. This is a very old myth —"

"A fairytale, that is."

A fairytale is a paramyth: *paramýthi*. "This is a true *mýthos*," Bell insists, "about a beautiful princess called Psychi who —"

"You mean her *name* is Soul?"

"Yes. Will I tell it to you?"

"Tell it." Kyria Sofia makes a face at the cover. "If that's what you call beautiful —"

"Well, in life Psychi was. She was so beautiful that the people worshipped her and kept saying she was Afroditi no less, an Afroditi in the flesh. Soon Afroditi herself hears about it and in her anger she sends *Love*, her son Erota whose arrows are poisoned with lust, to humiliate the girl by making her fall in love with someone hideous. No man on earth has ever yet dared to ask for Psychi's hand. Her sisters have both married well, but the fortune-teller foresees that the fate of Psychi is to be sacrificed on the high rock above the city to an immortal being, a sort of snake of fire —"

"The dragon. That is Satan."

"Well, a demon anyway, one that even the gods feared. Overcome with sorrow they dress her in a shroud and the wedding procession climbs with torches and dirges up to the high rock as if to a burial. But Psychi says she will accept her fate and go to her husband, 'even if he has been born for the destruction of the whole world.'"

"You see? Satan."

Kyria Sofia, busy at her lace, has her glasses on and glances up over the milky lenses at Bell. The cloth is the work of a winter of nights and covers her lap in white petals, circle on circle.

"Well —"

"Who else could it be?"

"Well, no sooner is she alone than a soft wind lifts her off and lands her in a valley with a palace of silver and gold, full of voices, and in the dark of night the man she has married comes to her bed and takes her to wife. He is gentle and she can tell without needing to see how beautiful he is. Every night he comes and by morning he is gone again, because if she ever sees him or learns who he is, he warns, they will be utterly destroyed.

"All this time everyone has been thinking that she is dead. Her sisters come to the high rock wailing so loudly that she hears and has the wind bring them down to the palace to see for themselves that she is well and in bliss. What they see drives them insane with envy, but they hide it well. Psychi suspects nothing when the next time they visit they say they have heard that her husband is a monstrous snake, swollen with venom; that the farmers have seen him at nightfall with the veil of the mist flaming all around him. They say he is only fattening her up to eat her alive, and her child too — Psychi is pregnant by now. Her only hope of salvation, they say, is to arm herself with a sharp knife and a lamp and kill him in his sleep.

"So, late that night Psychi, still torn between faith and terror, sharpens the knife and lights the lamp and lifting it high at last beholds her man, who is no man after all and no snake but a young god cradled in his wings. Her hand shakes, and a drop of the hot oil falls from her lamp on to his shoulder. He cries out in pain. Then the lamp goes out and in a black rush of wings he is gone and she is left crying to the gods to save her. This is when she falls into the hands of her mother-in-law, who hates her even more now if anything —"

"Like in the saying. The daughter-in-law's bread always comes out sour."

"Indeed." The saying is a popular one with the village women, young and old. "All the more so when the mother-in-law is none other than Afroditi and she finds out that her son has defied her: worse, he has succumbed to his own venom and fallen in love with a mortal woman. And of all women, Psychi, who is his mother's mortal enemy! In revenge Afroditi claims Psychi as her slave and sets her one terrible task after another. The last one is to run a message to the queen of the underworld. How can Psychi hope to get out of there alive? In her despair she climbs a tower, and is ready to jump and put a quick end to her torments when the tower takes pity and tells her the secret. She must take two sops of barley bread in honey water, one in each hand to calm the guard dog, and hold two coins in her mouth for the ferry there and back. Charo must pick them out with his own withered hand as he always does. And Psychi makes mistakes all the time but the gods let her off in the end —"

"Ach, I see. So it is a fairytale."

"Ti mýthos, ti paramýthi?" Bell shrugs: "What difference does it make? And they marry Psychi to Erota and make her an immortal."

"The Soul always is immortal, as everyone knows. You don't need to know letters to know that. I would have learnt many letters if I had my way as a girl. I wanted to be a teacher," Kyria Sofia says, "and if my brothers had not interfered —"

"Grigori told me. It was one of the first things he told me."

"I would have been a good teacher. Do you know that my brother — not the one in the village, my older brother who is forgiven — he lost an eye? Well, God put that eye out. Because he stood in my light," Kyria Sofia says.

"*Ela*, Mamma!"

"Yes! Yes, I tell you! He withheld the light from me, the light of learning. And so his light was taken. Not all. Half his light. One eye."

Kyria Sofia whimpers suddenly, so close that Bell jumps and in her shock slaps the book shut in her hands.

"What? Are you all right?"

"I think I must have gone wrong."

"Ah? Let me see."

Kyria Sofia holds the lace up against the light from the window, leaves and petals and hooked threads in a dark web.

"This is wonderful, Mamma. You were always golden-handed."

"But I will have to unpick it here. See the mistake? Look."

Peering close, Bell remembers an old photo, a failure she threw away, of these hands in a blur because the camera was too close, or shaking, or it was the hands shaking. A face as still as a stone and small, and these monstrous hands that filled the frame. No. She tips her head back in denial: there is nothing wrong with the leaf under the yellow fingernail.

"Yes, there is, look harder, there," Mamma insists, close to tears. Her glasses are two grey moons. She will pick and poke with the hook until her eyes are running, as Bell knows only too well.

"No, no mistake. It might be a bit tight, but that will iron out. Why not put it away for now? The light's gone."

To Bell's surprise she obeys, wrapping it carefully around the hook and sitting back with a tired sigh.

"And you? What are you knitting now?"

"Me? I have given up knitting."

"What did you do, *jánoum*, with the lace cloths I made for you that time?"

"Two are on the dresser and the others I have put away for Yanni when he marries," she says, and Kyria Sofia sniffs, satisfied, until Bell takes up *The Golden Ass* again.

"Erota!" she snarls.

"What?"

"There are decent books, Christian books, you could find to read in Holy Week."

"Didn't you like the story!"

"I was taken in, that's all. I thought it was a Christian story. You said the ass prayed to the Panagia. You said it was about the Soul."

Bell tosses the book down with a sigh. "Well, it is. It's a parable about the Soul."

"It is profane, Bella. It raises the devil high. If you want a parable there are any number of good ones in the Holy Scripture. Or I have the latest *Life*, now why not read that?"

Kyria Sofia pokes her glasses up on the bridge of her nose and blinks as Bell scans the pages of *Life* with sinking heart. Not the American magazine, of course, but a church pamphlet, and she *has* read this, in Athens and on the islands, or at least the front page, plastered all over the walls of bus shelters. It brands the Jews as the Antichrist who will bring about the realm of Satan and the death of the world in fire and brimstone. The Jews have been scheming for centuries to take over the world. Among their evil weapons are the credit card and popular music. The Jews are behind the music industry, all those songs which everyone knows carry messages from Satan when they are played backwards, and some are Greek songs, not only American, always at their work of evil, gnawing like rats at the foundations of our being.

She hands it back. "I have read it, Mamma."

"Already?"

"I read it in Athina."

"And the sermon about the Tree of Life?"

"No? The tree of life?" Bell stares. "You mean the olive?"

"What olive? The Cross, *kalé*! The Cross is the Tree of Life! What are you making big eyes for? And the fruit of the tree is light — the light of the world."

Erota, Bell thinks, Eros, Cupid, the names he is called. Monster, Satan, devil, demon, a *daimon*, Socrates said, a force of life. I know on what grounds he might be hated. Who doesn't? Eighty and she can still spit out his name with real hate. Everyone alive must have a grievance, a story they could tell about Erota, the power of Erota, if it were fit to be told. Maybe Psychi was never to look him in the face or know his name in case the spell would be broken and she saw the demon. But she doesn't, she still only sees the beauty of him, and this is true to life. Her lamp is like Eve's apple, only Psychi is allowed to regain her paradise. Which is not true to life, Mamma is right there. It has just enough truth in it to last. Some of which is below the surface. The prohibition, for instance. It's a strange thing, but as soon as you fall in love you can hardly look at each other, and the loved one's name becomes hard to say. It swells in the mouth, inflamed with too much meaning. Not only the first time; this happens whenever you fall in love.

On the mountain Grigori's name was Greg to everyone of whatever nationality, except me. He was Grigori to me from the beginning, and *agóri mou*, my boy, and *agápi mou*, my love. I had been Annabel, and Bell at home, and now I was Anna Bella, then plain Bella, and *angeloúdi mou, moró mou, katsíka mou*; my little angel, my baby, my nanny-goat; and in the bush in the sun once and his shadow was heavy overhead: you are a flower of the mountain, he said, *eisai louloúdi tou vounoú*.

"What will you wear, Bella?"

Already the old woman has the light on and her hands in the case with the airline tags still flapping on the handle, and to forestall her Bell grabs at a sausage of blue denim, her skirt, and drops the lid down smartly. Her brass Buddha is in there, wrapped in a jumper and forgotten until this minute. What if the old woman has seen! But it is the sight of the skirt that makes her head jerk back and her tongue click.

"Why, Mamma?"

"Tsk. Impossible."

Oh, come on. *Ela*. Bell sighs. Come on now. She shakes it out and holds it out, so full of creases that it looks pleated. It goes half-way down her calves, doesn't it? And it is too thick to see through.

"What else have you got?"

"*Ela*, Mamma!" Bell has her hand firmly on the lid of the case. "Just jumpers, underwear —"

"It won't do."

"This is the only skirt I have."

"I have a black skirt that should fit you."

"I want to wear my own skirt. That's what I brought it for."

"Yes, but not to church."

"What's wrong with it?" She pulls the skirt out wide under the lightbulb so that it looks like a blue tent with a lamp on inside, a wind tugging at the seams. "See how thick it is."

"But look at it, *jánoum* — blue jean! And not that jacket."

"It's a cold night."

"You look like a gypsy in that jacket. Have you a cross?"

Bell fingers the opal on its chain. "Only this."

"A jewel?"
"It was my mother's."
"What happened to the cross from your baptism?"
"That was seventeen years ago."
"Since we are going to church!"
"Does the Holy Scripture say what we have to wear?"

Bell has rolled her eyes and sighed, a mistake. Kyria Sofia rears up. "It's not only the Holy Scripture, it's the Church. An insult to the Church is an insult to God, because the Church is the body of Jesus."

"I thought the worshippers were."

"Bravo, yes, exactly. The living body of God. Don't you fear God?"

The bells ring out. Breathing hard, Bell turns and pulls her jeans off and her skirt on, and fumbles around for her pantihose. She finds Kyria Sofia waiting outside the iron door and they walk out together without another word. Their shoes clap on the road. The houses as they pass sink in the darkening cold mist.

Agio Dimitri's, and the pines surround with their high stiffness and gloom the square tower, blue-washed, where the stork used to nest. The lamplight stains the long windows and drifts with the gingery incense smoke in the nave and along the aisles. Men stand on the right, women on the left; but hardly anyone is here, only a group of widows at the front who turn with a smile, Zoumboulitsa among them, and wring Bell's hands with whispers of welcome. Zomboulitsa points out the families of the *papás* and the *psáltis* while Kyria Sofia, fumbling for change, lights a wax taper and pushes it in among the others bristling in the sand. She nudges her companion, who only rubs her forehead, biting her lips, and will not look her in the eye. They are standing up close to the ikonostasis, so close to one of the two candlesticks that the breath of the flame lifts their hair. These two candlesticks are new, she mutters in Bella's ear: the ones that stand for the pillar of fire and the pillar of smoke which led the people of God out of Egypt.

Bell hears. She smiles. There is a new *papás* as well, the rusty grey one having given way to a bushy young man who is one long flow of black, all hair and beard and flapping sleeves and hems, a stranger. Striding by in the glitter and rustle of his robes he booms at her warmly, he shakes hands and calls her Kyria Bella. He was a schoolboy when she was Grigori's wife, surely she remembers? Not Chrysoula's son from over the road! Well! And here comes Chrysoula herself to plant kisses on Bell's cheeks as the service begins. The new *psáltis* who is chanting the responses in Barba Nikola's place is also young, a tenor whose plainchant echoes and coils, soaring, pure as a clarinet, into the dome as if it came from the mouth of the Christ painted there to brood over the congregation, the Pandokratora, the All-powerful, at the height of the noon sun. The worshippers beneath stand in silence except for murmurs of *amín*. *Nin kai aeín* sounds and resounds, now and forevermore, and the ancient prayer of *Kýrie eléison, Kýrie eléison, Kýrie eléison*. Furled in incense, the priest paces among jingles and chimes in front of a wall of saints with fierce faces whose robes flap in the golden wind of another world.

Out in the wet dark among streetlamps, mud puddles, shadows, in the pine-bristling air she has to laugh. "So that was Chrysoula's little boy under all that black beard and cloth! Who would have thought he had it in him to be a *papás*!"

"If the beard and the cloth make the *papás*."

"*Ela*. He seemed to know what he was doing. He knew the liturgy."

"That is not to say he has it in him. A man is either born with it or not. He will never master the plainchant."

"No, not like the *psáltis*. What a voice that man has! He has a golden voice."

She smiles to herself. They were stationed as always at the back of the *psáltis*, inches away, and tonight there was not a peep out of the old woman. What a shame. They are the only ones taking this way home and their steps are loud on the shadowy asphalt. At the gate Kyria Sofia stops suddenly, raising her hand.

"Bella."

"Yes?"

"Tell me," Kyria Sofia says as they turn into the yard. "I really want to know."

"What?"

"What got into you?"

"What do you mean?"

"Not once did you make your cross. Not once, Bella. I was looking. All the world was looking. Not one candle did you light! A shameful thing. To be there and take no part in it!"

"I did, in my own way."

"Ah? What way is that, can you tell me? The Protestant way? The Catholic way?"

"Is that what all the world goes to church for, is it — to look?"

"Because there is only one Orthodox way, as you know very well. How do you think our Church got its name?" She waits for an answer. "You wear no cross, Bella, and you make no cross. You who have been baptised! Here! And you married here, and baptised your child! All the world knows who you are! All the world knows you are one of us and you belong to our Church!"

In the house there are cold foods to be laid out on the card table, picked at and put away, the last logs burning down in a sour smoke and no more to be said.

TUESDAY

In a waking dream Kyria Sofia is in a clearing among strangers who are digging open an earth oven and passing out lumps of food. Her share is a baby baked brown. Still warm, it lies calmly in her hands with its eyes closed. Its skull is a tight helmet. Gulping down her vomit, she creeps to a stone wall nearby, breaks the baby at the neck and hides the head in her apron. The body she will feed to the birds that have come flocking in low under the storm clouds. The meat is so soft, so perfectly cooked that it crumbles like new bread and she is tearing it into little pieces when she wakes up.

Bell creeps to the *méros*. She crouches above the seat in the glare of the lightglobe and holds her breath while the piss runs, knowing of old how it sets the deep smell loose. She was here when the *méros* was no more than a hole behind the barn, hidden with brambles and fertiliser bags. Once the cesspit was dug and closed over they threw in the corpse of a calf to start it working; she saw the annexe grow brick by brick and the whitewash go on. *Asvésti*, it was called: not what she thought of as asbestos, but lime, quicklime. A pit was dug by the gate to hold it. The old man put up a high fence and warned the grandchildren that if anyone fell into the pit the lime would eat him to the bone in no time. If no one found him, soon the bones would be eaten as well and no one would ever know what had become of him. The level of the pit rose and fell each time it rained. It drew the boys, the danger of it. They dared each other to climb the fence, standing close to the edge, closer, their feet on the white-splashed lip. The neighbourhood children hung around after school. Throw a cat in and watch, go on, she caught one urging, who looked guiltily around at her, warned by the faces of the others. The lime pit lay just outside the bedroom windows, too deep for the surface to show unless she walked close; then it shone, white-veiled. In the full moon it was like a sand bar or thawing snow and, fascinated, she stayed up one night taking a set of time-exposures of the white swirls and slivers of the moon. Fiendish children in her sleep threw a cat in and watched as it sank, swallowing a shriek under the scum of white, and the bones writhed. Didn't the cesspit have buried in it a whole stillborn calf that you could still smell under all the human sludge of shit? *Slaked* lime, whatever that means: there is such a thing. Was this lime slaked, and did that make it more or less harmful than unslaked? The pit fed and lay licking its lips. While the household slept after lunch she would come out and find a group around one or other of the bolder boys who would freeze, still hugging a fence post, at the sight of her; and the circle of awestruck onlookers would scatter. But their warped little faces would be there the next day, the shaven scalps bared like knuckles.

There is not a sound in the house as she creeps back to bed, and only the strange blank light at the windows, mist, a heavy sky. It reminds her of the snow light in this room the year she was pregnant with Yanni, how long ago? Eighteen years, towards the end of her time here: she left to give birth in Australia. There is the same light and silence now. In the rooms on the mountain in Australia where she and Grigori met, it was the same winter light.

Znow is *hióni*, Grigori said, teaching her Greek, and this was in 1961, thirty years ago.

Hióni. I hióni?

To hióni.

I love the snow. *Agapáo to hióni.* Don't you?

Me, no. Znow mek me sick.

It is beautiful though. *Oraío, to hióni*, she said, and he shrugged and answered in Greek. She could follow by then more or less, as long as he spoke slowly.

Not if you have animals to feed, and no food, no wood ... Me, I love the sun. The heat. The summer.

The lake was starting to freeze at one end and men were already out there setting up the lanterns in readiness for the night skating. The usual short cut, a brown path through rocks with a glassy overhang of shade, was clogged and frothy, blocked with snowdrifts, and you could only get to the lake by the road. They got a lift on the truck and went stumbling about on the shore where the ice was thickening. Her hands froze while she photographed the trees fading into the mist, the familiar rocks patched with snow and lichen, all their colours deep with wet. She sank to her knees, shivering, and her feet burned. When they came back he towelled them dry. She had a bottle of cream buried in the snow on his window sill which she mixed with honey and they ate it with a spoon, sitting folded together in his rug and the mist of their breath against the dim yellow wall.

The village has snow? she asked.

Yes, too much snow, and his mother fattened a piglet to kill every Christmas, he told her, and potted it under a lid of lard as firm as ice and buried it under the snow. That way it lasted all winter.

And do you make ski? No? She had to look up skating. *Patinage?*

In the village? No. Are you cold?

Yes.

One day we will have a hearth and burn wood, he said into her hair: Yes? You want?

I want. Later she went over this in her head and looked up the words he had used — yes, *tzáki* was hearth. She saw herself in a room of firelight, with Grigori. It has work, a hearth with wood, she said next time in her awkward Greek. Who will have the time?

I know. But my mother will help. And my father.

Have your mother and your father a hearth?

Sómba. They burn wood.

A *sómba* was a stove. A wood stove.

Where will we live?

Who knows? First we will find work and when we have children my mother will look after them.

But *I* will do that.

That is how it is in Greece.

I want to be the one.

The mother is always mother. My grandmother brought me up too but I love my mother more. I love my mother more than anything in the world.

What about me?

Then you.

That will have to change!

The mother never changes, Anna Bella. She is always mother.

"*Kaliméra*, Mamma."

"*Kaliméra. Podge?*" Kyria Sofia casts a thin smile at the saucepan.

"What? Oh, *porridge!*"

"As I said. *Podge.*"

"Mamma, you remember it all."

"All, all."

After breakfast Bell makes her bed and sits on it cross-legged with the Buddha on the sill, the shutters open but the curtain shielding him, breathing slowly, for as long as she can bear the ache and the stiffness. Even her breasts ache. *I lay awake remembering us in the snow,* she writes in her diary, *Grigori and me all of thirty years ago.*

Kyria Sofia, having stoked the *sómba*, slumps down on something hard on the divan and pulls out from under her black haunches a book of Bella's, the erotic one. Soul! she mutters. Love! Her lip curls. The cover is bent double, the picture creased of Psychi and the faces, and so what? It deserves worse. Bella should count herself lucky that her dirty book is in English, otherwise it might end up with the lavatory paper in the yard to be burnt. As she folds the cover back flat with both hands, something on the title page catches her eye: a mass of words that with her glasses on she can just see, though not read. They seem to be in English except for the Greek letters at the start of each line, A and T and B and P; and they are handwritten in ink as black as the ink in Bella's bottle. On top she makes out Anna, something in between, and a large M. Now who is this person who calls Bella Anna? That was the name she was baptised under, since it was the nearest Christian name to her own. Who would call her that, though? Someone in Australia, is it, some man? One thing I do know, she loves this book, the way she sits and moons over it alone by the *sómba*. M could be a Michali, a Manoli, a Menelao. Who knows how many more in her own tongue? Maria, for that matter — Martha, Marianthi, Marina, someone innocent, some friend. No, the black letters are in a man's hand, if I know anything. Even in English I can tell. I ought to burn this, if the truth be told.

I lay awake remembering us in the snow, Grigori and me all of thirty years ago. No time to her at all, at eighty. Μαμμά, όλα τα θυμάσαι, I said, and she gave me a look and said, Ολα, όλα. The yard, the swish of branches, olive leaves. Olive trees are everywhere and the village looks as I dreamed it would before I saw it. The plum tree is like a snowfall. Last time the sun had sucked it dry. Black plum skins left to hang.

The island houses are paved inside and out with the same grey stones as the streets, outlined in whitewash so that they seem to be in shallow water, a lazy thread of ripple. Here the bedroom floors are wood. The σάλα and the kitchen were tamped earth at first, then raked cement, and now cement tiles with marble chips and a scurf of white dust, and the woven rugs of winter.

We all went for a swim in the river, black and cold, the pool at the roots of the plane trees, when it was running deep and — this was in May, my first year — clean enough to drink. A red gold fin. The green of our skins as we crawled in under the leaf shade.

Her story of the saint tied to a fig tree with milk spouting from his wounds. At the full moon the young Gautama broke a long fast with a bowl of milk rice brought by a girl in a blue dress like water and then he sat under a fig tree with his legs coiled under him while he strove to be enlightened.

The plum has white flowers, bears black fruit. The olive. A fig or an olive tree she said the saint was tied to? The tree of enlightenment = the living fig. The tree of knowledge?

Together they walk through the silent school-yard to pay a visit to Kyria Sofia's living brother and the daughter-in-law who looks after him now in place of Magdalini who is forgiven. He sits quietly smiling at her, at Bella, at the neighbours who have followed them in. The television is on as always, though he pays no attention. It takes up half the wall in this *sála* kept dim behind the red velour curtains, where the only light is in the row of liqueur bottles cut like jewels, ruby, emerald, amber, luminous now in the light thrown by flames on the screen, spouts of fire. The niece brings in a tray with chocolates and glasses of water and pours Bella a glass of molten emerald so sweet it bores into her teeth. And how is our Yanni? they say. Is he a good student and when is he coming back? Or has he forgotten us? Of course not, how could he ever forget, Bella answers, one eye on the screen. The program is footage of the aftermath of the Gulf War and Kyria Sofia, disdaining all but the glass of water, takes a grim satisfaction in the way these fools can sit all in a row and smile and sip their jewel glasses of raki and munch their chocolates day by day on the lip of the volcano. No spring this year, by the looks of it, her niece is saying yet again. The whole Mediterranean is lying today under a pall of darkness, an announcer says in English, the sub-titles running in a white line of Greek over his collarbones. *Desert Storm*, he says again and again. A black beach glossy with pitch appears, a neck heaves up, a torn wing, and Bella is staring hard at gushes of fire on the screen now, the glass forgotten in her hand, as well she might. Is it just a picture show, that they pay so little heed? Is it a shadow play? — but if so, we are the Karagiozides, and the lantern at the back of the sheet is hellfire. This gloom day after day, this calm, what do they think it is, if not a warning to all mankind, a herald of the last storm, the day of the wrath of God? At the end of time the earth will turn black and the moon blood red, and the stars will fall like unripe figs as in the vision of Ioanni the Evangelist on Patmos, whom Jesus loved as himself. So he said on the cross: Woman, behold thy son! Fire, brimstone, and the first rumblings now of Armageddon to come. Already the wells of pitch are burning in the sand of the desert for the world to see. The smoke of their torment has made the sky black, and the rain, and the soil, and whatever is alive in air and sea. There will come rains of hail and fire mixed with blood. The solid earth will be lakes of fire, seas of blood. Then the angel will open the bottomless pit with a key and the great dragon, the snake, Satan, will be thrown down. That he should deceive the nations no more. And whosoever is without faith will be tormented with plagues and sorrows. They will all be crushed in the winepress of God.

Lord have mercy, she mouths, Lord have mercy, Lord have mercy. She closes her eyes. We shall all rise at the end of time clothed in our own flesh and blood and God will give us a raiment of air, of fire. Of the earth and her sorrows there will be no trace remaining, and no more sea.

The television leaves an after-image. How else to explain that on the way back home she sees nothing of the mist and the slimy length of the road, but only a fountain that sprang in the sky's summit, a waterfall, the flailing white arms of the water, and her darling, her Yanni who was doubly her son in that he was the son of her son, dearly beloved, struck down — he was sixteen years old — at the heart of the storm with the whole sea roiling, ink black and running in streams of fire, spouts and blinding showers, a white fire.

Zoumboulitsa is already waiting by the *sómba*. She has brought a dish of boiled weeds which she uncovers the moment they walk in and pushes into Kyria Sofia's hands.

"What is this now, Zoumbou?" Kyria Sofia peers, frowning.

"*Lápatha, kalé*. Fresh, picked this morning."

"What for?"

"For you. For your kindness."

Kyria Sofia sniffs the weeds. "Well" — she is on the point of relenting — "since they have no oil."

"They have!" Eagerly: "Salt, oil, they are ready to eat."

"You eat them then! You know I am fasting." And Zoumboulitsa's face falls. "What got into you, Zoumbou? You should know by now."

"Well *I* will eat them!" Bell takes the bowl. They have long taproots, dark red: docks, they must be. "*Amán!* How beautiful they smell."

Zoumboulitsa looks up with a stricken smile.

"Well, take them inside, Bella."

"And will we have coffee?"

"Not me," Kyria Sofia snaps.

"You, Theia?"

Zoumbou inclines her head to one shoulder in a shy gesture of acceptance, and Bell whips out to the kitchen, still so cold and dark that the refrigerator light makes her blink. She stirs the coffee on the little electric eye, as it is called — *máti* — a glaring red eye, and looks blindly through the window at the barn wall. The hens are squabbling in the yard. When she goes in with the tray, Kyria Sofia is absorbed in a pamphlet.

"How black you are." No sooner has Bell sat down than Zoumbou sidles up. "*E*, Sofia?"

"Am I?"

"Someone who saw you on the bus thought you were a gypsy!"

"Ah? Doesn't everyone know me by now?"

"Not the young ones. Or a fortune-teller!"

"I wish I was. They make good money."

"Indeed. You must have had plenty of sun on your holiday."

"Plenty." Shaking her head, Bell avoids meeting Kyria Sofia's glare of vindication. "And when I left Australia it was summer. We were in the water all day."

Oblivious, Zoumboulitsa salutes her with her cup and takes a sip. "Where did you stay, *kalé*? On the islands?"

"In rented rooms."

Having drunk her coffee to the dregs, Bell swills them and turns the cup upside down in the saucer to be read.

Kyria Sofia has a bitter little smile. "Mind you, she was not on holiday, Zoumbou. It was a job that took her to the islands."

"*Kalé*, what job?"

"To take photographs."

"There is money in that?"

"If I am lucky." Bell shakes her head and smiles. Her nose is blocked and, fumbling in her pockets for a tissue, she has pulled out her keys and the dangling silver hand. Zoumbou leans forward to stroke the fingers. "How beautiful," she says. "A lucky charm."

"Sort of."

"It holds a pen? No, it presses a shutter!"

"Do you think? With photographs, it's more the eye, though."

"Well, and you have both!"

"What? This?"

She fingers the opal and Zoumbou shakes her head, gratified. "*Málista*. You wear the mother's stone."

"The photographs are for another book," Kyria Sofia says.

"Not this time, no, a film. A videotape."

"You mean to make a film out of plain photographs?"

"Slides. Why not?"

Kyria Sofia sighs and Zoumboulitsa, looking sidelong, sighs too and lapses. She has her hands open in blessing to the heat of the hoarse *sómba*. Her cup is also upside down waiting to be read, and Kyria Sofia is the best *kafedzoú* in the village, but clearly she is not in the mood.

With the phone out in the *sála* and the doors kept shut all the time for warmth, Kyria Sofia is lucky ever to hear it ring. Bell has to tell her. Again and again she runs out to grab it — *Nai? Vaïa, esí eísai?* — and bangs it down crossly. Bell drops her notebook to sidle out and ask who it was. No one spoke, Kyria Sofia snaps. It might have been Yanni, Bell says. Why might it? And why would he not speak, if it was? There is a pause, Bell says, a moment of delay on international calls — something to do with space, the satellite, and Kyria Sofia sniffs. She knows that, thank you. Bell has begun to despair of ever speaking to her son. She accepts that she is not to ask to use the phone and offer to pay for the call. Nor is she prepared to betray Kyria Sofia by going behind her back to the public phone at the kiosk in the square in front of the neighbours and their knowing smiles: not yet, anyway. At last, lying in wait, she hears the phone ring and catches it just as the old woman's hand reaches out. *Yanni?* she says, and her son's cracked voice comes out of the autumn night of Australia.

"Yiayia? Mum! What's wrong with Yiayia? She keeps cutting me off."

"She can't hear. How are you? Where are you?"

"Dad's. What are you doing? What time is it?"

"Morning. Just reading. Is it cold there? It is here."

"Nuh. We just got back from a swim."

"A swim!"

"There's a heat wave. Who else is there?"

"No one, just Yiayia. Vaïa and Andrea and the kids are coming at Easter. How was your Easter, good?"

"We're waiting till this week, same as you."

"Red eggs and all?"

"I suppose."

Bell passes the phone to his grandmother, who shrills questions into the mouthpiece with a hand over her free ear.

You wear the mother's stone, *Zoumbou said. The mother stone. The opal is the stone of Ops who was* Δήμητρα, *the earth. And* *the moon is a mother stone, as are all mountains flowing with ice and snow, rivers of milk.*

FADE IN on an opal? Slow dissolve into water at sunset, evening, moonrise — the high full moon, silence. FADE OUT into the sea, full moon again and silence.

The old woman has company and Bell is free to go for a walk. She takes the road to the cemetery, picking blue grape hyacinths and rosemary on the way and reading the stones on the Civil War graves, the fierce epitaphs; and drops the flowers at the marble foot of the cross on his grave. Again the shock of the name, and she stares, shaking her head. There is something wrong. ΙΩΑΝΗΣ: they have left out an N. She takes her camera out and sits waiting for a stain of sunlight on the grave, a close-up for Yanni, and a few from a distance with the black oak trees in the background. The rosemary as she passes is full of bees. A speckled apple tree has started to put out its green crowns.

Kyria Sofia and Zoumboulitsa look up as she comes back in, and then sit back. Chrysoula is with them. The chocolate olives are out on the table, and a dry coffee cup. They were talking about her, these three in their black dresses. She can see it in the fox-brightness of their eyes. They remind her of the three nuns she found selling lace, who looked up into her lens in response to her flattery, cajolery, in just this derisive way, not for a moment taken in, but in a mood to be indulgent. Black hoods, white lace. The nuns, and the widows too, in their courtyards and on the shores.

"Kaliméra sas," she says.

"Kalispéra!" they say, *kalispéra* because it is afternoon now; and welcome, *"Kalós tiná!"*

"Sit, Bella, sit." Kyria Sofia sniffs. "I was looking for you."
"I went for a walk."
"So."

Chrysoula's eyes are busy on Bell, noting everything. I am in black myself, Bell thinks, for that matter, and I can hold my own as far as slyness goes.

"What do you see, Chrysoula?" she says, and Chrysoula puts on a wide smile.

"Are you happy, Bella, to be back?"

"Of course she is!" Zoumbou puts in.

"Very happy. Mamma thinks of everything."

"*Má!* You see, Chrysoula? Mamma, she calls Sofia. Well I never." Zoumboulitsa can still hardly get over it. "Just as I was saying. A mother who gets on with her son's wife is rare enough. But after a divorce! And how long has it been now?"

"Fifteen years. But I was here eight years ago."

"So I heard," says Chrysoula. "I was in hospital at the time. You were not here long."

"Eight days, and eight in Thessaloniki."

"You will have stayed at Vaïa's?"

"Yes, that time I did. This time I went straight from the train to the bus. Well, I went up the White Tower first, and after that."

"What for?"

Bell shrugs. "I always had a wish to see inside."

"*Má!* You went up the White Tower!" Chrysoula takes a chocolate olive. "I never have. A prison that was, under the Turks."

"Yes, it's all cells inside, a honeycomb of cells."

"In the old days it was known as the Tower of Blood."

"I know."

Kyria Sofia glances up scornfully from her lace. "The Boy Scouts meet there."

"Not now, it's a museum. You should see it, Mamma, Theia — the cells are full of holy ikons."

"As if we have never seen a holy ikon."

"These are age-old."

"*Kalé*, where would we find the strength to climb the tower?"

"*Má!* You say well, Sofia."

In the silence that falls, a log seethes and shifts in the *sómba*.

The women shift uneasy buttocks. Kyria Sofia is busy at her lace. With every movement of her withered hands the wheel of lace touches her clothes with a scrape that sounds unnaturally loud, like a moth at night on the pillow.

"Well!" says Chrysoula. "It is good to see you back. You have not changed as much as we have. The blackening suits you." Meaning Bell's suntan, and she pauses for a compliment in return. When none comes she sighs and stands up. "Does Grigori know you are here?"

"She asked him" — Zoumboulitsa jumps in — "and he said yes, go, he said, go and be with my mother."

"*Má*. Australians must live in a different world."

"My son is not Australian," says Kyria Sofia.

"Have you ever seen the like? Don't you think they are Ruth and Noemin all over again?"

"*Ade*, Zoumbou, now! And my son is alive."

"This is as close as I come to having a family. I was an only child. My father died when Yanni was little and then when my mother died," Bell is saying in a rush, "the same year as our marriage broke up, you see, I wrote to Mamma about all that. About my mother, and having no one now —"

"Sofia cried," Zoumbou bursts in. "Her eyes were all red."

Kyria Sofia shakes her head. "And then Grigori said Bella had left us a bit of money in her will. Us old ones, I mean." The three old women smile as one. "Not that we were likely to outlive — it was the thought, though, and how she felt about us."

"— and having no other mother," Bell finishes weakly, gaping, aghast, since she has never made a will.

"*Má!*" Even Chrysoula is lost for words. Kyria Sofia gives Bell a rueful smile and shake of the head. *Má!* And the fat tears are brimming again in Zoumboulitsa's eyes.

At last she can catch her breath in her room. She gapes again every time she thinks of it. Her will! Whoever makes a will at thirty-five? Did she really tell Grigori she was going to leave money to his parents? Well, she must have done! And Grigori, who can never keep anything to himself, will have rushed to the phone. What on earth did they think she had to leave? Part of what came to her from her mother, obviously, and now that she thinks back to those days, the thunderstruck first week after her mother died, she does vaguely remember something of the sort. Her will! So that's why they have gone on accepting her? Loving her? Under false pretences, for all these years! She had better make a will, then, hadn't she, the minute she gets home! She throws herself down on the bed, her head in her arms, torn between shrieks of hilarity and howls and afraid — someone will hear! — to let a sound out.

There is not a sound anywhere. She sits up, suddenly sober. Where are they? Still in by the *sómba*, probably. And while she was out, where were they? Might they have been in here? Surely not! She pats the pillow, sure that she can feel their presence, her flesh crawling. It has happened in the past and why not now? But she finds the thought hard to bear, that they might have come in and gone through her case, her clothes, even found — after all, they could hardly fail to find — the Buddha. Bell knows she is at their mercy. There is no safe hiding place. Under the pillow, in the bedclothes? The bed is hardly sacred, is it? Out of the question to lock her case. She can't, for the very reason that Kyria Sofia might come prying, find it locked and be scandalised, and rightly so. *I* give Bella the run of my whole house and look what she does! She locks her case! What an insult!

On the other hand, not knowing what she might find, would Kyria Sofia risk exposing her to Chrysoula? Not necessarily, but it depends. That woman! Little Golden One, hah! To think that she is the mother of the *papás* these days, Chrysoula! She has gone up in the world, hasn't she just — and the next world. No wonder she gives herself airs. Through no doing of her own, here she is, closer to God. Let Sofia be as jealous as she likes, and all the other old women who vie for the favour of the Church. Chrysoula has stolen a march on them. *She* has a blood tie.

In a strange way, being in the Tower was like being in church. A spiral stair around the inside wall opens into this maze of cells, brick vaults with wooden beams, low arches. The windows are narrow loopholes, deepset, with outer bars and inner glass: pigeons' nests in the space between, one with two shaggy chicks on it, the parents preening one another. Watched, they edged uneasily away. Glimpses as if from a lighthouse of the misty sea, the city walls, a faint red ship suspended. A lighthouse, a dome.

As if we have never seen a holy ikon. These are age-old, and how weird to see them all crammed in there on folded screens under lock and key — a warden even kept pace alongside, with a jingling of keys — when all over Greece they live on, kissed and censed in the candlelight. The higher up, the more recent the exhibits were, and the more cramped and small and dark, as if the Tower itself came to a dark point. It comes to a dead end, at any rate, the battlements being out of bounds. I thought I sensed in the ikons themselves a sort of shrinking from the pagan light, the hills and seas of the tomb walls on display on the ground floor, and all the mosaic skies and fields and seas of the heyday of Byzantium, into these dark little oils on wood, full of twisted ecstatic limbs, these interiors. Some have wings that fold over on hinges like shutters. Is this in recoil from the Turks, the hundreds of years in the full glare of Islam? A retreat to the dark, the cave and the crypt, candlelight. A faith like a bee in amber.

I have not lighted a candle or made my cross once since I came, and yet I came in good faith, fully meaning to take part.

For lunch Kyria Sofia has gone out and picked *lápatha* and boiled them in water with no oil. Bell puts Zoumboulitsa's *lápatha* on the table as well. When she dares to fork some on to her plate, Kyria Sofia asks if there is something wrong with her own *lápatha*. No, Mamma, of course not, Bell says, munching an olive: but yours will keep longer, being fresher. A sneer crosses Kyria Sofia's face. She thinks she understands. They all know how Bella shrinks from sharing. Since the day she first came she has put a serving spoon in the dishes when no one is looking, only to see them take it out and turn it to the light in puzzlement: whose spoon is this? She knows they accuse her of the sin of disgust, of pride; never to her face, but to Grigori. *Syhaínetai*? Is she disgusted? Do we disgust the *nýfi*, is that it? No, no, but if it has been dinned into you as a child that any shared food, one suck of a straw or bite of an apple, can cripple you, kill you? She tried to explain to Grigori. If you grew up in a polio epidemic and your parents were afraid to let you go out and play; and classmates of yours were away from school for months and then came back with their legs in irons, or never, and you only knew when their names were announced at assembly? And you went cold and sick in case it was you who somehow had made them die, you never knew. You might have got it. You might be next. So we have germs, is that it? he said. And you are clean, only you? Of course not. Only that custom was as heavy a weight on her as it was on them, and this was a prohibition that no effort of her will could shift.

Of course *we* grew up in one room with a dirt floor, he said later, abruptly.

OK. I understand.

Rats fed on the babies in some of those houses. Noses. Tongues.

"Since I told Zoumboulitsa I would eat her *lápatha*," she says now. "Would you want me to break my word?"

Kyria Sofia sniffs and will not look at her or speak for the rest of the meal and the dishwashing.

Kyria Sofia drops a photo in Bell's lap, Vaïa's family in a park in the sun. "Oh," Bell cries, "the new baby?"

"Hardly new any more."

For a moment there of utter derangement — it is not even born yet — Bell was seeing Grigori's new baby. But this is Rina's child, of course: Kyria Sofia is a great-grandmother. Vaïa and Andrea are grandparents. Andrea is holding her upright, his hands in her armpits. She is Rina all over again, as she was when Bell first saw her. "How time passes!" she says. She has photos at home of a Rina not much older than this, learning to walk in the shade of the grapevine: the old woman stands at the child's back holding her hands and steering her towards her grandfather, who is kneeling with his arms out. One of the photos is a close-up, a masterpiece, the golden face, the shadow of each eyelash, Rina with her thumb in her mouth, her eyes slanting away and down. Behind her in a blur of shadow the women of the family are spread out under the acacia tree with garlands of leaves in their arms, threading tobacco. Rina!

Sonya looks older than thirteen, posing here cross-legged with Rina and their brother, the other Yanni. Vaïa has grown stouter. Not Andrea, though, who lives on his nerves and tobacco. Almost bald, he has the same shabby, sharp-eyed face and rueful grin half-hidden under a grey moustache.

"You'll wear it out with so much looking."

Bell relaxes and smiles. "I just can't get over it. Who took it?"

"The baby's father." Kyria Sofia sniffs.

"You don't like him?"

"Another foreigner."

"I thought he was Greek?"

"Greek, yes, except that he is from Mytilini," she says, and now Bell sniffs. "The Red Island, as they say. And he is one. A big Communist."

"Really?"

"How else do you think they met?"

"And she is in love?"

"Sigá!"

"No?"

"She *says* she is, Bella, or so I am given to understand. Not to me."

"So where are they living?"

"He moved in with them."

"At Vaïa's?" She counts on her fingers. "That makes seven." In a flat that can hold three comfortably, five at a pinch.

"Well, he should think himself lucky, Bella. Both of them

have yet to graduate. As soon as *he* does he will have to go into the army. Vaïa will raise that baby, mark my words. And as many more as they have."

"More!"

"I hope so. Should they stop at one child?"

Their eyes meet.

"More," Bell says. "When they can't take care of one."

"With God's help."

Silence. By way of breaking the deadlock, Bell takes the photo over to the window. "He looks every inch a grandfather, poor Andrea." The skin of his face is sagging with tiredness.

"*Amán vre!* Who cares how Andrea looks?"

"I always liked Andrea."

"*He* is high up in the hierarchy. A Communist cadre these days."

"That's the reason you dislike him?"

"You think I am short of reasons?"

It is common enough knowledge that Kyria Sofia has never liked Andrea, and Bell is only being mischievous. She grins at the photo. Tall and blond, rawboned, he is a man of silences — one who has a heavy shadow, as they say here — intense, dour, almost as out of place in the family as she is.

"He has his good points."

"He is selfish."

Egoistís? Is he, though, Bell wonders. Dour, but he was a dancer when the spirit moved him, in those days anyway, a passionate, strenuous dancer, a Nureyev of the *tsámiko*, all the village said.

"He is a good teacher. Well, they both are, Vaïa too. He was always good with children. Their own and other people's."

She remembers a summer afternoon when Andrea hung a sheet across the back of the *sála* before there were any ikons and shelves of photos there, and cut out and painted a set of the cardboard Karagiozi figures for the boys, Yanni and Yanni, and a houseful of cousins. There was a handwoven sheet, which must be still around somewhere in this house where nothing is thrown out. It swayed and creased like water with the torchlight in it as Andrea, crouching out of sight in the corner, wagged the little jointed figures to cast the shadows, sharp and blurred, and drawled their speeches, which he knew by heart.

"When he was in the mood, at least," Bell goes on into the silence. "Do you remember his Karagiozi?"

Kyria Sofia snorts and sets her mouth hard.

"Didn't you enjoy it? Baba did. He said we were all Karagiozides. God's Karagiozides."

"He had no right to say so."

"And Grigori picked it up from him." Kyria Sofia bites her lips. She will not find fault with Grigori. "There was one about — I wish I could remember — Karagiozi and? — I know! Alexander the Great and the Snake. The Accursed Snake!"

"So what, Bella?"

"Just that he is a good family man."

"He has a nasty way of flaring up out of the blue. For all his cold blood. He goes wild."

"I know." She does. "Being the type to bottle things up. I think he is sorry afterwards."

"Ah? So long as he is sorry? And he will go too far and kill somebody one day, you mark my words."

"Sigá."

"From the time he flared up and hit the boy" — Kyria Sofia squints up — "there was never any question of liking him."

"What boy?"

"Their own Yanni, the time I brought him back to live in the city with them. You remember. Two years I had him here with me so she could go to work — you *know*, you were over here then, you two, together — and Yanni was *my* boy. So of course he clung and ran after me and fought Andrea off, and Vaïa too. But Andrea flared up and yelled at me to get out. I had to gather up my things — I took too long, it seems, with the boy wailing. Andrea slapped him to the floor to shut him up."

"But Mamma, this is ages ago!" The boy is a few weeks older than Bell's Yanni, going on nineteen.

"Yes, he was a boy of three. Not even three."

"He has probably forgotten."

"Probably. Children do. *He* has not, however. How do I know? Because when it came to Sonya — how they did it I have no idea — they kept her in the city with them from the day she was born."

"Was he injured?"

"If you had heard him scream! I had my hands over my ears all the way down in the lift. *Yiayiá mou!* And after all I had done. He knows, Andrea knows." She squints up sharply. "He is sorry afterwards, is he? Let the boy forgive him if he likes. That's up to him. But it was me the blow was really meant for and I do not forgive. Did Andrea ask me for forgiveness? I saw the truth that day. He had to hit the boy and do you know why? I tell you to know, Bella. It was for loving me more."

The sheet was tinged yellow wherever the light pooled in its folds, and hung from time to time with a haze of smoke, Andrea's cigarettes. At one edge was Karagiozi's hovel in lumpy silhouette and at the other a webbing of glassy panels, domes, a palace: the *seraï*, said Andrea. A monstrous winged snake was preying on the townsfolk, and the Pasha had proclaimed a reward for its head. There was its cave, and Karagiozi, no fool, jeering at a safe distance, as one by one his neighbours came and ran for their lives or were swallowed with terrible snorts and roars.

Mamma might scoff but the old man loved his Karagiozi. From the divan where Bell had found him close to death a few weeks before, he watched every move of the shadow play with glittering eyes and a wry mouth. Rina rang the bell to start and played the music on the gramophone; the three Yannakia, for once all together in the village, did the voice of the Accursed Snake whose fate is to sink writhing and groaning under the sword of Alexander the Great, in full armour, and even he has to rely on Karagiozi to pull him out of the Snake's gullet. Off he goes to the Pasha for the reward, leaving Karagiozi to play the hero and meet his downfall; because at the feast the town puts on for him, who should turn up but Megalexandros, brandishing the Snake's tongue. Karagiozi ends up with a thrashing and Bell remembers how fervently the old man clapped, sweating and wincing with silent laughter.

At the table afterwards Grigori was inspired to say that his grandmother once had a house snake. It was the first Bell knew of it. Yes, it lived in the ceiling, Grigori said. Of course we never said a word. She fed it, Yiayia Katerina. She gave it dishes of milk behind Mamma's back.

So did our grandmother. Have you ever known a house with an old woman in it and *no* snake? Andrea said, raising a laugh at Kyria Sofia's show of indignation.

At news time Bell tries the radio but a bus crash with a death toll of schoolgirls and an update on a sensational trial leave no time for Iraq and the oil wells on fire in Kuwait which will burn, as they said on television this morning, for the next five years. When she tries the television the screen fills with weaving lines like the sun in shallow water, and impatiently she turns it off. She only has to go next door, anyway, or to any house in the village, if she must watch television. Which is worse, to look on or not to look on at the torment of others? When even the desert is on fire! Sitting in front of the Gulf War at home one day, all day, on CNN, she must have pressed the remote control button without thinking, because suddenly the screen was a blue wall, a tall window, and then other windows looking out in silence, one melting slowly into another with painted shutters, and hangings, Matisse! — of course, his works in the time of another war, 1914 and after. Palms appeared, and shutters across a sun glare in the Midi, in Morocco, and goldfish, and women lolling on patterned cloths, and cool rooms with bowls and jars of water, the shadowy Seine, stillness. *Nature morte*, a dying world, and these mirrors of the unshaken mind had abolished the trenches, and they abolished the Scud missiles. One by one they shone out on the screen or folded one over the other until at the end there came the shapes of fish and seaweed, candles, a wall of light, the gold and blue-green chapel in Vence that is a hymn to water. "My chapel is not: *Brothers, we must die*," said the voice on the screen, in French, and the white words repeated them in English. "On the contrary, it is: *Brothers, we must live!*"

Tonight the church is gaudy, swarming with light. Lamps hang in front of each ikon, and the two dishes of sand by the ikonostasis have crowns of flame that thicken as latecomers, black widows and a few men in old suits, come up and light a taper, kiss the glass, make the sign of the cross. Every footstep and rustle echoes aloud and it seems to Bell that she can hear the breath of each new taper as the tip of another brings it to life, and that the air around them warps in the hot light. Her face is burning. The Bible is carried out in its gold case for the reading of the Gospel. Fingers lifted, the saints glare out as if from the portholes of an aquarium, incandescent, garish and crude — of course, in the village church — but still with a Byzantine suppleness and emphasis about them, radiantly suspended. The light flickers in brass and glass and again they ring out, the nasalities and broken rhythms of the plainchant.

Kyria Sofia nudges her. "Make your cross," she hisses.

To Bell, standing wooden, frozen stiff, it could all be a stately slow dance, intricate, full of twirls and back-steps on the offbeat, and they are waiting but she will go on standing there if they wait for ever. The thing is hopeless, and would be without anyone watching and glaring across. She is simply not free to yield herself to the music and lapse, and leap, into the dance. The phalanx of women stirs all around, a rustling of arms and whispers, all eyes on her now under the black scarves. All over the islands and in Athens, caught, steeped in the same light among the women, she made no move to cross herself, did she? No one looked askance there as far as she could tell. She shivers. Here no action is possible.

Bell steps in patches of shine with a star in them and it almost seems to her, making her way back alone, that when she opens the doors on to the gloom of the *sála* she will see the old man as she did in the first Easter week, though all she could really see was a hand spread wide, bone-white, and the gleam of a grinning face. He lay stiff on the divan, grey and wet, groaning. Not that she was alone then, thank God, Vaïa was with her and they were coming back with the baby, Rina, from visiting an aunt while Grigori and Andrea went to church to appease Mamma. Baba was as good as dead, Bell was sure, his eyes squeezed shut and his lips peeled back from his clenched teeth. Vaïa stayed, holding his hand in her two hands while Bell ran to the church — it was a night like this, after rain — and pushed her way in until she saw their heads, black and blond, at the front on the men's side. She whispered to a boy to tell Grigori she wanted him. Grigori leaned his head, attentive. She saw him glance behind until his eyes met hers, then turn to the front again. In disbelief she hung on, but he made no move and at last she had to send the boy to Andrea, who came straight away, thrusting his way out with both arms like a swimmer. What's wrong? he said, and listened while she gabbled and clutched his hands. Then he sprang back in for Grigori.

The two of them put the old man in the back of the bread van and drove him to the hospital at Agia Vrissi for one primitive operation after another under local anaesthetic, it was so urgent: a perforated stomach ulcer, the surgeon said, with blood-poisoning. He needed pints of blood, which they could only get by rushing to Thessaloniki and bartering their own. Bell's and Grigori's blood would not do, since they had had injections before travelling. Andrea gave his, and Vaïa cried when she heard, sure that it would kill Andrea to give blood. Relatives came forward with offers of more. It was a month before they knew if the old man was going to live, and most of that time Mamma camped in the hospital spoonfeeding him and doing the washing. Bell and Vaïa borrowed bicycles once and rode in to Agia Vrissi to find them transfigured by strangeness in the heat of the ward, a woman swollen with weariness on a spare bed, and a shrivelled old man trying to smile for the visitors.

This was in the early days, before Grigori had got his bearings again. In his ten years away the world had shifted under his feet: nothing and no one here was as he remembered. Everything jarred and caught him off balance, she understood how it was. But to spurn her like that so publicly, in church! It was some time before it hit her. There she was barging in, so he assumed, interrupting with some petty excuse, out of boredom or spite, or petulance, and he showed her what he thought of her, showed her in front of everyone in the village. There was no help for it, the thing was done, too small a thing to reproach him with, a whinge, proving his case, as he would see it. What good would his saying sorry have been, anyway? Does *sorry* mend the truth? Mamma is right: it's done in a flash. Andrea was a stranger I had only just met, Bell thinks; but he believed me, he came when I called for help, and the rush of gratitude and warmth has lasted ever since. I am on Andrea's side right or wrong. Just as Mamma has been against him from the day he hit her boy. She saw into the truth of him at that moment — there was no hiding what he thought — as fast as a camera shot, indelible, one flash and before we know what is going on the shutter blades have slid open and that truth is caught and fixed. We have been judged and we have judged. Every day we are betraying ourselves to each other like this in our small and large ways without our knowledge: betraying aspects of ourselves, anyway, since we are all half hidden, more than half. All we do is touch a surface here or there, we rub shoulders, mysteries to ourselves at best and to one other. And at worst, crude caricatures, lay figures, judged and sentenced in the heat of a moment.

It was a moment of truth, we say. How true is it really? The camera lies all the time. It tells half-truths. Don't we mostly see what we know, or think we do, what we expect? Never mind that the one who is judged might have had some other motive, some other factor unknown to us might be involved and the truly important action might be what is happening just off-stage, out of sight, while our attention is fixed on what has caught our eye. No, suddenly we *know*. We have seen into the depths of another soul, just for this moment. Beyond reason we trust in our moment of insight — even if at the same time we are convinced that there are no depths, that the soul and all experience are one flow of surface like shallow water, glinting and hollowing from moment to moment, never fixed, never graspable — which may, must, be why I choose film, choose photography to reflect my world. I must think about this. The false significance of the moment out of time.

Unknowable — what the Buddha meant by *maya*, illusion. What we see in the depths is that there are no depths. But we recoil, we have such a need to find the hidden meaning. So, in our need, we decide we *have* found it. Right or wrong, we cling to it. And we act on it, and the balance shifts. They are hinges in time, these moments. Our lives change course.

Something else jars her memory. Mamma was going to teach her to dance when she came to Greece. She had promised in a letter, naming all the dances, *syrtó*, *tsámiko*, *kalamatianó*, *hassápiko* and, yes, Zorba's *hassaposérviko*. But the only time Mamma has ever danced in front of her was the Sunday of that first Easter, in this yard by the plum tree. Baba was in hospital and Lefteri at sea, but the uncles had rallied round, welcoming Grigori home, and Andrea had set up two lambs on spits. Meanwhile the guests sat at a trestle table in the sun nibbling on *mezédes*, cracking red eggs. There was beer and red wine in demijohns from Agia Vrissi. The radio was on full blast, folk music. An accordion started up. A circle of dancers joined hands and swooped on Mamma, who sprang and twirled at the head of the line, one hand at her waist and the other grasping the handkerchief. *Yeia sou*, Mamma! Bell called out, clapping in time.

Shut up, Bella, Chloï hissed, red in the face.

Look how light on her feet she is!

Now other people were clapping, and others getting up and

tagging on to the line. Kyria Sofia beckoned her and Chloï joyfully in passing.

Shame!

Sout, Chloï!

Shame, I tell you. With Baba half-dead in hospital! Is that all she can do, dance while he wrestles with Charo?

It *is* all she can do. Baba is alive by a miracle. Easter is for celebrating the resurrection! I only wish I could dance.

Go on, then!

She is dancing out her pain. Like in *Zorba the Greek*.

Does it look like pain to you, Bella? Besides, Zorba was a man.

What difference does it make? Don't let Vaïa hear you.

All the difference. She will dance on his grave next.

As if she had sensed something, Kyria Sofia faltered in mid-leap and passed on the handkerchief. Panting, she sat down with her back to Chloï who was still red, swollen with venom, and received Bell's praises with a grimace. But when Bell poured her a full glass of red wine she drank it down, defiant, as the dancers wound past.

Bell gives the iron door a push and the catch slips, not locked, but she quails at the volume of the darkness inside, a density like water, the past waiting in the *sála* to swamp her and take her weightlessly up. She pulls the door to and sits down instead in the cane chair, Baba's chair, her arms along its wet arms, in a smell of whitewash and mildew.

Something else, something Mamma was forgetting, or not saying. There was an afternoon in the first summer when everyone came in together from the river field, which was sown to lucerne for the cows the old man was going to buy as soon as he came out of hospital, two cows in calf, a homecoming gift from Grigori and Bell, and wealth in those days. Everyone came in sunburnt and weary from gathering up the bales of lucerne and getting them under cover while the storm clouds gathered, flickering, and the thunder came close.

There was a late lunch set out, *makarónia* with oil and cheese, the house in darkness — the power was cut — and the kitchen acrid with male sweat. His face dripping, Andrea was wolfing down spaghetti in whole sheaves when a giggle made him glance up. Lefteri had his head an inch from his own plate and was aping him, and he made some remark to Chloï over the table — what? some jeering remark. With a face of stone Andrea answered with a great swipe to the head that sent Lefteri and his plate crashing to the floor. There was a cry, and then a hush of shock as Andrea stalked out of the house, slamming the iron doors at the very moment that the storm broke in their faces, and everything was bleached white, and the roof and the windows throbbed and swilled over. Lefteri picked himself up and tried to laugh it off as a joke that had misfired and it served him right; but no one could speak, retreating to bed in the great rush and roar of water, of thunder and hail, with the yard littered with balls of white hail the size of quails' eggs. Andrea was out there somewhere. Chloï had shut herself in their room with Lefteri and the baby. Vaïa is the one Bell remembers, the way she stood in the corner of the porch holding the baby to her, white and silent as the rain eased; the yard a lake by that time, sprouting little jets of mud. Two hours later when Bell woke up soaked in sweat, her own and Grigori's, and crept out for a glass of water she found the table as they had left it and Mamma quietly sobbing in the dark.

The hail, she said in explanation. Bella, it will have torn the tobacco to shreds.

Agriévei, she said today, he goes wild. He will kill somebody one day, you mark my words. *Sigá*. So might any of us, all of us. The first time Andrea hit a boy of hers, and she has not forgotten any more than Bell has. It was only that this is not to be spoken of. The wound is too deep. The house must be full of such secrets, unspoken, unspeakable: those that are known only to one or two or half-known, glimpsed; and those others that are known to everyone, open secrets, words said, deeds done and never to be undone. What was Lyka saying yesterday? Ghosts and secrets, *fantásmata kai mystiká*. Old wounds, old wrongs in its bones.

A cold blur of brass, the Buddha sits on the coils of a cobra whose hood is spread wide to shelter him. He is in the lotus position with a begging bowl in the palm of the left hand and the right hand reaching to touch the earth in the *mudra* of calling the earth to witness. *Idoú*, sings the liturgy: behold. The long eyes are cast down over an inward smile; the flow of the robe over one shoulder bares a swell of breast under the nipple. There is no inside window sill. With the light out, she has unfolded the panes to put him on the outer sill, a black shape in a rim of gold, the moon on his shoulders, and the streetlamp, and the slatted shutters at an angle — Matisse — so that she can see him from inside but no one will from outside. Closing the panes over for warmth she settles cross-legged on the bed with a rug over her shoulders. She can just see him. Her eyes half-closed, she breathes hard and strains to make her mind blank. There is no movement in the house, no light in the cracks of the door, no question of eating. In the end she unfolds her stiff legs with a shiver, slips the Buddha under the pillow and lays her head painfully down. The sheets encase her in ice.

WEDNESDAY

The morning air is muted, swarthy, or so Bell imagines. She wanders out to the yard with her coffee cup, hoping that none of the neighbours will see her and call out a greeting as early as this. The old woman must have gone out. Zoumboulitsa will be here soon, not that Bell is looking forward to it; she is in no mood for company today. A smell of smoke, diesel from the bus or a tractor, hangs in the air. Every blade of grass is as still as the fat hyacinths. They and the leaves of the olive saplings have a slick of shine, but they feel dry, cool and dry in her fingers. She goes in and makes her porridge and a second coffee with the light on in the kitchen, so little of the daylight comes in. *Moundós*, she thinks, is the word for this weather: sullen, scowling, burdened with snow, with rain and other things impossible to shed, smoke or ashes, or soot, an air of desolation swaddling the whole earth.

Zoumboulitsa is standing breathless at the door. Bell sits her down by the *sómba* and makes coffee.

Kyria Sofia comes home clutching a scrawled letter with an Australian stamp, full of photos.

"*Kaliméra,*" she says, waking Zoumboulitsa.

"Sofia! *Kaliméra, kaliméra.*"

"*Kaliméra*, Mamma. Has she had the baby?" Bell says too loudly.

Kyria Sofia scans the page through her glasses and folds it. "Not yet."

"She must be due."

"He will ring."

Without even glancing at the photos she presses her lips and the envelope shut and takes the glasses off. Bell is not to ask for a look, it seems, either because the sight might wound her, or because the mere fact of her seeing might bring harm on the new wife at this fine point of balance between two lives. Or for both those reasons. *Ekane to moró?* Her own voice rings in her head. Has she made the baby? Made comes closer to the truth of it, when you think.

"The new boat is ready. Did you know he owns half a boat now?"

"Half?"

"Half a fishing *kaïki*."

"Much good that is, half a boat!"

"A half-share, *jánoum*."

"All right, Mamma. I understand."

She squinnies without her glasses. "He says they painted the name on yesterday: *Sofia*. They are sending lobsters and shellfish alive to Asia by air. They have ten staff now in the restaurant."

"A pity it wasn't like that in my time, Mamma. It was us two on our feet all day and half the night with a baby and a wood-fired stove."

"I say it only because this should have been the fruit of *your* hands."

Bell shrugs. "Since I have other fruit?"

"Marriage is never easy for the wife. It takes work, it takes patience. If only you had had patience, Bella!"

"I did. I had no choice. I had patience."

I *made* patience, Bell is thinking: in Greek you make patience, just as you make a child. Patience which is the child of — what?

Kyria Sofia gives a heavy sigh. "Since you are good friends enough now? All you had to do then was sit on your eggs and wait for the hard times to pass —"

"That was *all*, was it? We are friends now but back then it was open war. What do you know? You weren't there. It was death to stay." Having gone too far already, she says what she has never said to a soul: "Listen. He threatened me with death."

"Well — well, as you said, Bella, yourself —"

"What!"

"You said he would never go through with it."

"It was life or death and that's all I have to say."

"And so it was life to go, was it?"

"As you see."

"As I see! Do you want to know what I see? A barren life. No man, a child who lives with you now and then. A desert."

"No —"

"What, no, Bella."

"It was war to the death. He thought he owned me body and soul. I had to work together with him, don't forget, just the two of us because we couldn't afford *any* staff at all. It was war day and night, nothing I ever did was enough, and on top of that I had a baby to look after. I was not as lucky as Vaïa, don't forget — "

"I know, I know."

Bell pounces. "Grigori wanted your help but so did Vaïa. You chose Vaïa. You looked after *her* son" — much good it did you, her look says, and the old woman's face concedes the point — "and I had no one to take the baby off *my* hands. My own mother was not well enough. Have another baby, you said, and then I will come to Australia. Instead I had a miscarriage. I lost —"

"I know."

"— two babies in two years."

Kyria Sofia has her haggard stare. She hangs her head. Bell has fought back too hard, brutally hard, to her shame, drawing blood, in front of Zoumboulitsa which makes it worse. And cheated as well: since when did she want Mamma or anyone taking the baby off her hands? Every word of what she has said might have been true — was true: the lie was in the essence. Not that the old woman knows. Bell has won, for once. No doubt she will pay for this, but she has silenced the inquisitor.

When Bell comes back from the *méros*, Zoumboulitsa is alone.

"Where has she gone?" Bell bites her lip.

"Back to church. She is great-souled, your mother-in-law," Zoumboulitsa says.

"Yes, what a good word. Great-souled she is."

"Great-souled and golden-handed and I am not saying that lightly. I only lived through the winter because of her."

"She is happy that you come here."

"She has had a hard life."

"I know."

"So you may, but not the way I know, after having lived alongside her all our lives. Nothing was easy. I tell you to know, Bella, it has been struggle, pure struggle."

"It is her nature, I think, to struggle."

"So it is, and that is why it's up to you —"

Why what is up to me? But Bell knows. Zoumbou is staring at the fat barrel of the *sómba*, tears in her eyes. The woman is a fountain of tears, for God's sake, and the *sómba* is burning too sleepily now for warmth. Bell grabs the hook and lifts the lid off.

"It wants wood, Bella."

There are two split logs on the metal apron. Bell drops them in and waits until they turn gold, the flames running in their jagged edges, before she drops the lid back on. *Megalópsychi kai chrysohéra*, as Zoumbou said, the lovely formal compound words of praise, so full and resonant, with an aura of the litany about them, and so commonplace. Everyday words. You hear them all the time. Bell was golden-handed herself one day, when Yanni was little and she was knitting him a jumper. They were out on the porch with a group of other women when Mamma grabbed hold of the sleeve and scrutinised the pattern of honeycomb and cable. It might be too big for him, but he will grow into it, she said. The others all wanted a look and Bell flushed red with pride as the jumper was passed around among the smiles and murmurs. *I chrysohéra i nýfi mas*, Mamma said, and Bell in her confusion took it to mean that she was a golden widow. Mamma, what an ill-omened word to say! she exclaimed, and they were all puzzled until it was straightened out. Because *híra* is widow, and even a divorcee is a sort of widow in Greek, a *zondohíra* or living-widow, alive in death. But she was neither, after all, was she — then. By the time she sent a photo of Yanni in this jumper of braided wool, playing in a riverbed of wet and dry rocks and shadows near where they lived, in the same town, only apart: by then she was. Is it the same river? Kyria Sofia asked in a letter. As in the first photo, she meant. It could have been, when Bell came to think of it, and besides the question gave her heart. Never the same river. It was a sign that Kyria Sofia was also on the watch for the continuities, such as they were.

"Now it burns well, Bella."

"Ah. Is the wood enough, Theia?"

"Enough, enough." Zoumboulitsa sighs and smiles.

"What if I chop some?"

"If she asks."

"There's an axe out in the barn."

"She might be upset."

"So long as she doesn't do it."

Zoumboulitsa jerks her head back. "*Jánoum*, where would she find the strength?"

"I'm not sure I could lift that axe, to tell the truth."

"No, well, then! There is a boy she can call on, Manoli's Yordanaki, he's a good boy. That axe, *amán*! The famous axe."

"The axe? Why?"

"It's the same one your Grigori held over his father's head one Easter to stop him slaughtering the lamb. That's how far back it goes. There was your father-in-law with the knife at the lamb's throat and Grigoraki brandishing this axe he couldn't lift. Both shaking with anger!"

"And who won?"

"Who do you think? Grigoraki was his darling. Yanni had to go out and buy a dead lamb. *Amán!* How we all laughed!"

"He would have no problem now."

"And then in the Civil War? No one has told you? Well, you know after the Occupation — the Germans, Hitler? — there was the Civil War? Yes, well, the *andártes* had their strongholds in the mountains. In these parts they were in the caves above Agia Vrissi, and they came down one night like wolves and looted every house in the village. They herded the men together at gunpoint up the mountain, leaving us women and children to starve. Any man too weak to walk they shot and left where he lay. My Christo was wounded. He would not have got far, only that Yanni and the old *papás* half-dragged, half-carried him and luckily it got dark quickly. Once there it was easy to hide the state he was in. Anyway, Sofia grabs the axe, the very same axe, *kalé*, and she walks the length of the village with it to the house of the leader of the *andártes*. In broad daylight, and not a soul to be seen. Your man has taken my man prisoner, she shouts through the shutters, and if he is not back here at my side by tomorrow, my lady, I will chop you into a mash, I swear before God."

"Wonderful! And was he?"

"He was, he escaped! No thanks to them."

"Just as well for the lady!"

"For everyone."

"What house was it?"

"The last one on the left on the road out, before you come to the bridge."

"The beekeeper's house?"

"You know it."

"Not the beekeeper? That gentle man!"

"No, no, his father."

"The beekeeper was his son? He came here with honey. He was a friend. He even helped dig the cesspit!"

"They were on good terms. Let me tell you something else. At the end when peace of a sort was made, that leader, the beekeeper's father, walked into the *kafeneíon* and hit your father-in-law full in the face in front of everyone. They all urged Yanni to hit back but he stood firm. The war is over, he said. Let an end be made to it.

"When he got away that first night, though, what he did was unwrap and oil the gun he had fought the Germans with and join up against the *andártes* — the village was a battlefield, can you imagine? — and we women gathered the children up and fled to Thessaloniki."

"And your Christo?"

"Yes, when his wounds were healed he got away as well, Christo got away and he fought together with Yanni here and in Kilkis and Agia Vrissi until the *andártes* shot him dead. In Thessaloniki they tricked Yanni and some of the others from here into laying down their arms and took them prisoner. When the wives and children were called in to see their men they had to pass between two lines, *andártes* and their families, who battered and spat on them. You can ask Sofia to know."

"No, how can I just ask, Theia?"

"Yes, why not?"

"It would bring back bitter memories."

"It depends. I think — don't we all want our stories known? They burnt the house down too, the *andártes*, did you know that?"

"I know. Grigori was there."

"He was, he was! When he was still a boy. He and his grandmother, Katerina. They got out through a back window. They saw the houses torched, theirs, ours, house after house in flames. She said it was the Catastrophe, Theia Katerina. Smyrni all over again."

"I remember they were saying the same thing when the Turks bombed Cyprus and we all thought Greece would be next, and instead the Junta fell."

"Yes, and no wonder. None of us who fled from Smyrni will ever forget. I was a child and I see it in my sleep to this day. When it was over and Yanni came back — the Civil War was over, I mean — he made the the new house with walls a metre thick. You only have to feel them and you can tell. It's a fortress. No eaves, no second floor, and that was because the fire caught in the eaves of the old one and spread upstairs through the floorboards. And the *andártes* looted first. Houses, barns."

"But you had all taken refuge in Thessaloniki by then."

"We had all taken refuge and no one was harmed, glory be to God."

In a glint of the sun, a street of branches with all their buds, fat red wicks. The kitchen garden, the *bahtsé*, is no more than this field of weeds, windswept, where the neighbour's hens strut and flap their combs. Bell has got her bearings by now. There are no beds of tobacco seedlings, of course, now that the fields are rented out; but more trees have gone as well, or else she doesn't know them by their skeletons. Even so, there seem to be fewer skeletons. The pomegranate that grew by the fence with the plum is gone. The weeds are deepest where the two old apricot trees were, on whose trunks the hammock was slung in summer. But there are spiky black trees further on that look like young apricots. And the corky limbs poking their long fingernails out of the ditch, those are the figs whose leaves were shabby with all the summer dust of the road, broad hands spread to a fire.

The way to the shop takes her past a muddy field by a high white wall where hens are straying and little boys have gathered to kick a soccer ball. She pulls up short, because this used to be the summer cinema, she is sure, before television, when the Junta sent a mobile cinema to all the villages in turn: a jeep manned by recruits with shaven heads who set up the projector after dark, mobbed by children. Everyone came an hour or so before the start, gathering in front of this whitewashed wall to spread their cushions and *kilímia* in the moonlight, slapping at mosquitoes. The film was a farce she had already seen with Grigori in Melbourne, with long gaps while the soldiers changed reels and the cigarette smoke rippled in the shaft of light overhead. This was in the days when no one had a car, when even a tractor or an irrigation pump was a rare and precious thing, so that the river ran high and as clear as glass. There was still only one phone, to which you were called by a loudspeaker, but they had electricity; all the houses were close to having pipes and a tap, and pure cold water laid on. The little ones have no idea, Bell thinks. At least half the population is too young to know the village as I know it.

The boys have called a halt to stand staring at the stranger. She moves on. *Hello*, one calls warily at her back, *hello, hello*, on two owl notes. *Hello*. She turns like Mr Wolf to face them and they freeze, panting, staring up at her with her own son's eyes, though the faces are not his. Any one of them could have belonged to Vaïa's Yanni, or to the other Yanni whose sins are forgiven, such as they were at his age: round faces, long-nosed, their olive-gold faded from a long winter. One of them smiles, the ball clutched to his muddy chest, the leader.

"*Hello.*" She smiles back.

"*My name is Jimmy, what is your name?*"

"*Bella. And what is your name?*"

"*My name is Argyri!*"

"*Very good. And what is your name?*"

"*My name is Yanni!*"

"*I have a son called Yanni.*" The boys exchange looks. "*He is older than you.*"

They could easily know him by sight, her Yanni. Their older brothers might even be friends of his.

"*How old is your son?*"

"*Eighteen.*"

"*He is in the army?*"

"*No, he is a student.*"

"*Is your son here?*"

"*No, he is abroad. In Australia.*"

"*Hello, my name is Lazaro!*"

"*My name is Taki!*"

"*You all speak very good English. Goodbye.*"

"*Good byee! Good byee!*"

Behind her someone punts the ball and a yell goes up. The hens at the edge of the field are squabbling over something shrivelled, a snakeskin, or a sausage-skin, she thinks, until the victor dashes across her path, spraying mud, with a condom in her beak. It occurs to her that Yanni must often have come here to play, all those summers he was in the village with his father: he and Vaïa's Yanni, competing as always. At first when they were only little it was Vaïa they had fought over, Vaïa's hugs and kisses and her bustling exuberance, following her around endlessly, calling, like magpie chicks: *Vaïa mou, Mamma mou.* But the other day when Bell had brought up Vaïa's fondness for him he denied it; she might have fooled him as a child, but he knew now that Theia Vaïa only loved her own. The same as everyone, Bell said, and he looked. Not you, he said, you left yours.

These days the shop is self-service and has rows of cans and jars from all over Europe. There are people she recognises, two or three, and the others have heard who she is by now. "How well you speak still, Kyria Bella!" the shopkeeper says.

"It is coming back to me slowly, slowly."

"How long is it since you were here last?"

"Eight years."

"Only eight?"

"Much longer since I lived here."

"*Má!*" someone joins in. "Here in the village? And did you learn our tongue at school?"

"No, I picked it up here and there."

"And she knows other tongues," one tells another.

"Well, so do you," Bell says. "You know Greek and other tongues."

"Of course."

"Yes, she says well."

With the groceries she buys bottles of retsina and one of the red wine that used to be sold from the barrel in Agia Vrissi. Smiling, the shopkeeper overcharges her and is casual when she pulls him up on it. All over Greece the same thing has been happening this time. Tourists are fair game, she accepts that, and has made a point of playing it by the Greek rules, her eyebrows lifting in scorn, or a grimace, a murmur of reproach — raising a song and dance, as her mother would have said, but with no show of anger. Among neighbours the rules are different: you save face. She smiles, she knows. Yes of course it was a mistake.

She drops the heavy bags on the table and the bottles roll out. Kyria Sofia goggles at her. "You went and bought wine?"

"Since Vaïa and Andrea will be here tomorrow. They drink wine."

"Let them buy their own!"

"I have to put in my share."

"Nonsense."

"Well, I do." She shuts the retsina in the refrigerator.

"What made you say tomorrow? They are coming on Friday." Kyria Sofia has emptied the bags on the table and is going through them, scowling with concentration.

"Oh, no!"

"Friday afternoon."

"Why so late!"

"They have school tomorrow. Is this honey?"

"Honey, but they only had German."

"Yes, the German is cheaper."

"The beekeeper might have some to sell." Probably not, she knows, at this time of the year, but now that she has been reminded of him, his house is not far, just before the bridge on the road out.

"What beekeeper, *kalé*? He has been dead for years. And there was no need to buy Nescafé. They bring their own."

"He was not very old! What did he die of?"

"Cancer of the lungs."

"No!"

"Poor man. He suffered."

That gentle man. Or if not gentle — how should she know? — sober, softly spoken, earnest in conversation. What was his name again? And now he is dead, the honey and the gentleness of no avail.

"Since he would smoke. Like your father-in-law." But Kyria

Sofia is holding another bottle up to the light, her mouth twisting in scorn. *"Amán!"* she says. *"Tahíni?"*

"Since I have eaten all yours. Will they bring Beba?"

"Who, Vaïa? They can hardly leave her behind, I suppose."

"I wish she had a name."

"What difference does it make?"

It makes all the difference. Having no name leaves her in a kind of limbo, known only as Beba, just as Yanni was Bebi for two years, and Bouli. If, God forbid, Beba died, the death would be announced of an unbaptised infant, *aváptisto vréfos*, as if this were no more than a stillbirth or a miscarriage. She is not a child of God until she has a name. The servant of God, says the *papás*, and then the name: *I doúla tou Theoú*. Bell shivers. They will wait for Grigori to come in the summer, she guesses, and have his church wedding. Then Beba will be baptised along with the new baby, his baby, if all goes well, the same as the Yannakia.

"I was just wondering what they will call her," she says into the silence at Kyria Sofia's back.

"Vaïa. Of course."

"*Will* it be? Not the groom's mother's name?"

"Tsk. Vaïa."

"Who does she take after, would you say?"

Kyria Sofia sniffs. "The mother. If you can call Rina that —"

"Does she? I can hardly wait to see her."

"— When Vaïa is the mother in all but name."

I doúla tou Theoú, *Vaïa*. But the one Bell is most looking forward to seeing is their Yanni. This is partly the old fondness and partly a rivalry that goes back to the first summers here: the days when there were three Yannakia, and whose was strongest, bravest, cleverest? These two were the closest, so much so that even now she thinks of their Yanni as her Yanni's other self, a dark one where he is light, her son's shadow. Yanni is sure to ask her for news. It is less than three years since he flew over here to join Grigori, just for the eighteen days of the school holidays, and Andrea took the two Yannis up Mount Olympus. Their long bodies in the grey slopes and crags of sunlit rock: she has them clear in her mind, from the photos. She was breathless with pride at the time — how many boys of fifteen in Australia have climbed Olympus? — and soon after, only a matter of months, with relief that these two had risked death and come through, when the third whose fate was tied to theirs that day in the church was struck down.

"I hope they remember the wedding photos," she says now.

"What wedding photos, *kalé*?"

"Rina's."

"Rina's wedding? They are here."

"Where!"

For once there are none on the wall of the *sála*. Kyria Sofia pulls them out of a bag with a show of scorn and Bell peers close. They are shots taken in quick succession. Thrown into shadow by the flash in the church and in the rainy street, the groom in the background is dark, thick-haired and heavy, while the bride is bleached white but for the dots of fire in her eyes, and a red smile. Her dress, like her long hair, is black, and a red rose dips on a stem from her shoulder over her heart.

"Any of these would be good on the wall. Let's put one up before they get here?"

"This? Look at her — shameless! In black for her wedding!"

"Was she in mourning?"

"Rina, in mourning?"

"I thought she might be." Her grandfather was still alive then, of course. "For Yanni?"

"For a cousin? What are you saying? And in a dress like that?"

The dress is black silk draped in folds across her breasts, not a low neckline but loosened a little, adrift in a stir of dark air around her, like the wave patterns of turbulence that are painted around a sitting Buddha, Bell thinks; not the wind but her own warm movements, as if she had been caught in a dance.

"It's a beautiful dress. She looks ecstatic, I must say," Bell says, though the photo she has picked is a close-up in which the marble smile could as well be one of helpless terror. "But too young to be married."

"Rubbish!"

"I mean unripe."

"Rina is as ripe as she is ever likely to be."

"I've read somewhere that in Greece, in the days before Christ," Bell says, "it was the custom to dress the bride in a shroud for the wedding," and Kyria Sofia casts her a hard glance.

"Why?"

"How should I know? To ward off the Evil Eye?"

Kyria Sofia puts her hand out for the photos. They are hard to see in the grey light. "If a girl should die unmarried," she says after a silence, "we bury her as a bride. Which amounts to the same thing, more or less, I suppose."

At the end of a silent lunch the phone suddenly rings and Kyria Sofia runs out to pick it up. Yes, yes, speak, she shrills. Yes, she is here. All is well, yes. Whoever it is has to shout so hard that even Bell in the kitchen with the door open hears the voice say then, in a little metallic squeak: "Is she fasting?"

"Yes." Kyria Sofia can say that, since Bell is not eating meat. "Yes, she is. Only what am I to do, she won't worship, *paidí mou*! She won't pray or kiss the ikons or light a candle or make her cross, she is scandalising the world —"

Paidí mou. It must be Grigori. Who else would Mamma be calling my child, my boy? No, it could be anyone she was fond of, *paidí mou*, said with that edge of impatience. What does it matter? Bell has cleared the table. Leaving the dishes she walks through to the *méros*, bolts the door and stands breathing in heavily in the half dark all the damp smells of lime and seepage and shit. Now they are even monitoring what she eats! The light that comes through the bars of a square hole high in the wall is enough for her to see the face full of drops of rust in the mirror over the basin. It is more her mother's face. More and more her mother's, as she peers up close, leaning forward, her brow wrinkled with worry that Grigori might not like the food, and nodding, saying, Was it hard at the Chalet, Greg, or were you used to Australian food?

We all shouted out our orders, Bell said. Remember, Grigori, at breakfast the first day —

It was thirty years ago.

Breakfuss, oh God! *Potch egg*? I say, hwat is? And *scremble egg* — hwat? and he threw his arms out in despair. Look, mate, you a bloody cook or no? chef say. I *cook*, I say, I bloody *cook*! Get a bloody move on then if you *cook*, you bloody Greek bastard, *he* say.

The chef was an Australian, was he, Greg?

Nuh! Nuh! Lebanese bastard! And her mother laughed, already won over, Bell saw, though her father munched on, grimly aloof.

Later outside they were shy with each other, she and Grigori, swinging by one hand on the trunk of the gum tree in the backyard at Murrumbeena, the tree that filled up every year with caterpillars like prickly tentacles, rainbow-striped, enormous, and yet they were invisible in the light of the tree; you only knew they were there when you reached out to grasp a branch and soft flesh was writhing in your palm.

Grigori? You are welcome in our house, she said slowly in Greek.

Good people, you parents.

They love you, she said, again in Greek, there being no Greek word for like. No half-measure. *S'agapáne*, which was a lie, in her father's case, but even he would have to come round in time.

You father very dignity man.

I'm twenty-one, anyway. My life's my own.

Good people. They know I em Orthodox?

We never talk about it.

Yeah? You *Christianí*, you? You parents? English church?

Scottish. Deep down I'm an atheist. *Sto váthos eímai — átheos*?

Hwat? *Atheos*! Och, my mother eat you!

The dishes are washed by the time Bell comes out; the kitchen is empty in the half-dark of afternoon. She puts her ear to the door of the room with the *sómba*. Slow snores. Relieved, she retreats to her room and closes the door.

I gathered grape hyacinths and rosemary for the grave. (The stonemason has left out an N.) Rosemary for remembrance. Rosemary = δενδρολίβανο, tree incense. I took photos close up and from a distance with the black oaks behind for Yanni. Day after day of this cold mist that hardly ever lifts, all day the same grey light, no way of telling the time of day or phase of the moon.

Stillness without calm. I sit in meditation. Flesh into brass into spirit, το πνεύμα. The breath and also the spirit. The holy breath.

She will never forgive me for the divorce, any more than she will forgive Andrea for hitting the boy. I never asked her to, anyway — forgiveness being beside the point. She could have cast me out. I have one shred of legitimacy left, I suppose: I married Grigori in church, which is more than the new wife has done so far. And bore him a child — a son! (If it had been a daughter?) And never remarried. I am at a loose end, and so she accords me a place as her grandson's mother. To give her her due, this is more than kind. Merciful. She gives what I did ask for. (I could have kept a daughter.) I want to respond. Why can't I? Because the gift is conditional on the cross and the candle, and there a wall of glass brings me up short.

Ιδού, and I obey: I behold, I observe. Observe and observance, the gulf between these, can it be bridged? How?

The *sómba* is stoked high and in the heat Kyria Sofia is asleep before she knows it, and standing out in strong sunlight on a platform, alone. She casts a shadow as thick as her black dress on the base of a wall on which are carved two ladders or lattices of sandstone as high as a bell tower, and woven around a rung here and there of each ladder a snake, a hank of red-gold stone, is falling headlong, the one immense, the other smaller and shorter. Their heads are not the flat spearheads of ordinary snakes but blunt and bug-eyed, fanged, monstrous. Level with hers, they glare down at the earth, into the earth, in a convulsion of rage and terror. The scales growing back towards their tails turn into feathers, or they are feathers all along, or flames. There is no one she can ask out here in the sun where the heat of the stone batters her, and the snouts stare, pitted rock with scales and folds that cast a thin shadow. And yet they are insubstantial, she knows, because she has been here before. They are air, not stone, as light as a spider on a ladder of glass.

The old woman snores on under the blanket undisturbed as Bell opens the door and closes it softly at her back. A log shifts in the *sómba*. The old pocket Greek–English dictionary is on the shelf next to the television, its binding frayed. The pages falling open release the familiar musty smell. They fall open at *elaía*, *eliá*, olive. And *éleos*, mercy. In the old days she was sure *eléison* had something to do with the olive. *Elaía*, *eléison*. They look and sound as if they must have a common root. There was a time when she went around looking up *elaía*, *eléison*, *elaiólado*, *efhélaion*, in every dictionary she came across. Not so, it seems; and yet the impression has proved indelible. At the back of her mind she still half-believes in it. *Kýrie eléison*. She is probably not alone in that. For any number of people her age and older, the ones expelled from Turkey and the ones who grew up speaking this or that Slav dialect, Greek has always been just beyond their grasp, fuzzy with such confusions. The old man was put to work in the fields at seven and only learned his letters when he married. Mamma was his teacher and how she despised him for it, jeering at his mistakes. Their first tongue was a polyglot dialect, half-Turkish, *trakatroúkika*. Their Greek was picked up haphazardly, in the street and in church as well, but there it was in an archaic form and chanted, not spoken, the holy tongue of gold.

A mole on the skin is an *eliá*. On Greek skin they are darker than ours, raised in a velvety mound, and some have a sprout of hairs.

Then there was the olive branch and the dove of peace that flew with it over the waters to the ark in token of God's, yes, mercy.

Once when the pupils had gone home I went over the road to the school and looked up all the *elai-* and *eli-* words in the big new dictionary until the teacher had to lock up. One that I came on was *eleiosélino*, defined as *agriosélino*. *Pansélino* I knew, the full moon. *Eleiosélino*, was that olive moon? And the prefix *agrio-* meant wild: ah, I thought, wild moon! What was that, the harvest moon, the waxing moon, the horned moon? Just as well I didn't ask, though, because as soon as we sat down to lunch I remembered in a flash. *Sélino* with a *ióta* — celery!

Ach, *sélino*! I said aloud. No, leek, someone said, and lifted a forkful. Can't you tell the difference?

All the same if you only heard *agriosélino* without seeing it written down it could just as easily be wild moon as wild celery — if you heard it in a poem or a song it could. Pandeleïmon could be All-olive; wasn't he tied to an olive tree, after all? A dry olive tree that burst into leaf and ripe fruit. Or was it a fig? For that matter the *Kýrie eléison* sung over and over begins to sound like *Kyría elaía* after a while, Lady Olive Tree. I knew of a Panagia Eleoussa, a chapel dug centuries ago into a sea cliff in the Mani. Our Lady of Mercy, which for ages I thought was Our Lady of the Olives.

Her ikons that I have on slides: the All-holy One, Who Gave Birth to God, Who Points the Way, Who Sweetly Kisses the Child, Who is Full of Grace: in the stable, in the temple at Candlemas, in the coffin shrouded in her blue robe, and rising like a jet of water out of a blue basin as the Zoödochos Pigi, Wellspring of Life, and Our Lady of the Passion who is wrung with sorrow at the foot of the cross. Our Lady of the Lighthouse, and of the Coppersmiths, and the Panagia Aheiropoeiti, the All-holy One Not Made With Hands, the ikon made by the angels in Thessaloniki and which I thought was Made of Hay, *áhyra*.

Anyway, why not Our Lady of the Olives? The trees were always in the gift of the queens of heaven. It was the virgin Athena who brought the olive to Greece in the first place and planted it on the Acropolis. This was long before the Parthenon. The city shall never be lost as long as the olive tree lives, said the prophecy. So the Persian army had the idea of setting fire to it, together with the wooden temple of Athena and the slender effigy of olive wood it housed. In despair the Athenians fled the lost city, all but one of the faithful who could not tear himself away and was still scrabbling and sobbing in the ashes of the charred stump when he came on a shoot, this man, a few leaves, living silver! — he ran to overtake the Athenians with the good news.

Shall I come too? Bell says, and tonight the answer is no. At last the bells ring in the dark and Kyria Sofia puts on her coat and scarf and leaves her free to go through the clutter of papers for the envelope. She stokes the *sómba* and sits by it with the photos in her lap. Awash in the yellow gloss of the lightbulb, most are of the two of them at the beach, though Yanni is with them in one, wading knee-deep. The new wife squints into the sun and leans back from the hips under her weight of belly, her shadow a black barrel on the sand. Bell folds the letter around the photos and puts the envelope back. The photos are public and there is no harm in having a look when they will take their place on the wall in any case. But reading the letter would be going too far.

If they have a boy what they will call him? A girl will be Sofia, of course, Sofia the Third, she thinks, as our son was the third Yanni. So far there's a Sofoula and a Sonya. What will they call the Australian one? Sophie? If it weren't for the miscarriages I might have had a Sofia. The doctor couldn't tell the sex either time, they were too mangled. Or so he said.

In the house, cold and heavy with damp, nothing stirs. She

turns on the kitchen light and puts out bread and cheese and olives, *lápatha*, an apple and a glass of the sweet village water which comes piped these days from a spring on the side of the hill on their land, where the old man grew wheat. He was never compensated for the tapping of the water. Grigori, Lefteri, Vaïa, they all wanted him to protest to the authorities, but he refused. I say I own the land, was his answer, the earth, but the water comes and goes as it will. Can anyone say he owns water? Who owns air and fire, and water? If it was his in law, then it was compensation enough to know that his water ran in every vein and artery of the village. He would have liked to know that there was going to be a new grandchild. Did they find out in time to tell him? She shivers. There was a lightness about these rooms while he was here, she thinks, or was it just that the past always seems lighter than it was? His absence has made a shift in the balance of the household, as it was bound to do, only Bell is taken aback by her sense of a vast displacement. It is not as if he was ever around the house much, after all, or said much when he was. There was something cowed in him, humbled, that seemed to spur the old woman into frenzies of scolding. She sniped and carped; she seemed to grudge the very bread he ate. What attempts he made to placate her or tease her into a better mood, winking and grimacing all the while at her back, always misfired. Mostly he smiled and put up with it in silence. The ring in Bell's ears of the silence now, the intensity of his being gone! He is nowhere here in spirit. The cane chair out on the porch that was always his is empty; the place at the table where he bent his tufty head over his plate, pulling off chunks of bread, grinning if their eyes met; the grasp of his hands, which had a black grain like old wood.

During the reading of the Gospel out of the great Bible bound in gold, her favourite part of the liturgy, a prickle of fury runs along Kyria Sofia's spine and she has to swallow down a sour gush from her stomach. Shall I come too, the woman has the gall to say! No, she shall not, I forbid it. Let her not cross the threshold.

Did she or did she not come to follow our Easter? That was what she told me. By what right does she stand aside now like something made of stone and refuse to take part? Did I need such a thorn in my flesh for Lent, is that it, have I been sent a viper for my bosom? Why does she have to haunt and hound me after all these years? She tells me a story. It is about the Soul and so I listen, but *her* Soul is in love with a dragon, her Soul is the bride of Satan and not of Christ. In my own house she tells me this and I listen. I hear the tale out. The wiles of the serpent are such that before you know it the fangs have sunk in. The venom, though, is slow to work. Too late I saw what an evil tale it was. Why else did I dream of snakes this afternoon, while she sat awake, yes, reading? I who never dream? And in the dream I had been to that wall before and seen the stone snakes or dragons. I never have, I know that, and yet even now, even here, the dream is too strong to throw off. I can shut my eyes and see them now.

I tell her the story of a holy life and what do I get in return? I give her bread and she gives me a stone. If a son shall ask bread of any of you that is a father, will he give him a stone? or if he ask a fish, will he for a fish give him a serpent? Or if he shall ask an egg, will he offer him a scorpion? It has always been like this with Bella. She has no bread to give, all she has is stones. And the worst of it is, she believes her stones are bread.

All the same, if a life alone is not good enough to make up for the life she threw away, it serves her right. If she is alone, that is, and not with this M, whoever that may be. For the sake of the boy I have to have her here no matter what, do I? She is still a child herself, for all her years, if she thinks she can have the pie intact and the dog fed, like in the saying. A woman of cold blood she has been from the first, a woman unable to dance and sing and pray — what would a son of mine want with such a woman in the first place? Not that the new one is much better. Well, I wash my hands of it. But she will drive me mad yet, this Bella of his, always there jingling around in her baubles and her gypsy trash. What happened to your cross? I ask, and she has the gall to stare at me as if she had just woken up with her head in the fire, red-faced, her hair on end and full of ashes. That was seventeen years ago, she says! What is that supposed to mean? I come and go but she stays put, having wormed her way in here. She is like the house snake my mother-in-law fed, if I had only known, that lived in the dark and crept out for its dish of milk and back into the heart of the house.

How she found it, the old wretch, and lured it inside I will never know. Did it breed, was there a nest of them? A wilful woman if ever there was one, a dry-head. Every Saturday she was off at dawn to the market at Agia Vrissi with a full flask of raki that came back as empty as her saddlebags were full, with the donkey in mud pantaloons up to its belly and her cheeks hot and her eyes running and red. The snake waited. It drank from her dish. Maybe it loved her in its way, as a dog or a cat does. Sounds I would hear in the night, a rustling like water, the wind in grass, mouse claws — all of them I put down to the snake, once I knew, always the snake, in the night. Even now I sometimes hear it shifting overhead, or one of its brood. Of course that was in the old house they burned down. Don't tell me the snake didn't get away alive. For all I know it moved to the new house with us. Sofia, it kills the mice, she said!

What if it had bitten someone? I said. Us, the children?

It was harmless, and the old wretch grinned at me.

How do you know?

I know about these things, my girl. It was a water snake.

She would say that. Her eyes shifted in their pouches of fat. She was lying.

My uncle Dimitri was no lover of snakes. A snake crawled to his cow not long before this and sucked her dry: within days, he said, the udder swelled and burst. It may even have been our snake. Anyway he came over and caught it for me after Yanni had refused, although even my uncle Dimitri was afraid to kill it once she had spoken to him. He took it across the river and let it go.

In I come from the dark and before I can even light a candle they are at me. Why have you come alone, Sofia? Where is Bella tonight? They are all dying to know. They stare. Ruth and Noemin, no less. Look what a bond of love they have in spite of everything, Zoumbou tells them all, for the woman to have come all this way simply to see Sofia. That may well be true. So what? No bonds are simple, least of all love. And love you or not, a viper is a viper, with a sting for a soul. She laughs and tells me a viper in Australia is a little hedgehog that eats ants. Let her meet a Greek one, that's what I say, and she will know what a viper is.

While the coast is clear Bell gets her tape recorder out and rewinds the tape she made in the church in Athens, standing among the women: a plainchant that soars gloriously over the rustles and murmurs of the crowd in overarching spans of pure song. Does the singing fall short? She thinks so, but it might only be because the *psáltis* here is out of bounds. How can she put him on tape when she is as good as banned? There is no getting past the old woman where she stands bristling at the church door, the guardian demon. If only Bell had thought to hide the tape recorder in her bag last night. Too late. The *psáltis* might even consent to be taped, if she asked. But that would mean going and being seen to go behind Kyria Sofia's back — so sly, so disloyal, no good could come of it.

There is to be no voice-over on the soundtrack of the film, Bell worked out long ago, and no voices except the chant, and no other music. What she has in mind is something that will be a sound montage in its own right, independent, not matched to or made to keep time with the changing images except at moments, chords: the elements of sound mixed, then isolated, as the images will be, and backing, advancing, unravelling in concert, counterpointed. All she needs is the few bars of plainchant she has, just snatches, the voice swelling and fading into the sounds of the earth, the sea and the sky. What does it matter which voice? Why be so stricken with regret, then?

Κύριε ελέησον. The church is flanked with saints on guard. Jesus overhead in his dome of light. Ιδού ο άνθρωπος. Ιδού, behold. Ecce Homo. Κύριε ελέησον. Κύριε ελέησον. The liturgy is preserved in the amber of nearly two thousand years, in the holy tongue of gold. Which is a male tongue. This is a music fused with the word and made flesh in the voices of men. No instruments allowed and no women, not even the piercing, eerie warbling of boys. Pure song in overarching spans, virile in its gravity and austerity of line. Behold the man. Man as the axis. Man's body and soul.

Kyria Sofia comes trotting in brisk and rosy after church to find Bella at the kitchen table hunched over a book and a notebook, an apple core gone brown in her free hand.

"Kalispéra," they say in unison, and Bella: "Here you are already!" She slides the book under the notebook.

"The *sómba*?"

"It has wood."

"And you have eaten? What did you have?"

"*Lápatha*. Have some with your tea."

"Bah!"

"*Ela*, Mamma, eat something."

"This is Wednesday. Great Wednesday."

"What did you promise Vaïa?"

"Yes, well. All right, if there are any *lápatha*." She takes the bowl out and stares. "I thought you said you had some."

"Zoumboulitsa's — so as not to waste it. There is water boiling."

She puts the bowl back untouched, and it is Bella's turn to stare. In the act of pouring the water over the linden sprigs in her cup she notices Bella's glass, still half-full. "Are you drinking *wine*, you?"

"Water."

She raises her eyebrows, dying to pick up the glass and sniff; not in front of Bella, though, in case it is water. She narrows her eyes. It could be just a shadow, the angle of the lightbulb, but Bella's lips look black. Blood, lipstick? But when she grins up, disconcerted, even her gums are black.

"Water, is it. Where did you find black water to drink?" she says, and watches Bella flick a black tongue over her lips.

"Black? Oh, my pen ran dry and I sucked the nib."

"Let me see your tongue."

It is felty and blue-black, a snake's tongue. Kyria Sofia sags over her bread in silence, dipping it in the tea and munching.

At last with the washing up done and Bella in bed out of the way, Kyria Sofia is free to savour the letter from Australia. She sits with it in her lap to draw out the pleasure, listening to the secretive shifts and creakings all over the house. Who was to know where a snake might go under cover of so much darkness? Any one of us, reaching for a handkerchief, a candle — there were no light switches in those days, it was all candles, lanterns — might have put a hand on it. Or going outside to the lavatory might have trodden on it. Or woken up — one of the children! — in the night and found its head on the bed, the pillow.

How the woman stared up when I came in, she thinks, with those eyes of hers like black lamps, and her mouth, and the house itself a blackness, after the lights of the church. A paper-mouse, she eats paper, she drinks ink. I wonder why she bothers with an ink bottle when she has ink for blood like all scribblers. *Kalamaroú*, Grigori used to call her a lot, I seem to remember. The kalamari grows its own ink and a glass pen for a spine. Andrea is just the same, another scribbler. Not that I have any quarrel with that as such. No, I love and respect letters. But not when they are a sign of weakness, and she is one of that breed, the summer always too hot and the winter too cold, because she is neither hot nor cold herself, is she? One of the lukewarm ones, a Laodicean, and I will spue her out of my mouth, not earthy and not heavenly either, a lukewarm water.

Not that she is soft. A weakling she may be, but not soft, however she may try to pass herself off to the world. I know better. She is not so weak either: more insubstantial, one who has lived too far out of reach. She has become all lack, and greed, a vacuum feeding on other lives. There has developed a sort of rubbery strength in her, a new power to resist, to lie low, to melt into the background. And cold ink for blood. An inkfish, that's our Bella, not a snake so much, more like eight snakes in one. She has the skin for it, the pallor and shine of the octopus, the skin that is one colour by one light and different by another, now clear, now mottled, all blushes and freckles and moles, though below the neck she is bone white, and bone thin, I know more than she thinks. And the eyes, swimming in ink, where have I seen them before if not underwater, in a head like an udder overflowing with black milk? If I had my way I would treat the woman as what she is. Slap her on the stones, lift and slap her down and mash her, and hang her out to dry in the sun.

It was water in the glass, not wine. You told the truth and just as well for you, my lady. Kyria Sofia fills a clean glass from the tap and drinks half, sighing.

It was war, did she say? Open war, was it? A lot you know about war if you can say that. War! Push anyone too far and you will see war, if that is all there is to it. You had your riots and massacres too, did you? You ate filth and lay in filth and fought the rats off your children? You woke at daybreak among the night's crop of dead and dying. You lost two babies, all right. None of your business, but I also lost two babies, in the real war. The one was born dead and the other the midwife had to rid me of if we were not all to starve. But you have *other fruit*, of course! And what might that be? Enlighten us, please. Two travel books? Those notebooks that you lace day and night with scribble? Black lace, where I make white, and we are two of a kind, if you think I sit and wear out my eyes for nothing. I am an old woman, Bella, what about you? Other fruit! And the world is hungry for it, I suppose. And your photographs, of course, let us not forget the film you are making out of *slides*.

She has gone and left the book, though not the notebook, never the notebook, on her chair. And yes, it is *The Golden Ass*, the love book, Anna's book. Kyria Sofia spreads it open at the inscription, squinting at the black pattern and, how she has no idea, but her hand reaching out for the glass of water tips it over and the water is suddenly swilling in long blue threads over the page. Quickly she dabs it with a paper towel, and another, but the stain has soaked into the page and even the pages underneath are crinkled, full of bubbles. I didn't mean that to happen, she says, hooking the lid off the *sómba* and holding the page over the yellow heat at the mouth. But I am not sorry.

The woman is everywhere. *She shall not come, I forbid it*, I swore, but she came anyway, a devil at my heels, to have led my mind so far astray from the liturgy. She might as well have been there; she stood in my light. And the truth is that I might as well not have been there; I saw nothing tonight while she stood like a shadow figure on a sheet between me and the light of the lantern. Does the figure stand and move and speak of its own will, though, when you come to think of it? How much is she to blame? There is a puppet master and he is Satan who lies in wait for us all with his snares of sin. And the light of the Lord is a lantern light thrown into the chambers of our hearts, as a father of the Church said; I read it in a *Life*. Nothing can stand in the way of His sight. What has He seen in my heart tonight? Anger, the fire of Satan.

As if in a dream Kyria Sofia sees, as God must, the masses and red hollows burning with inner light, strung like a lyre, their pools of blood and walls full of flame and shadow.

Lord have mercy: in the name of God the Father and of the Son and of the Holy Ghost she makes her three crosses and sighs, squinting through her glasses again at each of Grigori's photos. The baby will not be a boy, she can tell from the way the mother is standing, not carrying it high enough, although with a first child you can never be quite sure. I know Grigori wants a girl to call after me. A boy would be Dimitri after my uncle who is forgiven. Another Sofia, another chance. Sofoula is lost to me, and as for Sonya — it hardly counts, anyway, being a daughter's daughter. How will our Yanni take it, she wonders, having a baby sister at eighteen? Nineteen. Better than having a brother, probably. The children are all different. One thing you can never tell is how they will take it.

By holding the mirror up to the faint gleam of the flyblown globe that hangs in the *méros*, Bell can see behind the spots of tarnish a face with dark lips and gums, the teeth bared and yellow, though she has brushed them hard. Her tongue is blue-black, a lizard's tongue.

She squats and lets her piss steam out, holding her breath. When she has wiped herself she holds the paper up to the light in case there is blood, but no, no sign yet. The paper basket is brimming with crumpled paper smeared with shit, none of it hers, so far. The only sound in the world is the fine trickle of water, a thread of light like a snail stain from the sill down through the whitewash to the lavatory. This drizzle, will it ever lift? Will her cold ever be over? There seems no end to the cheesy mess bubbling up in the sockets of her skull and waking her in the night, half-stifled, with only half a nose, the other half blocked, numb and deadened, and no breath. The ink on her mouth tastes of metal, like blood, and won't wash off. The red spots on her hands refuse to fade. How is it that nothing in the world seems to want to heal, to change, to pass?

She is back in bed with the light out when the old woman's door creaks open and shut, and then her own door is cut in two, half a wavering light, half darkness. "Bella, are you asleep?" she hears the old woman whisper. She lies as still as the dead, counting each one of her own slow breaths, and after a moment she hears a sigh. The doorknob turns, bringing darkness, and footsteps shuffle to another room.

When it feels safe she crouches over fumbling for the torch in her bag and, still on her knees, clicks it on gratefully under the covers. The battery is low; only a trickle of yellow light flows into the tunnels of the sheets, ridged with shadow. No blood. There should have been by now. Not so much as a drop or spot in spite of the familiar ache in her breasts, the clench and heaviness of her womb in the last few days, the twinges of nausea. Just as well, anyway, she comforts herself: you could say it was a blessing of a kind, when you have nowhere to wash. She licks her dry lips, their black skin. Surely, though, it can't have come to an end so soon, so suddenly too, with no warning? It doesn't *feel* like a blessing. More of a curse. The onset of old age at one blow. As if the absence of the curse were itself a curse? — not, she thinks, that I have ever in my life called it the Curse or thought of it as such or wished barrenness on myself. Unless it's *her*! Bell gasps, sitting back on her heels so that the sheet works loose, full of light. The women of a household tend to bleed at the same time, it's a scientific fact, and even if they keep their periods a secret from each other, mysteriously their bodies will know and fall into step of their own accord. What if one of your household has stopped bleeding? What if she can dry up another woman's flow just by living with her? Bell hugs herself irritably on the cold mattress. Just by living with her for *four days*? Four days, all right, but considering I have been part of the household for twenty years? There has to be a bodily *proximity*. In which case, as soon as I have gone — if my mother bled until she was fifty-five, why should I stop dead at only just fifty? Unless there is some curse of barrenness on me. Grigori has a new wife to bear the children. I only had one, and look at me, blighted, like the fig tree. If there is a curse, it must have been *her*. Those red raw eyes, frilled like a turkey's, the way they glare! Bell's hand, absurdly, goes to the eye on its chain round her neck, dull and dark, its fires unkindled by torchlight, and clamps it. *It is her.* What is she always muttering under her breath if not spells? — prayers or spells, it's all the same to her. I know she believes in the Eye. They all do. She is a dry husk herself and she will never rest until I wither up like her. Stop it, you are being ridiculous, Bell tells herself, ridiculous, *you* know you don't believe any of it. All the same the fear gathers with the dark; something is there outside her skin, beyond her, in the house itself. Something, as she watches the shafts and plumes of light move on the walls.

The house in cross-section: the white skin, the scurf and dust and decay; the red flesh thick-knitted over bone; and the hollow within, the space, the silence. At the heart is there a pulse, a breath, a flame? Only drifts of dust, grey air and ash. As for Mamma, how does she see the house of her life? She is buried alive. Cold walls, a coffin of dark stone. She dreams of a retreat, the monastery on the mountain, a cell, a sarcophagus, a tomb. Not one to decay in like this but one where she will be reborn, a life stripped bare to the soul, empty of everything, even of time. More than anything, of time! Memory, the world. Αμάν! To leave time behind.

THURSDAY

This is only her second *Páscha* in the village, but her fourth in Greece, and she knows by now that Great Thursday is hard work. She makes sure she is up early to make her porridge. The honey she stirs into it, the German honey, is clear, a dark gold, not like Pandeli's. That was the name, Pandeli. His was grainy, dense, lazy to uncoil from the spoon, spring honey, the village made flesh: and it had to be early spring, this time of the year before the tobacco was in flower, or the bitterness would have tainted it.

Her mood has changed. She can take her time, after all, until the old woman gets back from wherever she is. Church, probably. Dawdling over the porridge, the *The Golden Ass* open on the table in front of her with a fork across it to keep it flat, she has still not finished the porridge when Kyria Sofia barges in with a loud greeting.

"*Ade*, Bella! Don't tell me you even read when you eat?" She drags her apron on. "It's bad for the eyes. Quick, we have work!"

"Coming." Smiling, Bell scrapes up the last spoonful and closes the book. It falls open at the first page, the inscription. She stares, not having seen until now that there is a water stain. "Bad for the book, at least," she adds.

"What do you mean?"

For answer she holds the book open at the inscription, buckled as it is, and dimmed in a haze of indigo.

"That book again."

"What?"

"It's dirty, I say."

"It's only water and ink. I can still read it."

"You would do better not to read it. Better to burn it."

"Burn a book! Who would do that?"

"Why not burn a book?"

Bell stares. The old woman means it. She has a fixed smile on her face, malignant.

"When you think of all the work that goes into a book! Mamma, it takes years of work. More than that! A book has a living soul."

"All the more reason then, if it has the devil in it."

"Because of Erota?"

"A book is the same as a man, is it, to you? Yes, I suppose so, to you. But I say, better a book than a soul in the eternal fire."

Kyria Sofia carries the wooden trough in, the *skáfi*: first of all the bread has to be kneaded. The lentils have to be put on to boil in onion and tomato paste, dried *rígani* leaves and salt but no oil, the lunch for Great Thursday. Stunned, Bell chops the onions and then escapes on the pretext of needing to change into something more practical to work in, picking up *The Golden Ass* casually as she goes and sidling off to put it out of harm's way in the lid of her case. The pages are dry and have no smell. It must have been water, although she has no idea how or when water could have got on it. It was all right last night when she was reading in the kitchen; yet it must have happened at some stage then, with the light so low, a mustardy glimmer overhead and the pages in her shadow, that she failed to notice. And the old woman was pleased: she was all grim satisfaction. Better to burn it. Bell sits on the bed folded in her own arms, wanting nothing so much as to crawl back under the blankets and not have to face Kyria Sofia again. What brought this on? When she liked the story! Even if she had reservations afterwards, she sat hunched over her lace, attentive to every word.

Bell had better change, having said she was going to. Besides, she is hot, panting — sweating, she sees, when she opens the shutters a crack, a gesture like lifting a blind, and a fuzz of grey light coats her skin all over. She looks smooth and clean enough, even sleek, which is not to say that she is. When was the last shower? And she is a child aching with misery. There was an old woman once, when she was six, maybe seven. A face, words, at the back of the mind: all she is sure of is the feeling. It was one of those long afternoons of summer when there was nothing to do but lie around the house in the dark with the blinds down, brown holland blinds, naked for the sake of coolness, her skin sticking to the lino. There was a hollowness to the light like the shuttered light in here, as if it were a reflection. Blowflies were blundering on the pane behind the blind with its flange of sun. In the pools of shadow lay a dank staleness from the melt water under the ice chest. The postman's whistle came and went like a bird. Now and then she lifted the blind to squash a sizzling fly and look out into the sun of the street. Looking out idly like this one time she was shocked to see a blur of white, the neighbour's little boy, run out into the middle of the road. Calling, she flung the front door open and ran out into the blast of light, grabbed him under the armpits and danced back on to the nature strip, the soles of her feet on fire. He was two and had run away before and got lost. He was naked too, and fighting hard, yelling his head off, until suddenly this old woman in gloves and a wide hat towered in front of them. Get back inside! she hissed. The grin of hate on that face: he froze in Bell's arms. You are a filthy dirty little girl. Their hearts beating, they shrank out of sight behind the trunk of the plane tree and held each other hard until there was no more sound of footsteps. Their bodies were shiny, mottled with the green light and shadow of the tree; as shiny and clean as the skin on a hard-boiled egg.

What is it about the house that draws the past out of her like the bitter juices out of a salted eggplant? Nothing in Australia seems to. There is nothing left there to dredge it up and no one who shared it is alive, as far as she knows. Not a trace, unless the house is still there, the old weatherboard room and the trees, buddleia and broom and oleander. As he aged, her father would never talk about the past, and her mother's memory was gone with her power of speech, ten years before her death, after a stroke. She left no photos, either, when she died. Even Bell's own photos are gone, the Brownie snaps of holidays at the beach and in the hills. Searching for the album to pack for Greece, the first time, she found it in a carton of books in the garage, dry, but warped and swollen from an old soaking. Her father had never expected the roof to leak, it was bad luck, he was sorry. She found all the photos she had taken since she was eight drowned in the grey pages, stuck in thick clumps which came apart to show the bare skin spotty with mildew and runny, melted in parts, a peeled head showing through here and there, as if a match had been held up close until it burned down to the flesh.

All the years of the old house that was dim by day and lit hot and harsh after dark behind the blinds, and fitted them like old clothes: the years in between, of the train to high school and university and back home again into the shower and an aunt's cast-off dressing-gown, green chenille, ready for dinner at six o'clock sharp. The three chamber pots, speckled green enamel scaly with yellow, sat out in a row by the gully trap all day and under the beds at night. Her mother and father used to wish for a little brother for Bell. Long ago her mother had gone into hospital for one, but she came home empty-handed. Bell would have to be all they had, a son and a daughter in one. By the age of twenty she was old enough in her ways to outdo the pair of them, dowdier, more furtive and hidebound. But then she shook it all off overnight. She left for a hard job on the mountain, for freedom, new youth, and a world, a life, Grigori.

When Bell gets back to the kitchen the work is well under way. The old woman only glances up — sardonic, those red eyes — from the dough she is pummelling and snatching with webbed hands on the smooth grey wood of the *skáfi* . The water has risen in a pink froth over the eggs in the saucepan. Bell minds them, fifty eggs all gathered in the last few days, and shifts them off the hotplate whenever they look like boiling too hard and cracking. As soon as they are a deep red she lifts them out and rubs them with a cloth dipped in olive oil while Kyria Sofia puts her risen loaves in the oven. On the soft dough of two of them she has pressed a carved wooden stamp. These ones are not to eat. These are *prósforo*, she says, when they are done, see, *antídoro* for church, and holds them out, one on the palm of each hand, so Bell can stroke and admire them before they are wrapped and go into the basket.

Kyria Sofia serves the lentils with warm bread. The sun comes out then, in the middle of the day and patches of it shine on the table where she has started kneading the *tsourékia*. Bell is given the little jobs one by one: to grate the orange rind, to wash the dull brass pestle and mortar and pound the spices with a clunk and chime. She dissolves the sugar in the warm milk, melts the butter, beats the eggs. When the dough is high, Kyria Sofia oils the table down and rolls out long ropes of dough, throwing and dangling and slapping them down as if they were alive, and stands breathless, smiling at Bell's admiration, a yellow snake in each hand. When she is satisfied she lays them flat, one long one doubled around a short one, and makes a quick plait. In the end she has four large ones and one small one rising in the oiled pans. She strokes them with beaten egg to make them shine, pushes a red egg into the heart of each one and puts them in the oven.

"*Amán!*" She subsides on to the divan. "*Amán*. This is the last year I go through all this. Such hard work" — fanning her wet face and stirring the sweet hot air — "and who cares one way or another? As if anyone will appreciate it."

"They will so! They do, Mamma. Where else can you get *tsourékia* like these?"

By the time the lunch dishes are washed, the *tsourékia* are done and ready to come out, brown and glassy in the late light. "Ah!" Bell says.

But Kyria Sofia is bent over the trays, stricken. "I don't think they are risen."

"They smell beautiful."

"No, look, they seem to have spread. Look, they are flat."

"But they are light inside." Bell taps one and, to her surprise,

Kyria Sofia breaks some off and hands it to her. Bell takes a hot bite, tender between the crusts, a springy bread as sweet and rich as cake; pale steam drifts from the torn golden substance in their hands.

"It's just right, Mamma. You try it."

Will Bell never learn? Kyria Sofia is fasting. "Not heavy? Not tough? All right, wrap them well," she says, "and help me put them away in the storeroom for Sunday. If I leave them out, I know Andrea and Sonya, the minute they walk in, they take and eat them like bread."

Bell mixes coffee and sugar in the *bríki* of water, a cup for herself and half a cup for Kyria Sofia. Too tired to move from the kitchen, they sip it with a glass of cold water among the flour dust and patches of oil, and then they clean up and set out for the bottom henhouse in the last of the sun. Blackberry brambles tear at their legs, and branches of wild plum in the ditches. The trees down on the river are still bare, but for a green haze in the light around them; the wheat is green and high here. The hens come running, red and brown and one dapple-grey, *psarí*, fish-grey, a mackerel hen, with the rooster on her tail. Kyria Sofia lures them in once she has all the eggs, and shuts the door: there is always the fox.

Back in the kitchen she washes the eggs carefully, five new eggs, and sinks them in the dye. The eggs laid on this day are the holiest. They are not for cracking and eating at the moment of the Resurrection but set aside to be kept under the ikon for as long as possible after Easter, for thunderstorms. If there is a thunderstorm, she explains, blinking with tiredness, you throw one of these eggs out in it.

"What for?" says Bell.

"To make it stop."

"Stop a thunderstorm?"

"Why not? As God wills."

A simper crosses Kyria Sofia's face and Bell holds her breath. How can she say that, as if it were so simple? Has she forgotten? No, it was a wince of pain, and now she is looking down and stumbling in the ruts of the path. Bell takes her arm and the old woman yields, for once, leaning on her.

Once there was a heat wave and the iceworks and the woodyard next to it down the end of Bell's street were burnt down. Everyone came into the street to see the pillars and knuckles of smoke go up with a roar and a gush into the sky like a copper of washing. Soon the beams upstairs broke out in black blisters. Little flickers went sliding like water along them until they crashed down into the ruins. The fire-engine came with hoses and everyone got out of the way in a hush that was heavy and dim like being underwater. A storm was coming with a muttering of thunder and flares of light on the edge of the sky. Where were the carts and the white horse? But no one seemed to know. In dreams this goes on for a long time and blends with an earlier memory, her first ever, a dream with a fire spitting and clawing at her toes and the mattress, which has been stood on its edge beside her on the hearth to dry, vomiting out smoke. A choking, charred thickness in the air, and a shriek, her mother. Bell is the one who wet the mattress and the fire knows. Fire is the death she has feared most all her life. For her mother it was lightning, and she would cringe at the first growl of thunder and hide shivering in the wardrobe during a bad storm. Everyone knew better than to make a fuss or, worse, laugh, because when her mother was little she had seen her own sister struck dead in the paddock by lightning.

Every storm is the same storm. Always the first storm, the shock, the sky lowering a belly of grey fleece on the rooftops, in a roar, in stabs of light. Drops of hot rain fell on the concrete, as heavy and dark as pennies, and ran down her hair and soaked like oil into her dress, a pink dress, with holes and seams of red cellophane appearing all over it. The house was dim inside and her mother was not there. Then suddenly she came out of the depths of her room, shivering, and held out her arms to Bell. Thunder is only clouds bumping into each other, she said, nothing to be afraid of; but, close-up like that, her eyes looked like two holes, red-rimmed, grey, in a face of bone.

When Yanni was killed not many who were there even noticed at first because a house on the beachfront, a villa, two storeys, was on fire. Was it also struck by lightning? That was not clear from Grigori's account. She would have liked to know for her own peace of mind, but for the sake of theirs she was afraid to ask. In her mind's eye it is white, this villa, bursting with smoke and flames, and on the beach at its foot a boy is lying in the pale water, the grey sky.

What sort of death does Mamma fear most? Does she fear it?

When the red water is poured off these last eggs of the day, Kyria Sofia lifts one out and balances it on the dresser.

"Oh, no! Broken?" says Bell, watching at her back.

"Only this one."

Yes, it has a fine crack.

"So! Is that the finish?"

"Yes, thanks be to God." Therefore, my beloved brethren, may you be steadfast, unmovable, she thinks, always abounding in the work of the Lord. "Have this one for supper," she says. "You might as well. Only be sure to burn the shell in the *sómba*. None must fall on the floor."

Bell shakes her head in agreement.

"Well, mind that none does."

And she shakes her head again. One by one she has polished each intact egg with a rag dripped in olive oil and set them all carefully on a platter; a warm breath of oil comes up into her face.

My son's son is dead and my son has torn out my heart. At his own father's graveside, to tell me I had to bear the blame! You accused our father of Yannaki's death, he said. I heard you, Mamma, and so did everyone else. Did you hear? he asked someone, and someone else: Did you? And it was the death of him.

I was too shocked to speak. The others tried to calm him but he threw their arms off.

Nothing to say for herself? Not Mamma! She won't turn a hair, and why should she? She is never to blame! She is like oil. However deep down in the water you throw her, she will be back up on top in no time.

There is no blood on my hands, I said in my confusion of mind, not meaning it how Lefteri must have taken it, because his face went black with rage and he walked away. There is no blood on my hands. If he took me to mean his father, there at the grave, no wonder. I understand him. I only meant that I was not to blame, my hands were clean. He must have understood me to mean his father had blood on his, that of the man in the brawl, or many in the war, who knows? Or Yannaki's. I have a sharp tongue. I make wounds I live to regret. I was beside myself with sorrow the day I accused Yanni. But he was my husband. He knew me.

Unless: no, the baby doesn't count, the blood of the baby never born, whose life I took, bartered, only for the sake of the ones already in life, Lefteri for one. *He* should try to understand me and know me better. He used to, before he married. His wife put him up to it, of course. She knows how I despise her. A woman who shuns work, a peasant — and the airs she gives herself! — ignorant, greedy, an animal. She was never a patch on my girl and she knows it. My girl is educated and she still has to work hard every day of her life, while Kyria Chloï sits eating the bread of idleness. And why not, when she has my son to batten on? In the sweat of his face shall she eat bread. And he would do anything, tear my heart out for her sake. If he hadn't already.

Oil, he called me, oil that comes back up on top of the deepest water. Is there any truth in it? God forbid, when all I have ever tried to do was hold fast to the teachings, the Word. I have to speak my mind. It is my nature. Is that a crime? What can we do but be what we are? The devil can find a way to put even the good in us to his own work. He plants the seeds of sin in every human heart. Only when we have confessed and put our hearts into the hands of God are we safe. Sin is inborn, the devil is everywhere, and what can we do in this world but act in good faith? I have always acted in good faith. Lefteri, if he could hear my thoughts now, if he could see into my mind, he would be wild with anger. I can just hear him: look, she is at it again! My child, the oil can only do what God has made it to do, according to the nature of its being. The fishermen pour it in the water when the waves turn rough. It spreads a pane of glass over the fish, the squid, the octopus and lets the men see in. Only how far down do they see? Not far at all before the light gives out; and water, anyway, has thicknesses and colours of its own that distort things the further down you look. You hardly ever see as far as the bottom. Lord, let the scales fall from our eyes. Lord, have mercy on us who can do no more than blunder about half-blind in the daily world.

When it comes time to eat, Bell lifts the stone out of the brine, stabs a block of feta and lifts it dripping on to the board. It is as white and brittle as chalk, and the fine slices splinter under the knife into white honeycombs, like thick lace, salty and so pungent — she squashes the crumbs on her fingertip to be tidy and nibbles them — that her eyes fill with tears. She makes a meal of salty feta with the last shreds of Zoumboulitsa's green *lápatha*, the dark taste of iron softened by the oil, and some of Kyria Sofia's, and the egg with its red wound. Where has Zoumboulitsa been all day? In church, perhaps, with the other old women who have no strength left for cooking, or no one to cook for. The *sómba* has gone out when Bell lifts the iron lid off, reaches in and drops the shells in a downy nest of ashes.

So many eggs, fifty altogether for dyeing. Eggs everywhere, bone white and red. The one I ate had a long red vein. The white was rubbery and loose on a hard little yolk in a grey skin, ash grey, but powdery yellow inside, an egg like any fresh egg.

She stewed a pot of lentils and baked bread: four τσουρέκια and four plain loaves in all, two for the house and two with the cross on them for church for Communion. Πρόσφορο, she said, her voice as sweet as a bell with pride: αντίδωρο, holding them out, newly hatched, keeping them warm. Mothering the church, giving it this day its bread. Lentils, sourdough bread and ταχίνι have a taste of earth.

The bread stamp is a mandala carved out of of olive wood with a thick cross on it and a corded edge like a large coin. Byzantine letters run in pairs down the cross. ΙΣΟΥΣ ΧΡΙΣΤΟΣ ΝΙΚΑ, she told me years ago: Jesus Christ conquers. The arms have no letters, only a triangle pattern, and a fan opens in pleats out of each of the four corners, like spokes of a wheel or sun rays.

While Kyria Sofia is out Bell takes a half dozen careful slides of the bread stamp from close up, angling the shadows for depth — olive wood as brown as a new loaf, sleek, rough-hewn all over with those black slits — and puts it back in its place on the shelf. Not that there was any need to hurry, when she will be here all night on her own; tonight is the women's vigil in the church. She wanders through the *sála* to the door of the storeroom. Though the shutters are always closed, the handle turns when she tries it; so she opens it wide, switches the light on and hurriedly lifts the lid of the old crate of junk that has been in here since she and Grigori brought it.

The room is bleak, abandoned. She cringes. She is not welcome, she knows by the way it shrinks shut against her in the dusty grey of its light as if she were a stranger, a sneakthief. In its hoard there are things she must look at again, all the same, things that belong to her, or used to. The cold walls can accuse her all they like. Only let Kyria Sofia not come back early and see from the street the shuttered light in a window that should be dark, and stride in and confront her. Her hands are shaking as they fumble down through folded summer clothes and linen. Near the bottom they come on cardboard and paper, a book! She knows what it is. Now she can straighten the linen, close the lid. She has chanced on something she thought was lost for good, the first book Grigori gave her: the red book full of black and white photos of his city, Thessaloniki forty years ago, the streets of the past.

So stricken that she feels numb, sits on the lid to riffle through the pages. This is the Thessaloniki she saw before she came to know it, a play of lights and shadows, sunlight on withered stone. It could almost be the Thessaloniki she came through only a few days ago. Here is the broken span of the Kamara of Galerius with its load of grubby carvings; the wharf crowded with masts and cranes, freighters, island ferries; the church walls full of saints that stare through soot and candlelight into the everlasting dark. Here are the sandy shoulders of the Walls of the Seven Towers, with the Great Gate on the hill and a *kafeneíon* in the open air high over the first lights of the harbour. They have not changed. The walls keep their secret, as walls do. They are Byzantine ramparts so thick that only cannon fire has ever breached them, so thick that they can hide another world in their depths. It is another name for hell, a Turkish name, Gendi Kule, Seven Towers. Steeped in the sun and with golden illuminations at night, the old stone blocks are honeycombed with tunnels and caves that crawl with rats, cells where an open sewer runs and chained men live and die.

He took her to see the quarter where they had lived then, and found the old slum still standing, the door open on to a mud floor and gaping roof, chairs — someone was living there. He was lost for words at finding himself, after twenty years, back at that door. One look at her shocked face, though, and he was hustling her away. No, he said, no, too much I shame. He should have been proud. It was a monument.

This house, too — think of the pits and underground caves and burrows of the lives that intersect here: each one is a well whose lid, if you lift it, will only reveal a black length of space and at the bottom a whiteness, a stone, a staring face. There are whole cities in the earth and underwater and immersed in ash and pumice, royal tombs and caves, figures of bone and clay and rock. Day and night the ferries and ships cross and recross the Aegean over the drowned green marbles of streets and walls as they move, swelling, shrinking in the shallows on the edges of islands. The seabed is littered with anchors and amphorae and hulls that burst open to the water and weed centuries ago. Of the people, no trace. Fishermen on the islands say they have seen ghost cities that shine out at sea in the dawn light, and towers underwater, and armies of ghosts on the clifftop that vanish in the sun, the drowned and the smothered; as if the soul, or an image of the soul, one moment of its being, were bound forever to the place where it had lived most intensely.

First we go in Thessaloniki, Grigori said when she unwrapped the book, and after in village. Is one tower there, white tower, near in sea. We go.

A white tower? A lighthouse? She looked it up: *Fáros*?

Fáros? Nuh, nuh. One white tower of stone. Turkish using for prison before.

Prison?

White Tower, yes. Tower of Blood, they calling.

Can we see inside or is it still a prison?

No, not now. Is another prison now, Gendi Kule. Seven Tower. My father was there.

What for?

Big fight, many men, and one man he break his head and die. Accident was.

Were you allowed to go and see him?

With my mother few times. If we hev we take food. Bad times. We went with empty hands, he went on in Greek, waiting while Bell made her way through the words. It was when he worked on the wharves. I saw my father buried alive. Gendi Kule is another name for hell.

He bought her this book in English full of photos of his city and turned the pages until he came to the city walls, Gendi Kule, and the White Tower, a barrel of stone with barred loopholes and battlements and the water at its foot. There were open boats for hire, their awnings flapping in the sun glare.

He said, I work in one *tavérna* near White Tower before. Here. See? One day we go.

His was a childhood shuttling between here and the village while the Italians invaded, and then the Germans. His father had enlisted and no one knew where he was. In the Civil War Grigori — he was ten — was with his grandmother in the village when the *andártes*, relatives of theirs among them, and neighbours he had known all his life, swarmed down off the mountain and burnt the house. He saw the howling faces, firelit. In his dreams he sees a red tower thrust into the starry air high over the roofs of the village, a tower of fire and blood.

Footsteps crunch along the wet road, a man laughs and there is a burst of men's voices. Recalled to herself — what business does she have foraging in the storeroom and the crate? — Bell switches the light off, shuts the door and hurries out. She slips the book into the lining in the lid of her case. It is her book, of course, and has been for thirty years. Grigori gave it to her and she has every right to it, as Kyria Sofia would surely concede, if she were asked; only Bell baulks at asking, at the thought of the grim look of injury, of inevitable offence, of accusation. She gives an angry laugh. This *is* my book! she says aloud. It makes no difference. A sneakthief, say the blind walls, and the word hits her with the force of truth.

"Have you eaten, *kalé*? What did you have?"
"Cheese, egg. *Lápatha* again."
"I wonder when you will try my *lápatha*."
"I have tried it, Mamma, look. Will you have a tea now?"
"I don't know that tea agrees with me any better than coffee."
"*Ela*, you must eat something."
"Everything gives me wind." She peers up with a sly smile. "Mine are better than Zoumbou's. Even without oil."
"They are, but don't tell her. Where was she all day?"
"She also has her preparations for Easter."
"She is good company in the mornings."
"Yes. She has a good heart. It started when they brought the forgiven one home to be buried. She came and sat with me day and night. She never left my side."
"Where?"
"Here, *kalé*."
"Here!" Shocked, Bell spreads her hands.
"Not in this room! Out in the *sála*. By the time the cold weather set in she was in the habit of coming here. We had a hard winter. Has the water boiled? Well." Kyria Sofia presses her hands to her white head. "I should have a tea. I suppose. *E*, all right, a bite of bread."

After the meal Kyria Sofia asks if Bell minds spending the night alone. Her voice has a wistful note to it, or so Bell imagines. "No," she says.
"You can always read, can't you?"
"I have work to catch up on," she mumbles and a sneer crosses the old woman's face. With a coat over her shoulders and the door wide open as a show of willingness to be intruded on, just in case, Bell lies across her bed with a fan of papers spread

out, until the iron door slams shut and the footsteps fade into silence.

If only she could catch up on her work. The bulk of it will have to hang fire until she can see the slides, in two or three weeks. It might help if she could make notes, working blind in the meantime, even rough out a tentative sequence or so: apart from dates and exposure lists, technical jottings, she has nothing to speak of. Not that speaking is the word. There are to be no words in the film. The job is precisely to pass into the mind a flow of images and sound without words, bypassing the word. Which is not to say, all the same, that notes might not be useful beforehand, as scaffolding. The few she has made are too disjointed to have much bearing on the film in her mind. They may play a part. No knowing at this stage. The film will only begin to come into being when the photos do: a photo mosaic put together out of the flesh and blood photos that are here in embryo, wound in their little cases in her bag.

The wake and long rolls of water nudging at the hulls of ships off Piraeus. A headland, a skeleton temple, a dry tongue of land. Then mist, the span of oil-slow water, far capes, mountains casting their shadows on reflections, a lighthouse on a grey cliff.

A port at night, the ship sliding out again, a looper caterpillar of gold light out in the dark under the moon.

Blue doors and shutters in white walls, blue and yellow panes of glass. Black hoods, white lace. Sun shapes on a path of silver stone. Tall fennel with flowers like yellow sponges. Goats, belled and hobbled, and spotted kids. Olive trees in the wind, an almond, flying flakes of white, a red spot at the base. Fig branches, the beaky yellow buds of leaf pricking out. Dry grapevines in rows worming out of the old ground. Anemone, blue iris, red poppy, snapdragon, the blue of the bell-petals as clear and fine as a jellyfish mantle.

The shore of pebbles, brown and white, glassy veins in them, swollen under water — scuds of dark wind over the bay ruffling it, moving out to sea. The standing rocks and the blue islands.

On her rounds of the house on Paros, a Buddhist nun, tiny and red, yellow-rimmed, a shadow in the sun underwater. She has to duck under the arch to go in, and her robes fin out. She stoops over the oil lamps and the water bowls where the flames are reflected. They flicker on her face, her hands, the rosary. Her head and back, a dark bell against the yellow robes of the enthroned Buddha.

Ikons on a church wall. Domes and apses, mosaics on gold. Domes, white on a dark sky, ultramarine blue on a white sky, lace silhouettes of bell towers and bells hanging in cloisters. Broken columns. Blank stones, pitted surfaces, stains and trickles in seams, darkening as the sky reddens. Black and grey and sandy gold, stones in the late light, their skins weathered and raddled with old oil and wine, old blood. Bone, clay and stone figures with eroded faces out of graves, all bulbous, great with child.

A snake. It lifts a staring head and moves on like water over sand.

A girl who dips her face to water. One hand holds her long hair back against her throat. Strands float through her spread fingers, black ripples, water. A honey flow which darkens to wine or blood running over and under and between rocks, great thighs, a cleft.

As she thought, the notes are no help. No sequence, only an idle memory comes to mind, a statement, words heard once on television: After a storm the sandstone dries fast. The one sentence sounds in her head, in an English voice, quiet, oracular, which she misheard at first, thinking he said "sunstone". Why that, of all things, when there is no sandstone here? Unless it was seeing the walls and towers of Thessaloniki. The film was about a desert, she is sure, cliffs, a wasteland of sand and stone. The Gulf War, Desert Storm, was it that? But the image that the words bring to mind at last is one of great knots and braids of resplendent stone.

She sighs. This is no mood for work, or for meditation either, though for once the impediment seems not to be what the nun at the *gompa* on Paros called monkey mind, no such onslaught of leaping and chattering thoughts. We call it a butterfly mind, she remembers having said. She was Dutch, this nun, ordained in India, in Dharamsala, and her English was perfect. She ran a quick hand over a scalp like a brown suède cap, and replied: Tibetans say a waterfall of thought.

The nun said Bell was welcome to stay for Easter if she wanted, and lent her a book when she left, on the understanding that she would post it back, from here or Australia. A travel book, Bell has been ready to say if she was caught with this one: yes, another travel book, Mamma. And so it is, more or less. It maps by stages the progress of the soul from the corpse through an otherworld of shadows and bodies of light to the foetus in its new incarnation. The foreword is by the Dalai Lama, and the body of the text a translation, with notes, of an eighteenth century Tibetan work. The pages bristle with underlinings in pencil and ink, not hers — she has barely skimmed through, anyway — and train and ferry tickets, which are hers. The cover is a photo of a snowy dome out of which rises a stepped tower in the form of a headdress woven in sunlit stone. Looking out between the dome and the tower are two gilded, heavy-lidded eyes with the slumberous inward gaze and intensity of a tiger's eyes, rimmed with blue.

> *Those born within the realms of desire and form must pass through an intermediate state, during which a being has the form of the person as whom he or she is to be reborn. The intermediate being has all five senses, but also clairvoyance, unobstructiveness and an ability to arrive immediately wherever he or she wants. He or she sees other intermediate beings of his or her own type — hell-being, hungry ghost, animal, human, demigod or god — and can be seen by clairvoyants.*

If a place of birth ... is not found, a small death occurs after seven days, and one is reborn into another intermediate state. This can occur at most six times, with the result that the longest period spent in the intermediate state is forty-nine days.

Colour
The Sutra ... *explains that [the body's colour in] the intermediate state of a hell-being is like a log burned by fire; of a hungry ghost, like water; of an animal, like smoke; of a god of the desire realm or a human, gold ...*

Mode of exit from the body after death
One who is to be reborn as a hell-being exits from the anus; as a hungry ghost, from the mouth; as an animal, from the urinary passage; as a human, from the eye ...

As an external sign of the dissolution of the eye sense power, one cannot open or close the eyes.

As an external sign of the dissolution of the visible forms included in one's own continuum, the lustre of one's body diminishes and one's strength is consumed.

The internal sign of the dissolution ... is the arising of a bluish appearance called "like a mirage". It is like an appearance of water when the light of the sun strikes a desert in the summer.

Question: What example is there for the existence of such an intermediate state?

Answer: Nowadays when we go to sleep, the four signs [mirage, smoke, fireflies, and flame of a butter-lamp] as well as the four empties [empty, very-empty, great-empty and all-empty] of sleep dawn like those at the time of death, but only briefly. The clear light of sleep [which is coarser than that of death] dawns, and when we begin to rise from that, we do so in a dream body ... Having risen from the clear light of sleep, a dream body is achieved, and we perform the various activities of dreamtime. Then, when we begin to awaken from sleep, the wind body of dream dissolves from the outside like breath on a mirror ...

When male and female become absorbed together ... [t]he heat melts the white and red drops, which descend within the empty insides of the seventy-two thousand channels. Through this, body and mind are blissfully satisfied and, at the end, during a period of strong desire, a thick regenerative fluid arises. After that, these drops of semen and blood ... are mixed in the mother's womb. The consciousness of the dying intermediate being enters into the middle of this, which is like the cream formed on boiled milk.

Womb-born humans of this world are said to have the six constituents — earth, water, fire, wind, channels and drops.

If the child ... in the womb is a boy, he dwells crouching on the mother's right side and facing backward towards her backbone. If a girl, she dwells crouching on the mother's left side and facing forward.

At the channel-centres there are white and red drops ... white predominant at the top of the head, and red at the solar plexus. These drops have their origin in a white and red drop at the "heart", which is the size of a large mustard seed or small pea and has a white top and red bottom. It is called the indestructible drop, since it lasts until death. The very subtle life-bearing wind dwells inside it and, at death, all winds ultimately dissolve into it, whereupon the clear light of death dawns.

Mother and son clear lights
The clear light of death is the "mother" clear light, whereas that which dawns through the power of meditation during sleep and in the waking state while on the spiritual path is called the "son" clear light.

Tired of scribbling, she closes the notebook. But the book holds her spellbound. You could copy it all down word for word and still not have taken in the half of its meaning. It reads like poetry and resists the grasp of the mind. The clear light dawns, it says, on the last dissolution and is "an appearance of very clear vacuity" like that of "a dawn sky in autumn, free of the three causes of pollution — moonlight, sunlight and darkness." That, coming out of an ideal world, makes her smile. Why autumn, when it is a season of mists and mellow fruitfulness? Autumn, the scholar explains, is when "the summer rains have suppressed well the rising of earth particles into intermediate space, and the sky is free from the obstructions of clouds". So it may be in Tibet, in a desert of sand and gravel, stone and frost, a higher world, crystalline.

Whatever is reborn through the *bardo*, the intermediate state, is not the flesh; nor is it the self, the soul, of the previous life: the *bardo* being is like the flame as it passes from candle to candle. What proof is there? None is needed, the *bardo* being an object of pure faith, like rebirth, like the resurrection in the flesh for Christians. Faith lives in a realm of the mind, an ether, where doubt has no air to breathe.

The old man died in the autumn and where is he now? Does he rest in peace? The scholar would say he was in a womb, at the quickening by this time.

The *bardo* is a realm of images and sounds, with no words. Yet words in a book and words said over the corpse are believed to be enough to guide the being safely on the way even, perhaps, to enlightenment. Better not to need the words: better, that is, to die forearmed through long meditation on the visions and sounds themselves, of beauty and terror, soon to be encountered. Failing that, however, the words are the way.

She tries reading out loud what she has copied down, since that is what it was meant for: as a mantra only comes alive when the words are embodied in breath. And still her mind can't get a purchase on this. It is smooth and slippery, opaque, impenetrable, a shell she will never crack.

We see the world, she writes, *through the lens of the past. Are we condemned to do so by the nature of the mind, or are there ways to live the present moment pure and uncontaminated, undistorted, unburdened? My hope of meditation, practice, the clear light: that my eyes be stripped bare. Is that enlightenment, when the scales fall from the eyes? Is this why the stupa has eyes?*

The dome is part of a tall stupa. The peaked golden tower stands for the element of fire, the dome underneath for water. Where is the stupa in the photo on the cover, Lhasa, Dharamsala, Kathmandu? The dome sits like a great egg in the sun, stained with small shadows, ragged prayer flags in lines of flight, as small as swallows. *The wind body of dream*. The surface is crisp with a nap, silken pleats, runnels and cross-hatchings, the creases of wind and water over white sand.

The house is full of shadows, creaks and small, private rustlings, absences. Too uneasy to go to bed alone, she goes out, driven out. A sneakthief, a spy, she creeps with her tape-recorder on RECORD around the church of her baptism. The only light is that thrown out by the windows and the white stain that is the moon in the clouds. The people of the desert must have looked up in the Gulf on the night the war ended and thanked Allah for a sky with no planes or missiles, only the stars and the moon. Or was there nothing to see for the smoke of burning oil? In the desert a veil over the sun might be bearable, even a blessing, but over the night sky? The moon was full, huge over Greece, the sea, and she took photos of its rise those nights not even knowing the war was at an end. The late summer/winter full moon of February.

A murmur of voices, a bird screech. A white shape, an owl, a barn owl? *Koukkouváïa*. *Koukkouváïa* is owl, but the screech owl has a name of its own, a beautiful one, *klapsopoúli*, weeping-bird. This is the night of the bread and wine, the cup of death in the garden and the traitor's kiss. *I doúla tou Theoú, Anna*, the priest said, the slave, the servant of God, Anna, and sponged her with water and green oil. *Elaía, elaiólado, ef-hélaion*, fruits of *elaïs*, the holy tree. The soapy water from her first bath after this was holy too, and had to be saved in the *skáfi*, the copper dish, for Kyria Sofia to tip into buckets and carry here in the cool of the twilight and pour at the roots of the pines, holy oil to holy ground, these roots, here at Bell's feet, cold under the rust-red needles. Straight after she was baptised she had her wedding, a wife of nine years in her own eyes, but the Australian registry office counted for nothing in those days. Yanni was two that summer. He stood with his cousins, all licking ice-creams, and the pines rang with cicadas.

The Junta had fallen only a month before. A new dawn for Greece, people were saying. The marriage had two years left to run.

I doúla tou Theoú. And *i ieródoulos* is almost the same, the holy slave, so close in meaning that you could easily confuse them and yet that is the prostitute, *pórni*. It must go back to the worship of the Goddess, her temples, her priestesses. With my body I thee worship.

The next week Yanni had his turn in church, with his cousins. Mamma gave them all a bath out on the porch first, soaping and sluicing them one by one in the copper dish, shrieking whenever one twisted free or shoved at the other. One by one they were given the grandfather's name, dunked in the font and daubed with oil, wrapped in towels and passed on to godfathers draped in barbershop white sheets. Each new Yanni shone in the candle-light, wet and convulsed with howls while a young godfather — three young boys, strangers to Bell — wrestled to thrust him into a brand new suit of clothes. She was at the back. The custom was for the mother to be banned, and at a baptism in Melbourne she had seen a mother driven out by scowling men; but Vaïa and Chloï were there and so was she, taking the photos that are on the wall. On that day a trestle table was set up and waiting in the cool of the *sála* for the family and the guests.

Three such fine boys! the world said, three *pallikarákia* to take the City back for us.

God forbid, she said. May they grow up to be men of peace.

What are you saying, *kalé* Bella? These three will go into the army together.

For their national service, that was all they meant, no harm in it, only this was a few weeks after the invasion of Cyprus, the call-up that brought chaos and despair to Greece and then brought down the Junta; dead young soldiers had come home mysteriously in body bags to the villages, and the border with Turkey bristled with mines, destroyers, troops. Grigori, Lefteri and Andrea were all called up. Lefteri was being kept in the navy. Go into the army? God forbid, said Bell and they stared.

Bella is a hippy, said Grigori. He smiled. Never mind her.

She went through it all willingly enough back then, the rites and responses, and made her cross and swallowed the bread and sweet wine. So why not now? But since she was not in good faith, however willing? Because until she was married in this rite their Yanni was officially a bastard. It was for his sake and even more for his grandparents' sake, so that he could take his place in the family, she thinks, and be baptised in his fatherland without the stigma of illegitimacy on his papers. Did the world know that she believed in none of it? Would the world have cared? If you have joined the dance, the saying goes, you have to dance, and belief is beside the point. Or so she chose to see it, deceiving herself, perhaps, but can you ever know the truth of anything you are doing, the whole story, at the time? The past is like a dream when you look back, with whatever wisdom you can muster, of hindsight. Hidden bits of the past may come to light, but how much has sunk out of sight meanwhile, changed or forgotten? The only difference with memories is the illusion we have of sharing them with others who were witnesses. Like a dream also, a memory can flare in the mind like a match only to burn down to a thread of soot in the time it takes you to open your eyes.

Here one New Year, the whole of the region snowbound, she was a belly in repose, great with child. Great with child. Yanni began here. He quickened here, and was born at home in Australia. The shutters were dripping with icicles all day. She would just lie in the bed and stare. A belly warm in its rising like the floury dough. A snowy dome with a blond nap of hairs, a ripple of movement, of life. In the four nights she has been here in the house where it was common knowledge that she was to raise her children and grandchildren and care for her husband and his parents into old age, growing old, dying, when her time came to be buried in that graveyard out among the wheat and the vines: she has not had one dream. Not a flicker of one, or not as far as she knows. The nights are darkness and cold, oblivion.

Nothing flows, nothing but piss and mucus — no blood, no tears, no dreams, no action. I came to — behold? A condition of stasis, she writes in her diary. *Apógnosi,* she adds, a word with no English equivalent that she knows of, but close to despair. Although *apelpisía* is our despair.

We old women and a few young ones are in the garden together inside a wall of black pines, folded in silence while the flowers of light simmer all around us in their pools of oil. We have made ourselves beds out of rugs. We are here to keep watch and to sorrow and to pray on this the last night of the life of our Lord among men. So did his holy mother mourn, on a night like this of the Passover, among the women, and weep and pray to the Father for her son in his agony. This is the night they were gathered to feast on the Passover lamb and eat for the first time the bread of the body of Jesus and drink the wine of his immortal blood. We have our rugs spread and our candles alight. Some are falling asleep. Here is Zoumbou fast asleep already, and Chrysoula is swaying. Our eyes are heavy. Lord, let me not enter into temptation, grant that I stay awake in obedience to your command. My soul is exceeding sorrowful, even unto death: tarry ye here, and watch with me.

And he came out, and went, as was his wont, to the Mount of Olives; and his disciples also followed him. And when he was at the place, he said unto them, Pray that ye enter not into temptation. And he was withdrawn from them but a stone's cast, and kneeled down, and prayed, saying, Father, if thou be willing, remove this cup from me: nevertheless not my will, but thine, be done.

And there appeared an angel unto him from heaven, strengthening him. And being in an agony he prayed more earnestly: and his sweat was as it were great drops of blood falling down to the ground. Where was the holy mother then, to wipe his brow, and why do the Evangelists have not a word to say of her? And when he rose up from prayer, and was come to his disciples, he found them sleeping for sorrow among the olive trees of the garden. And he said unto them, Why sleep ye? Rise and pray, lest ye enter into temptation. The spirit indeed is willing, but the flesh is weak. He went away again the second time, and prayed, saying, O my Father, if this cup may not pass away from me, except I drink it, thy will be done. And he came and found them asleep again in the cool of the olives: for their eyes were heavy. And he left them, and went away again, and prayed for the third time. Then cometh he to his disciples, and saith unto them, Sleep on now and take your rest: behold, the hour is at hand, and the Son of man is betrayed into the hands of sinners.

Restless and wide awake, Bell stands in the *sála* with the light off, looking around. Here is the centre of the house, the no man's land that all the other rooms open into, by far the largest room and the coldest, with a mosaic floor of grey ice. It has the smell of a room little used. The oil lamp is still burning among the ikons, but its flame only makes a tawny smudge with no more warmth than a breath. In September of course it would never have been as cold as this. But in September it would not have mattered how cold it was, or not to the old man. As if the dead felt the cold, so obvious, so silly, and yet her heart is suddenly grasped as if by a hand, with astonishment and dread. Here Kyria Sofia knelt over him and lifted his hands, his feet, to push them into his best suit among the candles and incense and the green branches. She rolled a scarf under his chin to keep his mouth from falling open. She pressed his eyelids down. Here in the *sála*, where in the good years the overflow from the barn was stored, the tobacco bales, and sandhills of barley at blood heat, the summer still in them, so that you were always having to crunch over a scattering of seeds and pick them off the soles of your feet. There were crickets, bunches of grapes turning brown and mouldy, apples, in a cloud of gnats. This is where she laid him, blue with the cold, and where the familiar hands, one with a tight ring, held and sponged and moved on his flesh.

The soldiers woke them, tramping in with torches and swords to take the Lord prisoner and they lying in a stupor all that time in the dark of the garden with the bread and the wine warm in their bellies.

When Yanni's hour was at hand the doctors knew better, didn't they? They kept saying all he needed now was rest, the operation was a success — well, he awoke asking for the priest. And in came the hospital priest bearing incense, holy water and wine but no bread, not so much as a crust. And what an irony, when the Church has had from our hands, from our earth, a mountain of bread over the years and yet not one crust can be found to go with the wine when it comes to giving Yanni his last rites. Is this what you in Kilkis call a Holy Thanksgiving, Father? he asked, and rightly so. The blood of Christ without the body?

He saw a dream while he was under the anaesthetic. He was walking across the bridge, he told me, on the way out of the village. I had not gone far, he said, when I thought it was time to turn back, but when I got to the river again, Sofia, the bridge was down.

There was no bridge?

No bridge and then I knew.

He had another dream that he told no one but Grigori. His mother had come to him in his sleep, Kyria Katerina, and said she loved him and was waiting for him, but he sent her away; he said he wanted nothing to do with her. So I fear it will be when my Lefteri's time comes to die. My darling, who would have thought it? You will send me away like that. But if that be the will of God. Lord in your mercy only let me die at peace with the world. How strange life is, the way you sometimes see another pattern from the one you knew, a deeper, broader pattern under the real one, and looser, more free, utterly strange.

Yanni was not in any pain by then, he was so far gone, and they had given him morphine. He rested quietly once the priest was gone. I held his hand while he slept, or seemed to sleep. I thought he looked smaller in the bed, the way a corpse does, as if he were already shrinking. I thought he might be dead. I sat still, afraid of alarming him if he was still alive and I moved or called out. Once or twice I must have fallen asleep myself, my head on the bed. It lulls you to sleep, this hum of the voices rising and falling and the soft movement of the golden lights like the interior of some great beehive in the full sun. What does that remind me of? A story. I know it has something to do with the holy bread. A bee in the church flew off with a crumb. And no sooner had she eaten of the bread of God than she built a church of wax in the hive, perfect in every detail. What made me think of the bee? The Garden, was it? Gethsemane. I am too sleepy to remember now. What am I trying to remember?

Bell crawls into bed, there being no point in keeping watch here by herself, and changes the tape to one she made on the islands, on Paros. It begins with a loud hiss, not of over-amplification or wear, but a warm salt wind as it flails in the olive leaves, an unsteady, shifting hiss like waves over sand. Bell closes her eyes. When the sound softens, this is when the sirocco abated enough for her to fight her way to shelter under a dry-stone wall and catch her breath. A fig that grew hard against the wall shook soundlessly, having no leaves, only a thousand thin grey lifted branches, light as cork, darkening with wet and drying fast. And she remembers now in the hot wind's hiss and stir the way Kyria Sofia once ran inside out of a storm, the door slamming at her back, half the *sála* awash, and stood to catch her breath with her cupped hands held high, full of dark figs. A milky rain ran down her bare arms.

When Bell turns the tape over, there are the cries of wild birds, owls and crows, the croon and cackle of hens, a rooster, pigeons. Goats and goat bells, a donkey wheezing and sobbing. Then comes the chanting of the liturgy, hollow, an old voice among rustlings and a murmur, the jingle of the censer in a stone chapel. A chime of bells in triads fading into a dirge in the same tempo, a few bars of a woman singing a *moirolóï*, wavering, jagged, harsh.

She only has to lift the bedcovers to be flooded with a sour smell like urine in hot straw: sweat, with something else, no sweetness of blood, not a drop, still not, but something sooty to it, tarry, like the ooze that coats the barrel of the *sómba*, and the smoke that seeps out day and night from every chink. How long is it since she had a shower? Not that any mere shower will be enough to wash this off. She can see herself arriving in Australia — *there's a heat wave* — and dragging on her bathers to run to the beach and soak, for the hour or two that it will take to get clean, in a bay of salt. Then into the shower to finish the job. Ah-ha, she sighs, and the sourness floods up, a hot breath around her ears that makes her choke.

Only a week ago the islands, the sea, Athens, were the whole world, and what is left of it all now? — nothing but a few sharp images and snatches of sound in her mind. Some are on film, she hopes, and on tape. Which is more than the house will be, and the village, Mamma, all of this, in a few days' time in Australia. But that is no consolation.

*Ο κάτω κόσμος. In the cave of the Mysteries of Eleusis at midnight Lucius in **The Golden Ass** saw the sun shine out of another world, underworld, the place of death, **as if it were noon**. The sun on its way back east, the black sun, the sun of the south of the world, fire and glory. A heat wave. Fold on fold of sand, water, wind.*

The skin of the moon is soot black and only looks white to our earthen eyes caught in the sun.

Holy Thursday, and the votive lamp is the only light. The pleats of its glass are enlarged in shadow and light over all the house. This is the night of the Last Supper and the Agony, when Jesus found his disciples sleeping. They lay there among the olive trees. For all their tiredness the women will keep watch in the church until daybreak. Sing and talk and read aloud, sleep only if they can't stay awake — the one time that their voices are allowed to be heard. No wind, a still night, a watery sheen on the window panes of the village. Streetlamps and the shadowy trees printed on walls. They have whitewashed trunks and the blossom has no scent, paper flowers. Now and then a drift of chant, a bell chime, a bird's pipe note. A street of windows with one lamp in a glass mantle of light. A furtive puppy squatting in a puddle. At midnight I saw the long windows alight in the pines and heard a murmur, voices of women reciting, singing in low voices. What are they doing, Mamma (how many years ago now)? Καλέ, μοιρολογάνε: Lamenting, mourning, bewailing the dead.

GREAT FRIDAY

On Great Friday morning Kyria Sofia sleeps in. It is half past nine when she stumbles to the kitchen, where Bella is drinking coffee. *"Kaliméra,"* she yawns.

"*Kaliméra*, Mamma."

"You have just got up?"

"No, I have been for a walk. What time did you get home?"

"Five? Six?"

"I'll make your tea."

"No, no, tonight we have the *epitáfio*. There will be no eating, no drinking."

"You must, Mamma. Where will you find the strength to walk all the way around the village?"

"You say well."

She sprawls over the table, her eyelids hanging open and raw, pressing fine crumbs of the grey *halvá* on a fingertip and licking it. But sipping the hot tea she looks sharply up at Bella and spits out what has been sticking in her craw.

"I wonder what you came for."

"What do you mean?"

"You wanted to follow the whole of our Easter week, you said. But you are missing the heart of it — *ná*, last night — "

"How can I, when I scandalise the world?"

"Make your cross at least. Then you won't scandalise them, will you! *Ná!* It's your egoism."

Bell rewinds last night's tape and, pressing PLAY, hears again her slow footsteps on wet pine needles, the unseen walker in the dark; rise and fall of the faint singing within the walls; a bird's chirrup of surprise, a sharp rustle; the barking of dogs in a long sequence, in yard after yard; a donkey's rhythmic sobs and gasps, as soft as pigeon coos; a cock crow; a vast depth of silent sky.

O egoismós sou einai. Lost for words, she hovers over her diary. She came here to take part in a ceremony and a grief. Now look at me, she thinks, a woman of fifty skulking in my room after a fight over — what? — my clothes, my behaviour in church, as if I were a schoolgirl. *It serves me right*, she has written, and, *I have to stand up for my freedom. A mind of my own. Hier stehe ich!* Ridiculous, but there it is; and it serves her right for letting them both in for this, as if she could crawl her way back into the womb, a grown woman, like a hermit crab backing itself painfully into a shell too small for it. Yes, come, Mamma said, there is room for you, of course. Taking me on in good faith, no child of *her* womb either, no reason why she should, and no wonder she feels let down now. She is within her rights — and her house, and her Church. The body of God! Isn't the whole earth the body of God, so long as you believe in God? *I believe in earth*, Bell writes, *the holiness of earth*. Look at us, two more stiff-necked and sullen old village women at each other's throats. This *is* the village, given time, all its life sealed up in a few dim rooms and postures and attitudes, in cold stone. *(To think I was here for years and dreamed of a life here!)* she adds with a flourish.

The whole world, ὅλος ὁ κόσμος, everybody. Ο κοσμάκης, in the saying, the little people. The small world. And ὁ μέγας, the great.

Q: I wonder what you came for. Απορώ γιατί ήρθες.
A: Ο εγωισμός μου είναι.

Μεγάλη Παρασκευή. Good Friday morning. The passing bell rang clear across the fields from the next village down river. Low knuckles of the vines alongside. Now the ground is green with a sprinkling of white stars and grape hyacinths, σταφύλια του κούκκου, grapes of the cuckoo. Rosemary in blue flower and a white pear tree. Women and children bent over lighting the candles at the graves. Hum of bees and flies, small cypresses, the oaks dark, their corky trunks speckled silver and gold lichen like beaten foil. They still have the old brown leaves.

Finding her drooping in the yard, Kyria Sofia observes that Bell would do well to have her Easter bath this morning, before the house fills up with people. A bath, Bell says, would make my cold worse. Any excuse, although it is true that at night her nose fills up with snot as if from a well between her ears so that she wakes up dry-throated, gasping for breath. How long is it now since she had an all-over wash? Since Athens, seven days. A further disgrace, if she is not washed and clean by Sunday, let alone Easter Sunday. The question of turning on the *thermosíphono* does not even arise, of course, what with the price of electricity; and since in this gloom the solar panels barely take the chill off, Kyria Sofia suggests putting saucepans of water on the *sómba* before she goes back to church. Thank you, Bell says, and blows her nose for effect, but I think I'd better not take the risk. She shrinks from the memory of the years of washes — you could hardly call them baths — in the *méros* with its thin skin of cement blocks and the wind hissing in on her as she stripped naked, in the candlelight at first and then in later years under the lightbulb, to soap and sluice herself time and time again, shivering until the copper *skáfi* rattled on the grit of the floor, and filled and overflowed. In one, two, three, four, five days I can have a shower in Australia, after all, she announces, watching the old woman scowl and bite her lips and bustle around putting the saucepans on anyway. In case you change your mind, Bella.

Sorry, it's my egoism, Bell mutters, to the wall since the old woman has gone again. Since I have the name I will have the deed, as the saying goes. Besides, the tub is blocked. On the other hand, her hair could do with a wash, clamped as it is in a cap of cold grease on her scalp and lank beyond bearing. After all, once the others arrive she will have lost her last chance of having the *méros* to herself. So she makes up her mind to it, mixes the water that is bubbling in the saucepans by now with icy water from the tap and, locked in the *méros* with the copper dish, rinses and soaps and rinses her hair. She sighs aloud with the pleasure of it, the flow, warm and heavy, of the golden water over her scalp, and the sigh comes back, a cave echo from a wall of hair. Kyria Sofia arrives home while she is towelling it dry on the porch in a gleam of sun cast up in a hand-mirror. She catches the old woman's mocking look, her black figure dwindling, shapeless, a black candle by a fire. Straw-bright hair glows under the brush and hairs float out here and there as loose as smoke. Falling. Let them fall, the grey ones, and at this rate I can go on shedding my age hair by hair, Bell thinks: grow a young curtain of straw-gold between my eyes and the sun, steam rising, the flame, the wisp of smoke, the phoenix.

Her clothes are wet at the neck and need changing. She shivers in her room, looking down at the mixture of young and old that her body, like her hair, has become. The breasts are still young. Longer than they were, softer; small, but not shrunken; they were never much larger than this, except when she had milk. The belly is smooth, white; and the thighs. The calves are better hidden, so veined and loose, so scraggy. And the arms, and these yellow hands, gloved in chicken skin. Elbows shrivelled to the bone. Years ago, when he was only little, Yanni caught sight of those elbows and asked in horror what had happened. Even then she was a young woman and an old woman in the one skin.

The grey hairs renew themselves, says the voice of reason, thick and fast. You only have to look in the mirror to see how the old woman is gaining ground. She is bound to win. Provided she lasts the course, that is. Bell pulls on the black clothes she travelled in. Yes: but you only see the flat grey fuzz on the outside when you look in the mirror. It looks all grey. You have to be inside it to see what a shower of straws of glass and rain and spider thread it is, how bright.

Kyria Sofia is not tired, only weak, so weak — and this is early morning — that she has to lie down. The *sómba* has gone out. No wood, no kindling. The hard work never ends. Bella has washed her hair and the *sómba* can go out now for all she cares. My lady is too busy adoring herself in the mirror. If you adored the ikons half so much you might see beyond the flesh into what is eternal, like the Empress and her ladies once upon a time: for the ikon is a window for the eyes of the soul. The court Fool creeping into the harem one day caught them all adoring their ikons and kissing them. And these were the days of the Ikonoklast Heresy, when the high and low of the City hid their ikons for fear of being dragged through the mud, and worse, for idolatry, as it was called. Off went the Fool full of glee to the Emperor, who stormed into the harem. The Fool is mistaken, the Empress said calmly, we were just admiring ourselves in our mirrors: and the Emperor was satisfied and withdrew. Who was the real fool in the story? For the ladies were free to adore images to their hearts' content, so long as they were of their own selves, and not the saints.

This winter that never ends — might I be better off if I made my home with Vaïa after all? Maybe I will next winter. Time to think about next winter when it comes. This is no home now, she thinks, and no fatherland of mine ever, these villages and fields of mud or brown stubble, the stork landing and lifting. Zoumbou can look after the hens for me if I go. But not the grave. Only I can see to the grave. All those graves in the cemetery, so old, so many, and yet we are the ones whose tread is light on this earth, the newcomers, the first of our lines. Our forefathers and mothers are scattered all over the old Turkish lands. How many were left to lie in their own blood, not in the ground but on it? They burst in the sun like ripe figs under the walls, forage for the crow. We were children of Konstandinoupoli, we three, my brothers and I, born in the City. But our parents were strangers there, newcomers whose home was on Lake Ohrida, wild *kléftes,* rebels who had harried the Turks until they lost patience and uprooted them all, the whole village, and sent them out across Makedonia, across Thraki, on foot with their mules and pigs into the deserts of Anatolia, exile on exile. Transplanted there under the eyes of the Turks our village was put to work running the *karavanseraï*.

But not our parents, who gave them the slip in the City where my father who is forgiven had a cousin who owned a carpet factory and took them in. We Refugees only know by hearsay who we are sprung from, our year and not our date of birth, since the records were lost in the Catastrophe. Turkey was all the home we knew. As for our fathers, mourning for the old lake land, bear land, wolf land, Lake Ohrida where they belonged, they had no love for Turkey, neither the golden City nor the desert, my uncle said; and nor did he. Do I remember the City? A street in a purple light in the heat, a harbour of red and gold water, a room with a lamp. One daybreak a woman came, a Muslim, young, I could tell, with her face hidden in a white cloth and in her hands another white cloth that was warm. There was bread wrapped inside, flat bread. I can still feel the bread in my hands and mouth. Or was this in Smyrni? I no longer know if I really remember or have heard the story told, or if it was a dream. Our parents I remember as a grey photograph, a wedding. They died of fever within days of each other when I was seven and so it was that my mother's brother, Theio Dimitri, came for us. He took us to the desert where we burned and froze, half-starved. When the Greeks failed in their invasion and were slaughtered, we were herded past the dead and the dying, and the Turks ripped and tore them with bayonets and yatagans and the crows fed on them where in the past they had fed on the flesh of kings and the flesh of captains. It was with us as with the Armenians before us, and the Kurds and how many others since? How will the Turks answer for these sins at the throne of God?

A column, we walked out with the mules and donkeys, those that lived, as out of Ohrida, on the return journey, across Thraki to Makedonia. Yanni and his mother were on that exodus; his father was dead. We who were the village had taken ship out of a city of fire, Smyrni, and on Greek soil at last we crossed river after river and the last was the great Vardari into which our river flows. The Vardari was our Jordan, a new life. We settled on this village for the sake of the river, the elders said, and the many trees. We were not wanted here. At first the villagers attacked us.

Later they shunned us. Only now are the young people starting to make friends and intermarry. How could they know what we lived through? I dream and when I wake I can hardly call it to mind, the crowded harbour of Smyrni. Boats in the water, and heads, bodies bobbing and nudging the hulls of ships, the great ships of the Great Powers in a sea of blood and fire while the city burned. Hands grasping at ropes, at oars, hacked off, babies spitted with bayonets in their mothers' arms. But our uncle carried and dragged us three on board a ship that took us with a cargo of salt to Greece. For years we talked of one day going back to see the City, what it has become. A stockade of minarets the sultans built, towers of marble, towers of blood. A pilgrimage, Grigori said, one day Bella and I will take you on a pilgrimage; but something would always come up, the Junta and then the invasion of Cyprus, and in the end he and Bella separated and now we will never go. Nor to the other City of God, Jerusalem the Golden, where it is every Christian's duty to go once in a lifetime. Why, when God is everywhere in His creation? Because in the flesh He was only ever in Israel. But it has not been given to me to see Bethlehem and the Jordan River, the Mount of Olives, Gethsemane and Golgotha, at Easter, in the footsteps of the Lord. I have only the one pilgrimage left in me, one river, and the land of death is nearer now than any city. The fatherland of death. I am most sorry, all the same, never to have seen the Agia Sofia, the temple of the Holy Wisdom, the heart of Christendom on earth, whose shell is a miracle of the Lord in stone. And the lake lands where our parents belonged — there is a monastery in a fir wood on the shore where water and air are one and souls are saved, or there was once, they say, before Communism. Can we really be said to belong to any land until we have lain in it?

Ashamed, Bell on the porch remembers the copper dish suddenly, still full of water and suds on the rush stool in the *méros*. If Kyria Sofia sees it she will empty it herself, heavy as it is, beyond her strength, and Bell runs inside. The old woman is asleep under a blanket in the half dark; both *sómbes* are still unlit. The dish is where Bell left it, precariously balanced. Relieved, she puts her arms around it and totters forward, bent double, her wrists shaking and her face almost on the scummy surface of the water. Perched on the rim of the lavatory bowl it lurches as she tips it, carefully spinning it out to avoid a flood, down into the dark throat. A wave of froth rises and then, thank God, sinks down, rising and sinking, and loosening the corpse-reek from the depths of the cesspit, a puff of sweet, warm rottenness.

Dark sky, μουντός, thunder and thick rain. Sun, birds, the storks settling and folding up. Everyone is hoping for fine weather so they can spit-roast their lambs and kids outside on Sunday.

The village is all gardens, roses, and only hers is a wilderness. A little row of hyacinths, two olive trees, gaunt trees and weeds with a broody hen (dapple-grey, ψαρή), pecking out, thin — the eggs are in a manger in the shell of the old barn next to the house.

Ψάρι is fish and ψαρή is fish-coloured, in the feminine, silvery. Ψαρόνι is starling. Plain grey is φαιός and a grey-haired woman is a φαιομάλλα, γκριζομάλλα, σταχτομάλλα, ash-haired one, or ψαρομάλλα, fish-haired one. Pale or light is open, ανοιχτό (whereas dark is a borrowing from Italian: σκούρο, obscure). The idea in Greek of open colours, as if shade from the beginning of time has been a matter of apertures, the lens, the iris.

Her hair in its topknob still feels damp and, shivering, she loosens it to the open air to dry off. She still has it spread out in a curtain all over her knees — *the ruddy limbs & flaming hair* — and over the notebook on her lap when Vaïa, Andrea and Sonya arrive with the baby. Bell offers them her room, but they prefer to make up their beds in the one warm room with the *sómba*, and the basketware cot can go at the foot of the shelf that holds the television set. Kyria Sofia will sleep on the divan in the kitchen. She can light the *sómba* in there as well and have it burning all day and not be cold, since they will need it for cooking in any case.

Taking the baby for a hold, Bell asks after the mother. She is coming, surely? But Rina and her husband have arranged to have Easter — make Easter — on Mytilini with his family. And the boy, their Yanni? He went with them to Mytilini. "What a shame. I would have loved to see him," she says. "My Yanni sends regards."

"Did you bring photos?"

Moving slowly with the baby, Bell gets them out, passing them around while they exclaim over how much he has grown, how his face has ripened and become more Greek, until Kyria Sofia mimics spitting in the Evil Eye.

"I burst with pride," Bell says, "when I heard how Andrea and your Yanni took him up Olympus."

"We had a good time," Andrea says, with the quirk of the lips which is his smile, and holds out his arms for the baby.

The *mother*, though! Retreating to her room for a breathing space, Bell shakes her head in disbelief. To think that Rina is the mother, when she was a baby herself in this very house not all that long ago. I can't keep up, she thinks. Look at me looking on, a ghost, an old self, condemned to walk these rooms. She hugs herself. And the baby! She is the mother all over again, her white skin and blue eyes, long-limbed, and so light, no weight at all. Of course a baby always feels lighter once it can sit and hold its head up, Bell remembers, or thinks she does. That was in the days of the long summer afternoons spent submerged in the *sála*, cross-legged on the floor threading the tobacco leaves on lengths of string. There was a year when the grain harvest overflowed here, red-ripe, and then the grapes, fermenting in a fog of gnats. Now it fills with more visitors, their talk and smoke, relatives also here for Easter who have seen the car and come for a coffee, and Bell has to be on hand to greet them. They dandle the baby and Vaïa laughs. Her hair is cut short, springing all over her head in crisp black curls with a few white glints and strands showing under the lightbulb. Yiayia Vaïa, they all tease, does the baby call you Yiayia, Vaïa? No, of course not, she says Mamma! She is grandmotherly enough anyhow, Vaïa, stout and slow-moving, young though she is, or younger than Bell at least, at forty-six. Bell herself is far from grandmotherly. Spinsterish is more like it. She sees herself as they must all see her coming out of the cold kitchen with the glasses of water, a snivelling drudge, yellow-faced and gaunt, whose words slur from disuse, having to be pushed out one by one through a wooden jaw.

"Sonya is learning English at school," Vaïa says when all the visitors have gone except Chrysoula. "Now what did you want to ask your aunt?" She puts the baby in Andrea's arms. "I have to go for the milk."

"Oh, where?" Bell stands up.

"To the aunt's down the road. She has goats. Sonya?"

So Sonya brings out a magazine in English all about a pop group Bell has never heard of, New Kids on the Block, and flops down next to her in a whiff of chewing gum, and meat, or something raw, fleshy, with rust in it. *Yanni would probably have heard of them*, Bell says slowly in English. *I love New Kids on the Block*, Sonya answers and with Andrea looking on she reads aloud slowly while Bell helps out with the hard words and then with filling out the application form for the fan club. Then Lyka runs over looking for Sonya. Lyka loves New Kids on the Block as well. Their hair tossing, they run back over the road.

Theia Kalliroï is soon here and the chatter that starts up again over a coffee with Chrysoula turns derisively to someone called Kyria Yorgaina, but as if Bell should know her too, until she is driven to asking who this Yorgaina is.

"You know," says Andrea through his cigarette.

"Not the one in the song?" There used to be a hit song of that name on the radio day and night, in the seventies.

"No, don't be silly. I forget her name now," he says and Bell stares in consternation.

"Yorgo's wife, *jánoum*!" says Theia Kalliroï. "Zoumbou's new daughter-in-law. You *know*."

"Her name is not Yorgaina."

"Well, it is now. You marry a Yorgos and you become a Yorgaina, it's as simple as that."

"You mean you *call* her that?"

"Why not?"

"Do you call Vaïa Andreaina? Was I ever called Grigoraina? I think that's awful."

"What do you mean?" Chrysoula frowns. "He says well, Andrea. This is silly talk."

"Awful! Not only to lose your surname but your Christian name as well!"

Kyria Sofia, hurrying through to the kitchen for her apron and the scraps for the hens, shoots her a look. She heard that. "Will I give you a hand?" Bell is quick to lean in the doorway and offer.

"What?"

"With the hens?"

"Tsk." The old woman's head jerks back, abrupt in rejection.

"Mamma, where *is* Zoumboulitsa today? Everyone else has been here."

"Exactly. Do you expect her to come with everyone here?"

"Won't she be cold?"

"She will stay in bed. I will call in on the way back if I have time before church."

At nightfall Vaïa brings in a billy of milk which she strains through gauze into the saucepan. No one is in the mood for more talk. This is the time of day the old man would always trudge in and sit without speaking, rolling a cigarette, or stretch out on the divan by the *sómba*. Bell helps with the food, *makarónia* again with feta and spring onions stirred in with the green oil, always Andrea's favourite meal in the summers they spent here together, and tonight he eats two plates. The milk wrinkles and puffs up, and falls loose again.

The baby is still asleep. Vaïa grasps the chance of a moment alone to make a coffee she finishes in two gulps. Then as always she swills the soft grounds up from the bottom so that they coat the sides, and turns the cup deftly upside down over the saucer.

She has adjusted now to the smallness of the house of her childhood. Every time she sees it she is taken aback all over again by how much it has shrunk. It always takes a while for the image in her mind to match the new scale, with the rooms little again and bare of magic. No matter how far her childhood recedes, once she goes away the house reverts to its true size and power in her mind. While her attention is on it, like now, the house stays as it is. Once her attention wanders, the house is vast again, dwarfing her. It takes over. It will feel too small in the first moment of return even when she is an old woman, as old as Mamma.

I am the daughter of the house, she thinks, turning the cup over at arm's length to see what shapes are hidden in the coffee dust. All she can see at first is a clod, a shapeless dark mass, death, earth of the grave. But to one side there is a shape in feathery lines, a ship's mast, a bird with a long tail, a leaf, what is she to make of it? A mast or a cross? Two deaths, and there is a third to come, but who, and when? A cross, though, is supposed to be auspicious, especially now, and a leaf ... Her eyes are watering with the strain. If only she could ask! Now Mamma has taken it into her head to refuse to read cups. A sin, she calls it, an indulgence of the godless. Sighing, Vaïa gives up and rinses the cup out.

The baby coughs in the next room. Vaya holds her breath to listen, but there is only silence. The daughter of my daughter, she thinks, is my daughter twice over, so the saying goes. Three times over, the daughter of the house. With her coming we have brought new life to the house, cancelling out the death.

Bella has left her packet of photos on the table, Bella who is back yet again. There is something not right about the way Bella persists in haunting the village, the house. What does she find here after all these years to draw her back? My brother has made a new life of his own and so should she. Why must she always be in black as if he were dead? Fifteen years alone in the world!

Was there no one else in her life she could have loved? If that was the case she might as well have stayed with Grigori and still had a place here, at least. If it means so much.

Idly Vaïa picks up the photos and shuffles through them again. Ach, Yannaki. Slouching on a jetty with his hands in his pockets, Yannaki on a sandy shore, Yannaki at a desk of books, his eyes a point of flame. How like Grigori he looks, blond though he is, and how Greek! His eyebrows have thickened, that must be what it is. He should come over more often now that his father can afford it. When he was little he came every year for summer, the full three months, and the boys were the Yannakia to the family and to the village at large, meaning the three of them, inseparable. When did it come to mean only the two? Grigori and Bella's Yannaki and our one. It was Chloï who kept Lefteri and the boy at a distance. In no time he became a stranger to us, their Yanni, stilted when we all met on family occasions, and shifty somehow, not hostile so much as unresponsive. He was null, cold, a presence that was more like an absence, as if he were a trespasser, already not in our world, so that after the first shock — I could never say this aloud, not to a soul, the shame would strike me dumb — his death made no real difference.

Except to the old ones. Baba took it hard. Vaïa takes down a photo of her father in the cane chair in his ragged work clothes, his arms loose on the arms of the chair and his head held high in the pose he always assumed, however tired, however ill, for the camera. Grigori's camera in this case, and she watched him take it. That was the day they drove up from Thessaloniki to find Baba digging the garden in the full sun, the hens all around him as bright as fire, planting the olive trees.

He was about to go into hospital for the operation. He had only days to live and he was planting olive trees. Like in the saying, when you plant an olive tree you are planting it for your children. The olive being a slow tree. There was a story Mamma used to tell, one of her stories of the Hodja, or a Karagiozi, whatever, about three young men in the flower of their youth walking along a road, who jeer at an old man they find planting an olive tree. He only shakes his head and says that no man knows the hour of his death. Rounding the bend in the road, still laughing, the young men are run over and killed instantly. As to the old man, the story has nothing to say.

The trees are thriving, so slender and long-leaved, years away from bearing and yet they will bear. They will have their beaded flowers and their abundances of grey-green little berries to ripen in the dark of winter, blacken and grow rich with their own oil.

He had no inheritance, our father. Nor did Mamma. They came here empty-handed, little children, herded on to the ships while behind them Smyrni bled and burned. The land he was allotted in the village he had to clear stone by stone with his bare hands. He built the house in stone, twice, because after Germans had cleaned it out, the grain, the animals, and retreated, Greeks burnt it down. War and more war, half the village at war with the other half and the cemetery filled with their graves. This house he built to last, after the peace was made. I was born when we had no house, in a slum in Thessaloniki, the only daughter. He raised it with Grigori on the corpse of the old house, in the ash and stone of the foundations, with the corpse of a cockerel thrown in, as if there were not enough blood spilt on the land. But the custom is meant as a blessing on the house, to make it stand firm and fruitful for all time. We moved in when the house was nothing but a shell of stone and we all slept in the one room in those days, as now. Mamma and Baba, Grigori and Lefteri and I and Yiayia Katerina. Strange how I have clung on, when the custom was always that the daughters cut their ties and clove to their husbands while the sons stayed, pillars of the house. For the old people, the *children* are the boys, and girls are not to be mentioned in the same breath. And yet I have been the one, with Andrea. We two are the pillars. Man and wife: however much they may, in the flesh, fall short, they are the doorposts, the two candlesticks. They are at the heart of life. Even Andrea — such a hothead, a fiery ikonoklast to this day, up to a point — even he has never wavered. He is unfailingly loyal. For our children and now our grandchild this is their home. Little enough, after all, and why not cling on? Nothing will change while Mamma is alive. You only have to look at Mamma to see that she is half air already, hollow, a shadow walking. What will happen then? We three will somehow have to share it, my brothers and I. The one in Australia and the one at sea.

She drops the photo on the table and the old man gazes proudly up, having planted olive trees.

So why only two?

In her room with the door left ajar for the sake of politeness, Bell can hear Sonya whining to her mother in the *sála*.

"Must she fart the whole time?"

"*Sout!* Shame on you."

"Why? She's out, isn't she? She has to let the world know. A belch, a fart, a screech, a fart —"

"She has wind. She is suffering a great deal."

"So are we. It stinks."

"*Sout!* Do you think she wants it, Sonya? She doesn't even eat."

"I can't stand it."

"People who live alone tend to forget themselves. This is her house, don't you forget."

"Mamma, I can go over to Lyka's for a while, can't I?"

"Ask your father."

"He said to ask you."

"Why at this time of night?"

"There's a good show on in a minute, all rock videos. Yiayia's television is no good. Mammaka? Please?"

"And after that?"

"We thought we might look the disco over, have a Coca Cola, you know, see the boys."

"You won't go to the *epitáfio*?"

"I will. I'll go."

"Don't forget."

"What time are you going?"

"I'm not this year, I'm minding the baby. Don't you be late!"

And the door scrapes and then slams shut.

Why is it only we old ones who come to worship now? We are the faithful who keep the light burning, we old women. It was not always so.

When you were crucified, Christ, all creation trembled at the sight of it. The earth quaked to the foundations in fear. For on this day when you were raised up, the people of the Jews were cast down. The veil of the temple was rent, and the graves opened and the dead rose from the vaults.

How did you bear it when the nails went in, and your blood burst out over the holy wood of the cross and seeped along your limbs when they raised you up high, jeering, and the flies swarmed. The Evangelists say nothing of this. I have read the four Gospels and not one tells of the hammer blows of the nails into the flesh of you who were a carpenter. You were God's carpenter. Life is full of such strange patterns. Irony of ironies. And those who loved you and stood by at the foot of your cross while you fought for breath were helpless to lift a finger.

Those who were there on the day of his death saw the sky strike at the sea a white stroke, a gong shaking with reverberations and afterwards, in the hollow light, swimmers were seen afloat in the shallows with their white bellies up like fish that have been dynamited. Men who were at hand ran in and dragged them out and laid them head-down on the shingle. There was a screaming. The rescuers clamped them and blew and sucked air into their lungs, and thumped their hearts until one by one they awoke. All but the last, and that was our boy, our own Lefteri's Yanni. And he was not burnt, not even struck, no one was; everyone had seen where the white forks plunged a long way out into the deep water. He was waterlogged, but had not died by drowning. His heart must simply have stopped, the doctor said, out of the shock of the blast.

I am old and ready, Lord, for death. May you not forget the least of your living ones, as we who live do not forget our dead who are in your keeping. My eyes are awash, I shudder with the cold, in your house I am in a sea of golden sparks and depths of water. Lord have mercy, Lord have mercy, Lord have mercy.

The Roman captain saw the omen and he shuddered. Your own mother stood there, and weeping like a mother cried out, How should I not lament? How not beat my breast when I see you hanging naked on the cross like a felon? Glory be to you, Lord, crucified, buried and risen again!

They took my clothing from me and cast a scarlet robe about me. On my head they placed a crown of thorns. And a reed they put in my right hand, to dash them in pieces like a potter's vessel. I bared my neck to the scourging. My face turned not away when they spat on me. I took my place before the judgment seat of Pilate. And I bore the cross for the salvation of the world.

All creation was transfixed with fear at the sight of you, Christ, hanging on the cross. The sun grew dark and the foundations of the earth were shaken. The very world suffered with him who created it. Glory to you, Lord, who freely took this upon you for the love of us!

When on this day the spotless virgin beheld you on the cross, you the Word of God, a bitter wound struck her heart and like a mother she lamented. And as she sighed in the depths of her heart, her strength was taken from her by such pains as she had never known in childbirth. When he gave up the ghost they took him down off the cross and laid him in her arms to hold, her son, as naked as the day that he was born and she cried out, loudly weeping: Woe is me, divine child! Woe is me, light of the world! Why did you vanish from my eyes, Lamb of God? Therefore were the hosts of the disembodied spirits seized with trembling and cried out: Glory, glory, Lord beyond all understanding! Amen.

In the kitchen Andrea, rocking backward and forward with the baby in his arms, is singing the old lullaby, Vaïa's lullaby, *náni náni*, over and over. He breaks off to make a frog face at Bell as she walks in.

"Off to church again, are we?"

"Not me, are you?"

"Me? Religion is the opium of the people."

"Ah. Is it still? You look a bit tired."

"I need an early night."

She opens her arms and he gives her the baby, who kicks and strains away to her grandfather. Bell passes her back. "No, she doesn't want me. What a beautiful eye," she says with a sly smile, fingering the bead of blue enamel pinned to the baby's collar, not looking at him.

"Of course the eye isn't religion."

"No? What is it?"

"Superstition."

"Ah. You remember once we all went to the Meteora and up to the monasteries and stayed the night at your mother's house?" He frowns, but then he shakes his head, he remembers. His mother has been dead for years, and Bell was only there once, but she can see a house with a courtyard in Kalambaka, almost at the foot of the high pinnacles of rock and mist where the monasteries sit like old storks' nests, eagles' nests. "Such a peaceful house," she says and he rocks the baby, listening. From there the Meteora are blue spindles, canyons.

"It was, yes."

"She was a woman of peace, your mother, I was so sorry to hear ... You men went to the *kafeneíon* and we women were in the courtyard when all the children burst out crying. All of them together, Yanni and Yanni and your nieces, and they wouldn't stop, so your mother sent for a wise-woman —"

"Theia Asimina."

"Was it? Oh, I laughed, I loved it. They brought her a glass of water, and she put a drop of olive oil in. It sank straight to the bottom in one drop and rose again. There, she said, the Eye. It was green and gold, shining on the water. Otherwise the oil would have scattered, your mother told me — is that right?"

"How should I know?" Andrea says, but his lips are twisting to hide a smile.

"So she cast a counter-spell —"

"And they stopped."

"Yes! All at once they stopped!" The sudden hush, and crickets, the night wind, a trickle of water. She sits down. "The crying stopped as if she had cut it with a knife, your aunt — Theia Asimina? The relief! No one but me was even surprised."

"Faith works miracles. Ask our mother-in-law."

"You know, all right, the opium of the people and all that, but the people have lost their faith. Lost interest in the church. Hardly any men go any more. You only see a few women now, widows."

"Well, you know why *they* go. The *psáltis*."

"Sorry?"

"They're all in love with the *psáltis*."

"*Ade!*"

"Of course."

"Well, not all!" Their eyes meet. Not Kyria Sofia! Well of course Kyria Sofia! Andrea gives his brief grin.

She poses. "He has this operatic voice —"

"He's their New Kid on the Block."

"— and it seems to come out of the dome, out of the mouth of the Jesus Pandokratora. Really, you should hear it."

"No, thanks."

"*Ade*, Andrea, in love! The man has a wife and three children."

"All to the good. No harm in dreaming, is there, then?"

The village gathers in the churchyard to wait for the *epitáfio*, children running, men wandering from group to group, smoking. At last the great wooden cross is carried out of the church, a wreath on top, and three candles, and then the bier, its carved wood woven with carnations and branches of bay. Everyone falls in behind, some cupping a lit candle against the wind of their passage through the village. Bell, losing sight of Kyria Sofia, walks with a neighbour who knows who she is and asks after Yanni. No other wind, but a drizzle of rain starts, and the line of wet hands glows out like printed hands on a cave wall when a match is brought up close. The *papás* blesses the crossroads in a chant, and the children join in.

In the porch of their house as the procession passes, a flame is moving like a firefly on the yellow walls, Vaïa, it must be, minding the baby.

Back in the churchyard they put down the bier and scatter under the pines. Bell is on the point of going when suddenly a bonfire bursts out in an open patch alongside. Sparks fly out through a funnel of smoke, then a rocket whooshes, showering flames. The bier is on fire, and she gasps, but no, the flames are only reflections on the wet wood and leaves. "What on earth?" she says aloud. There are yells in the dark as crackers go frisking and backfiring along the ground.

"What are you frightened of, *nýfi*?" a voice says into her hair. She turns and stares into a man's face hollow with fire, a cousin.

"I thought the fireworks were for tomorrow night."

"They are. Tonight they are burning the Jews."

"I see. The next best thing to a Scud missile?"

"Ah. *Operation Desert Storm*," he says in English, and smiles at her surprise. "Like you, we watch the news."

"I don't, here. Our television is broken."

"Well, the war is over now, anyway," he says, "and this is not like that. No need to be afraid."

"Father, forgive them for they know not what they do."

"I agree," he says, "that it has its insensitive side."

When the fire has died down to a few black branches in the drizzle, the four bearers raise the bier shoulder high at the church door and the worshippers, linking hands, duck their heads underneath as in a game of Oranges and Lemons and dance back inside.

Vaïa stands out of the wind on the porch, the candle dripping on her hand. The *sála* at her back was full of such candles only six months ago, burning all around Baba as he lay. Candles and death. For a long time this has been the house of death, with the chill of the *sála* at its heart. Now she has brought new life within these walls, brought the baby for her first Easter, and the house is reclaimed for the living.

The fear is still there, however. When was the first time she felt the force of the fear of death? The time that comes to mind is the hot day she and Bella were riding on bicycles to Agia Vrissi to see Baba in the hospital, riding and singing aloud all the Theodoraki songs banned by the Junta, while they had the breath to sing, when she was suddenly thrown off on to the road. In the great thunderclap of that pain, her head reeling, pasted with dust and sweat which she thought must be blood, she knew how easy it was to die. Baba might easily have died back then. He looked as if he had. Last year, newly dead, he had the same face she remembered from that Easter; and then, in the *sála*, a face that had no likeness to his at all, a mannikin of grey putty lying in the candlelight.

Who is the next in line? The third. If the cup is to be believed. God protect us, maybe Bella is. She has the look of death in her. Even her voice, so low, so soft, and her dusty hair. Her eyes glow in the hollows. Her smooth skin is the only thing not old about her. Even her clothes are the same, her moonstruck clothes and that eye she wears, of all things, at her age! Does she think she might still be the target of anyone's envy? The poor thing is a relic of another age, a woman with no real weight, light-minded, without roots in the world. She lives in the past and that keeps her coming back to us. Would she go back to Grigori, I wonder, if he would have her? As I understand it, because no one ever talks about it, they went too far and broke up too bitterly to think of going back. Perhaps I was wrong before and it *was* better to leave and go off alone if she no longer loved her man. Would I, if I stopped loving Andrea? Or he me? But that will never happen. It might have once, but we are out of danger now, bound until death with strong bonds. And child after child.

There is no sign of the others when Bell gets in. They must all be in bed. She grabs her towel and hurries out to the *méros*, pisses, washes her face and brushes her teeth. Groping with wet eyes for the towel, she grabs a white cloth instead and is warned off at the last moment by the smell, a rusty, sweet smell of meat, of blood. She has picked up a pair of knickers: Vaïa's, or Sonya's — they are too small for Vaïa. The blood looks dark but is still damp and thick, and she holds it to her nose, breathing in deep. Oh let me have mine, she mouths. Let it come back to me. The door handle rattles. Bell throws the knickers down, mops her face and comes out into the kitchen, the light.

As ill luck would have it, it's Kyria Sofia, just back, breathless, and surprised.

"You are here! I thought I saw you in the procession."

"I was, but I came back."

"So early?"

Bell helps herself to a glass of water. "Yes, they were burning the Jews" — she looks over her shoulder — "while we stood by."

"The Jews who betrayed the Lord. Not the real Jews."

"We stood by and cheered and laughed."

"What else are you good for, Bella? All you do is stand by."

"Since I was not dressed to go in — "

"I told you you could have my skirt."

"I brought my own."

"You call that a skirt? Blue jean!"

They both speak in a fierce whisper, so as not to wake the others.

"I wore this in Athina."

"Not in church!"

"Yes, and there were lots of others in blue jeans, both men and women."

"And where did you go to church in Athina, you?"

"In the Plaka. The Holy Archangels. And on the islands. Every Friday at nightfall they —"

"Yes, yes, the *hairetismoí*. Every Friday in Lent?"

"As many as I was here for — here in Greece for."

"In that skirt."

"In Athina half the women there were in trousers, and in blue jeans, what's more. No one minded me."

"A foreigner, a tourist? As soon expect them to mind a cockroach! Why would they? Here you are not a foreigner, though. What you do here reflects on us. The world has expectations."

"In Athina I suppose they let God be the judge."

"Who cares what they do in Athina! I suppose they don't light their candles in Athina? They don't make their cross?"

I am Bella and sometimes Vaïa, and as often as not, καλέ, my good one, my dear, or τζᾶνουμ, soul in Turkish. Refugee families sprinkle τζᾶνουμ right and left to express affection with just a hint of impatience. Αυτή is offhand, hostile: an all-purpose this one, you there, whoever you are. Κρασί πίνεις, αυτή? Are you drinking wine, what's-your-name? As for cockroach. Μια κατσαρίδα. And in the same breath — Εδώ δεν είσαι ξένη: here you are not a stranger/foreigner.

You have to let me go, she said, we can't live like this, I'll go mad: that was all there was to say in the end, over and over. Some time in those last days — the terror of the delay, she remembers, the stalking, the drink — he grabbed her hair and held a knife stained with meat at her throat, only letting her go to stroke the blade with his thumb, which he thrust in her face. An iron knife that smelled of blood, it had made a gash in the hump of skin above the nail.

You my wife.

Yes, if you want to go to prison, she said.

One year, two year, hwat is? You don't know nothing.

What about Yanni if you go to prison? For *murder*? His *father*?

Hwat you say?

How would it be? *You* should know.

You say thet to me? *Putána!*

A father who killed —

You bitch. Go if you want.

— his *mother* —

Go while you can. Go on. Piss off! Go! Now he lowers the knife. You can forget about Yanni. I look after him. *Mother*! You not fit *mother*.

Sonya is at a wedding, at the long family table with her parents and grandparents. Yes, Pappou is back at Yiayia's side, when he died, and everyone knows that, but he is as solid as they are. There is water and wine in carafes, black wine, but red in the glasses, and one falls. It soaks the white linen cloth and the fine dresses and the ground. Rina just laughs. She gets up and dances, spinning, a blur of red and black under the chandelier. There are woven loaves of bread by their plates and Sonya breaks some off and eats it warm, and then more. The others sip their wine but no one will touch the bread. This is good bread, she says, straight from the oven, have some, but they glance at each other and she sees the horror in their faces, horror of the bread. A vampire hates the taste of bread: her skin chills. Go on, she urges them, eat. Her mother pretends not to hear. So do her father and her grandfather. Yiayia is crouched with her sour smile. I have been to hell, she says, and what did I see? All the beautiful women came by laughing and dancing in a line and the one at the end reached out and dragged me by the hand. Sonya stares as the sour smile spreads on face after face.

Bell lies transfixed, wide awake. The best summers of her life are hived in here behind this whitewash which turns yellow in the sun, and rough, like a calico sheet. Five summers, the last one fifteen years ago and yet no part of them is lost; all she has to do is shut her eyes. Five summers of the hum in the grapevine over the door, the moment of blindness and a shiver at the first step inside on to cement mosaic and then on to the warm boards where the slats of shadow from the shutters circle for an hour or so and vanish. The stillness in the heat of the afternoon where nothing is moving, only hens in the dust, the papery scrape of feathers, the flame in a comb; sleep in every house and the cattle all away on the hill. In this room she woke in the early evening to a patter and the smell of water sprinkling on sheets hot from the sun or the iron: the smell of the dust of the yard, where the old woman must be shaking water out in skeins from her hands to settle the dust, shaking drops in the sun like the *papás* with his sprigs and holy water on the first day of the month blessing the house for a small fee. Soon the cattle will come trotting through the dust. Figures are gathering in the *sála*, the family, with coffee in the lank brown shadows, in a shine, the sweat of walls and flesh. And the hiss of someone hosing the plants in the olive oil cans, whitewashed, against the long shade of the porch.

SATURDAY

For as long as anyone can remember, Saturday has been market day in Agia Vrissi. Early in the morning those who are going, Vaïa and Andrea and Bell, like so many times before, make a quick Nescafé in the kitchen and drink it standing up. Mamma is still curled up under the blankets, so they keep their voices down until she sits up, her hair loose.

"Ah, *kaliméra sas*! Are you going? What time is it?"

"*Kaliméra*, Mamma," Vaïa says. "Not quite eight."

"And is Sonya going?"

"She's asleep. You don't mind, do you? We'll be quick. She can give you a hand with the little one."

Kyria Sofia throws her a scornful look, stretching, running her hands through her hair.

"It's like a waterfall," Bell says, "Mamma's hair."

"Yes, beautiful," Vaïa says.

"You've all seen it before."

"Not loose."

"*Bah!* It wants cutting."

"No, no!" Bell says, and Vaïa: "Don't you dare!"

"Are you drinking coffee?"

"Coffee. Will I make you some tea?"

"It can wait."

"Might there be a bit of *tsouréki*, Mammaka?" Vaïa wheedles. "To have with the coffee?"

"Is there something wrong with the bread?"

"*Ela*, Mamma!"

"What makes you think I had the strength to make *tsourékia*?"

"You say well. Never mind, we can pass by the baker's."

"*Má!* Is the baker's *tsouréki* fit to eat?" says Bell, catching Mamma's eye. Andrea has his head down, munching bread.

"It will just have to do," Vaïa sighs.

"No *tsourékia*, I said, until after Lent."

"*Ade*, Mamma. We know you've hidden them."

"From tomorrow you can have —"

"*Ade!*"

"— all the *tsourékia* you want."

Lined with wild plums in flower, the new road to Agia Vrissi follows the river upstream through two huddled villages of domes and blank windows framed in blue. That other Easter they had to go on the bus, jolting over stones in the dust, the same old blue bus thick with smoke, crammed full. Some of the men had a lamb or a kid at their feet, tied with rope, whose white-edged eyes and feeble blatting kept the village children amused. This time the little red car, Vaïa at the wheel, has plunged into the crowded streets of Agia Vrissi in no time and squealed to a rest in the mud of a narrow laneway. An eye of thick blue glass is swinging from the rear-vision mirror, which is just as well, Bell thinks, considering. She wants to get her bearings again while the others do their shopping, and so they arrange to meet back at the fountain on the *plateía* in half an hour for coffee.

Sound fades when you are up on the *plateía*, and today even the traffic noise at the crossroads is misted over in the drizzle. The whitewashed trunks of the great old plane trees, the pride of the town, have an oily sheen of wet. Under the woven boughs, nothing but silence. All the buildings, old and new, have a warped, melted look. Agia Vrissi has had an earthquake since she was here last, and she knew that before; all the same it comes as a shock to see so many shabby buildings all around, their overhung balconies adrift and façades sagging, the jagged cracks patched with scars. Even the *plateía*, intact at first glance, is faintly askew, although the columns and arches of the plane trees still stand, their furry pompoms and dead leaves fallen in the scatters of rusty chairs and tables outside the *kafeneía* and in the empty basin of the memorial fountain. It is cracked in two, the basin. For the first time there is no sound of splashing, no heave and gush of black and white water, no crust of foam in the shade. The stringy wisteria woven through the boughs is bare grey wood. Is it dead? And the planes themselves? By Easter there ought to be leaves, and wisteria everywhere overhead in watery bunches like pale grapes.

"*Raus, raus*," a man mutters at her back, having taken her for a German. He is young, shabby and his friend sneers. She turns her head. A policeman down at the crossroads is directing a traffic jam with shouts, and now the horns blast back.

"Bloody Wogs," another voice says in her ear, Andrea, breathing smoke.

Taken by a surprise, Bell gives a snort of laughter. Bloody Wogs! It was their catchphrase for a summer of travelling and camping a long time ago, humpies in the pines and shelters of branches hastily rigged up, the only shade, and they the only people, in those early days before the tourists flooded into the north of Greece, on a long line of white beaches. Bloody Wogs! It all began at a market like this when a brawl broke out and they joined the ring of watchers at the side of an unmistakable Englishman. What's going on? Bell asked him in English, and his head swung sharply round on a turkey neck. Euh, God knows, he drawled, bloody Wogs.

"*Amán*, yes!" Bell cries, falling into step. "Bloody Wogs!"

A car hoots, missing her by an inch. She reels back into a *papás* who staggers, clutching at a red plastic bag with a lamb carcass in it as tall as he is, and begs his pardon until his glare softens.

Only the wine to go now, Andrea says, and Vaïa is meeting them in the shop. This is convenient. While Andrea is still deep in thought over a row of bottles, Bell buys a dark, opaque red from Naoussa: "For old times' sake," she says, and he nods in agreement, smiling up as Vaïa comes in.

"Here you are," she says. "When did you get glasses, Bella? Oh, how silly. What made me think you had glasses on?"

Bell only grins and shrugs, and goes back to reading the wine labels. Of course, Vaïa thinks, she always had those round white lids and a grey half-moon of skin under them like the nap on a hard-boiled egg yolk, thick like eyeshadow. Only now they are hollow with a black rim, and shiny: they did look for a moment as if she had glasses on. Her face is brown otherwise. Vaïa remembers going through Bella's toilet bag behind her back once, giggling, with Chloï, when Bella first came and Chloï was an ally, as long ago as that, twenty years ago or more, and if Bella owned an eye-shadow it was well hidden. We were all so young and silly then! No, Bella did well to come, Vaïa thinks with a rush of warmth. There is a line of blood which is a family. Like the red thread that is the story, as the saying goes, unwound by the teller for the listeners. She is one strand of our thread. She has given us a son. But how she has aged! Much more than we have. It might just be the ashen hair. Or the hollowness of the light in here after the rain.

"More rain on the way," she says.

"The streets are so slippery I nearly knocked a *papás* over." Bell nudges her: "The one over there with the Lamb of God."

He is waving to someone at the bus stop now, and Vaïa laughs. "I hope you kissed his hand."

"*Sigá!*"

"Bad luck, that. To meet a *papás*." Andrea hoists the carton of bottles. "Let's go?"

"Bad luck for *him*. *He* got knocked over."

Vaïa has fallen into step beside her. "They tell me off, you know," she suddenly says, "about the new one —"

"What new one?"

"— for not being as close friends with her as with you."

That new one.

"But what can I say? I try but we just *are* closer, even now."

"I think — those were years when we — " She lapses. Her Greek is not up to this.

Vaïa shrugs. "We were young together. And silly."

"I know."

"With her we can't talk — my English is nothing much and she refuses to learn Greek."

"Refuses?"

" 'Well, *Bell* did,' she says, 'and you saw what happened. The marriage broke up.' "

"Good luck to her! Young and silly is right. Remember the day you got a loan of two bikes when Baba was in the hospital here? And we rode in from the village and back?"

"We still could if we had to."

"Yes, now that it's asphalt!" Bell is dying to laugh but she holds it in, as she must. It was a hot day on a stony road, in shower after shower of dust. Without ever admitting as much, they made a contest of the ride, as they did of everything. They were at the outskirts and still neck and neck when Vaïa caught her wheel in a rut of the clay road and pitched off in front of a cartload of gypsies, who cheered. Vaïa dusted herself off, hissing up at them: You put the Eye on me! Softly — Bell was not meant to hear. The fall never happened, that was understood. No one was to be told, not even Andrea. Bell broke, of course. She just had to tell Grigori, rolling on the bed and muffling her squeals in the pillow for fear of being heard in the other room. I must not laugh, she tells herself. "Those were the days," she says instead. "We sang Theodoraki songs."

"*We* still do," Vaïa says stiffly.

"Well, I still do. Why not?"

By the time the wine and the bags of shopping are safely in the boot of the car, the drizzle is a steady rain and Bell has given up hope of a coffee under the trees. Instead they take their newspapers into one of the dim *kafeneía* stale with smoke, give their order and glance through the pages.

"This is on me," Bell says when the coffee comes.

"No, no."

"Please. Just look! This isn't spring!" She throws her hands open to the desolation beyond the panes.

"What did you say?" Andrea mumbles.

"What has happened to the spring?"

He looks up from the front page. "Yes."

"No sign of spring."

"The Gulf War again. It says so in the papers."

"Oh no! Again!" She peers across. She has only one thought: her flight out of Athens on Tuesday at dawn, unless she is stranded.

"No — the weather. It's the Gulf War. You know that the Iraqis set the oil wells on fire when they left Kuwait?" He sucks his coffee to the dregs and folds the paper over. "Five hundred or so. It's the smoke that's shutting out the sun."

"Even here."

"*Málista.*"

When Andrea says *málista* in a monotone, instead of plain *nai* for yes, he is losing patience. "In Greece," Bell persists.

"A blight over the land. The whole Aegean, they say."

"It sounds like Chernobyl!"

This is not a safe comparison to make to Andrea, but he lights a cigarette and answers mildly enough. "With the difference that this was not an accident. There was no negligence. They systematically set fire to the oil wells."

Vaïa signals the waiter for more coffee. "You've come at a bad time, Bella," she says.

"Oh. If I waited for peace —"

She is finding it hard to breathe in here.

"Yes, you could wait forever."

"What does it say there about the Kurds? Andrea?"

"Another massacre." He taps the grey photo she is pointing at, a scarved old woman clutching a bundle, her mouth wide in a howl. "The triumph of the West. We sent a frigate, I'll have you know."

"Australia sent two!"

He throws up his hands in disbelief.

Sonya's mouth is dry and her heart beating after another dream so terrible that she is scared to open her eyes. She has forgotten she is at Yiayia's house. The baby murmurs, shifting in her sleep, and only then can Sonya look, her face stiff with fear, at the cot on the floor, the dead *sómba*, the shutters and the singed lace of the curtains in the cold air.

No one else is here. There is no sound in the whole house. They must have gone to Agia Vrissi already and left her here, alone with the baby! It's not fair. She won't get up until she has to, anyway. She can't even think about going out into the *sála* yet, because that was where the dream was. She shudders. There is no way out into anywhere in the house except through the *sála*. If only they would take the photographs down! I really hate this house, she thinks. I could have been on Mytilini now with the others only I wasn't allowed. *When you grow up you can go where you like.* It certainly won't be here. No one's going to make me. I hate the place, it gives me the creeps. Yiayia is horrible the way she keeps cramming that wall with her saints and dead people. The place is more of a shrine every time we come. I really hate old people. All the old people here in the village. They make a nest for themselves out of dead things, a tomb, not a shrine, what's the word? Mausoleum. And they potter around farting and peering, burning their incense, lighting their lamps. The living are only nuisances as far as they're concerned.

My mother wants her to come and live with us. Where, on the floor? She can't, that's all. She was at our place once and we were watching a show, just the two of us, when suddenly she got up and switched it off in the middle of a videoclip and started raving at me about how the singer was nothing but a whore and I was no better. Let her dance with her veils. So did the witch, Salome, the murderess. Writhe your body too, she said, go on, gloat over yourself! How long does beauty last? But the flames you light are enough to burn your soul in eternity. I was only dancing along. Maybe I am inclined to gloat. After all, I can hardly avoid knowing I'm pretty, can I? I didn't speak. I didn't answer back. The woman is a burning fire, Yiayia shrieked, and a woman in her beauty is more bitter than death and her heart is snares and nets and her hands are bands. She is the tongue of the serpent Satan and his vessel who sucks men's souls from their bodies! Does she? I had to laugh. Well, I said and switched it back on, that's something to look forward to, then. Yiayia flung herself at the set and pulled out the plug. Snarling, she turned and slapped my face, once, hard. I should have hit back, it would have served her right, but I never did, and I never told on her either. My father would never let her get away with it if he knew. I just pulled my jacket on, with her dragging me and shrieking like a madwoman, and slammed the door in her face and went to my friend's flat and watched. I never said a word about it, just as well for her. Neither did she. She's mad, but not that mad.

I doubt if she will come and live at our place. If she does I'm ready for her. Why *not* do us all a favour and go into a monastery and die to the world, if that's what she wants? Only my mother has to argue and start yelling, and Yiayia yells back, and in the end they fall into each other's arms and wail their hearts out. I wish she *would* and be done with it. What's stopping her? As if this house isn't dead enough! The cold smell and the stale incense. It should suit her down to the ground.

There are birds outside, and people moving around, trees, and in here I am alive, and the baby, breathing, rustling, I can hear our breaths. Only the *sála* is silence. The *sála* is the well of silence on the other side of the door. It is just like a church out there and the wall is the screen, the ikonostasis with the secret room at the back for the priest and the boys to come and go, their holy of holies, where women are not allowed. It makes you wonder what she keeps behind hers; and Yanni who was killed is in so many of the photos, I don't even know how many, I can't look. If I go too near I know his eyes fix on me. Like when he kissed me at their house, when he cornered me behind the bookcase and opened his fly and muttered, Look. All I saw was hair — it was dark — and a red knob, his hand on the stem. You hold it, he said, and he made a grab at my hand but I pulled away. No. I said, I won't. Leave me alone. He had fine hair all around his lips and it tickled. I feel him looking out of the eyes in all the photos of him and his anger, like a storm in the air. It's me he is angry with because I won't look and I won't let him. No! So leave me alone.

The wedding in the dream was in a long cold room and that was the *sála*. I am just aching to tell someone, ask someone, but who can I? Even if they were here, just imagine: Mamma, Baba, Yiayia, listen, I had a dream that we were all at the wedding, at a long table, all the family in the *sála*, all of us, and none of you would eat the bread because you were vampires. Is it true that they hate bread? Oh yes, dear, and then what happened? The wine was spilt, black wine, big splashes of it over the cloth and the dresses. And Yiayia said she was in hell with all the beautiful women and they were dancing. Yes, imagine saying that out loud to anyone! Unless it was someone who was not there. Not in the dream. Who, though? My aunt, Bella? She is like the walking dead in real life. In fact if anyone is a vampire here — no, no, this is madness. Maybe Lyka, then. Except Lyka might laugh and turn the whole thing into a joke. Vampires! Only there was nothing funny about it. And what if she says something in front of *them* and they hear? Imagine that. Face after face — Sonya's hair prickles and she shudders — curdling in a smile.

The travail of Agia Vrissi, ruin and drizzle, a hopelessness. Will there be spring this year? No wisteria over the πλατεία, just the grey hanks of the withered vine.

A strumming of wings — the stork has landed on the nest. To λελέκι, or ο πελαργός. What is the feminine, πελαργίνα? She stands with one leg lifted, her beak sunk on her white bib. The swallows have a mud nest under the porch light. Three little black heads pull hastily in at a footstep. In the cane chair Andrea is singing the baby to sleep with Vaïa's old lullaby, νᾶνι νᾶνι: warbles and quartertones, like the plainchant.

Sonya and Lyka have written a comedy show and spent an hour rigging up a theatre in the white space under the plum tree by the henhouse and dragging the old cart out of the barn to be one of the props. The car being another, they commandeer it as soon as the shopping is unloaded. The rehearsals involve a lot of door-slamming and such screeches of rage and laughter that eventually the whole household comes out on the porch to watch. Kyria Sofia, who has her lace spread like an apron on her lap, puts it aside with a good enough grace when Vaïa passes her the baby. Bell runs in for the camera and takes her photo in the cane chair holding the new great-granddaughter upright while she dribbles and kicks. The old woman's face shrinks in an answering laugh that, hiding her flayed eyelids and brittleness of movement, makes her seem almost young. All the same she is quick to hand the baby back. Two generations of babies I took to my bosom and what thanks do I get? she thinks. They loved me as babies, and I loved them all only to see them taken away for ever and brought up strangers to me. She smooths the lace, a weave of petals in her lap, white and black interwoven. I have done enough. Leave me be.

The rehearsal is over. Sonya and Lyka bow and start again from the beginning as one by one the audience drifts inside.

Vaïa brings the baby into Bell's room and sits on the edge of the bed. "Am I interrupting?"

"No, come in!" She shuts the notebook.

"What's this we hear about you making a film?"

"Not a film exactly, a slide montage on video."

"Will it be like a real film?"

"Well, like a documentary. More static than some, I suppose."

"Is there a story, though?"

"Not as such."

"What's it called?"

"I don't know yet. That comes last."

Vaïa grins. "Come on, what's it about?"

"Greece."

"That is to say?"

"Well, Greece. Just aspects. Images. A mosaic. The land and the women, the old goddesses —"

"Not the young ones?"

"Yes, the ones that were young in their time, and the old ones."

"And they speak Greek?"

"No, nothing. They are silent."

"You mean, not a word?"

"One sings part of a *moirolói*, but the words are not clear. Oh, and the Church speaks."

"How?"

"In a man's voice. Chanting, but again, no clear words. Look, it's hard to explain! I know it sounds vague. I'll send you a tape if you like."

"Will you? Good. Yes."

"Not that *I've* seen any of it myself yet." Bell shrugs: "Seen the slides, that is."

"What!"

"Yes, there wasn't time to get them processed."

"Beba, come here." The baby is tangled in the folds of the blanket. Vaïa lifts her free and plants a fierce kiss on her head. "Ach! I love them when they are little like this." She rubs her head in the baby's belly. "Why do they have to grow up? I'll eat you, *jánoum*! Yes, I will, I'll eat you all up!" and the baby squeals, grabbing at tufts of hair.

"Look, Beba." Bell hands her a red egg, and she lets go to clasp it with both hands, staring open-mouthed.

"Where's the video camera, may I see?"

"There isn't one. I can borrow one back home."

"You mean to say you have nothing on video and no idea what's on the slides? What if they don't come out? What will you do?"

"How should I know? Cry? Scream?"

"*Má!* Have you taken enough?"

"Three thousand."

"Three *thousand*." Vaïa is awed, or shocked. At any rate, far from convinced.

Over three thousand, in fact, if they all come out. Every one of them hidden, so far unseen: seen only the once, that is, in the moment before the shutter slid over and the moment after that. Which is as it should be, working blind. They have to be given time to settle and shuffle in the mind, sink to the bottom or loom larger, mix, dissolve and eclipse each other, be superimposed and come back up to the surface.

Sonya finds her mother lying on one side of Bella's double bed, and Bella on the other, with the baby in the middle fumbling in the folds of the blanket after a red egg. They all look up and smile as she spins away.

Kyria Sofia, squatting down to pick docks and nettles and dandelions powdered with a white drizzle, has remembered to snap off a handful of the hyacinths to take to Yanni's grave. In passing she drops some on her sister-in-law, Magdalini, and one on the old *psáltis*. Yanni's mother is close by, the name almost weathered away. ΛΤ ΙΝΑ. The lamp is long gone, and the candles. Kyria Sofia shrugs. I did my duty by her, she says aloud. I was a good daughter-in-law. I nursed her all those years although she ruined my life. The old fool, she told me herself how she put Yanni up to it. Didn't your own father take me by force, she said she told him, at Lake Ohrida, and didn't he break into the church on horseback and throw me over the saddle in my wedding dress and spur the horse away before they could lift a finger? We left the bridegroom standing there like a Karagiozi. You think I loved my husband any the less because he took matters into his own hands? The old fool. As if we were the same, she and I; as if all the fingers are ever the same, as the saying is. And Yanni was a young fool — so young, not much older than our Yannakia are now — not to see until it was too late who was the hero and who was the Karagiozi in our story. Well, and are you paid back now, Kyria Katerina? I owe you nothing.

As always, though it makes no sense at all, it is with a start of surprise that she comes on the new grave at the far edge under the oaks. When will she ever be used to it? She leaves the hyacinths at the foot and in the muddy grass by the grave she lights the candle and the lamp. He has no framed photo yet. Vaïa is always forgetting to bring one. He was a handsome enough man in his day, a man that a woman might very well love, for all that he had never learnt letters and barely knew how to speak. He was not a man I loved or ever could have loved, she thinks, once he was foisted on me. I already had a man I loved and whose wife I should have been but for my brothers, and whose child I should have had, but for the hard work they made me do, so that it was lost in a flow of blood, the one that should have been my firstborn, a son, his son, before anyone even knew I was carrying it. Then the whisperers went from house to house. I had no dowry apart from my beauty and the work of my hands, sheets and cloths, aprons, blankets, embroideries, and my man's family were against me from the first. But Yanni's mother had already sent a matchmaker, knowing that my brothers were in a great hurry to marry and could hardly wait to get me off their hands. For fear that Yanni would hear the whispers and change his mind they married me off to him out of my sickbed. I was eighteen, he twenty-one, and I bled on the wedding night. He made sure that I was black and bleeding by morning. Well might the bride at such a wedding wear a shroud, if what Bella said was true, like the Soul in the tale, who was married to the demon. Erota is a demon, is he? Well said, Bella, for once. Erota was my demon and I cast him out. If I could do it, why could Yanni not? I did my duty as a wife to the end. He was a good enough man, Yanni, a good father and householder most of the time, until the War and then in the city the demon took him over. If he could not make me love him then he would make me hate him, brawler that he was in those days, and jealous and violent without cause, so that in the end a man's death was laid at his door, our door, and they sent him to Gendi Kule with the dregs of men, the forsaken of God. The hardship I had then on my own, trying to keep us all alive, taking in sewing and washing, day and night!

All for nothing, since he knew as well as I did that I was a faithful wife. The only man I loved I had never so much as set eyes on since the wedding. I heard that he died in the German invasion, blown to mincemeat by a German landmine. Buried at Agia Vrissi.

He came to his senses, Yanni, but he took his time, and for his sin God took the boy who was his namesake and my son twice over, the son of Lefteraki who was the child of my heart. Why else would such a fine boy die? And so I told Yanni to his face. God has taken our grandson to pay for your crime, I said at the grave, for your sin, a life for a life, and when we came home he went out to the barn and wept aloud on the hay.

Husband and husbandman. Our times of calm and increase and of almost love were all here in the village. I was the garden and he the gardener, I the earth to his plough, as a woman is to a man, and what he sowed then, God willing, was his to reap. He was of the land, a tree root nothing could pierce. He fought with the strength of five. He saved his skin through ordeals that killed thousands of men, even the black pits in the city wall. A man like that can only rot from the inside out, and then if anything could have healed him it would have been this earth, his earth, this air and water. As it was he lived to a good age, considering how he defied the doctors and went on drinking coffee, even ouzo, and smoking. Andrea smokes like a chimney. Vaïa, watch out. Life in the city would have been the death of Yanni if we had stayed. I thought it would be in Thessaloniki, the death of him and of us all, the years of hauling loads all day on the wharves and all night drinking and smoking hashish in the dens and dancing alone like a dervish, only one possessed of a demon. He would stagger home at daybreak wringing wet, stinking. Vaïa, why do you think I would accept to end my life in the city that ate up my youth? At table he would sit wall-eyed like a bull, lowering at the children as if he had never seen them before, a heavy puzzled brow of curls low over the plate. He slept where he fell and when I hauled him on to the bed his slobber soaked into the pillow. If he woke it was only to hold me down and jab at me, moaning, shuddering. The children heard it all. Yiayia Katerina heard.

His hair of clay, his stone eyes. How still he lay among the branches on the floor of the house with the candle flames darting, hanging on threads of smoke, as the mourners came and went, so that the pits of black ran like water over his face and I saw a glow, his eyes, and my heart was in my mouth. All night he filled the room. One or two who dozed off screamed when they saw him standing. He glared from the dark, they said, and we were all immersed in a vast anger.

And now? What is he like now in his liquefaction? Like any corpse when the grave is opened too soon. He has his flesh still, black by now and bursting off the branched bones. His hands are folded in his ribs, lying in wait. And his last wish, that they bury him nowhere near his mother. Nowhere near her, he said at the end, my curse on you otherwise. Now here he is at the roots of the black oaks, waiting as he used to, flat out on the bed, surly, heavy, for the day when they dress me again and lay me at his side, again.

Cross-legged in front of the hooded form of the Buddha, trying to clear her mind, Bell is buzzing with thoughts. It seems to her that this is all the old woman wants as well: to empty out her life, like the *sómba* in the morning, the past, ashes and debris and soot, like her womb, a dry husk. And just at that moment along I come, Bell thinks, in search of a womb to crawl in. Mamma, let me in, let me in! Is this like something in a book once? Of course, in the first Greek book Grigori ever gave me, the Kazantzaki novel about an Easter passion play, after we had been to see the film of it, *He Who Must Die*; as we all must, anyway. Silly title. A very old man, one of a starving band of refugees, goes knock-knocking on the ground with his stick and calling to the earth, *Mother, let me in*. He has a sack on his back with all the bones from the ossuary. The Turks have burnt their village. *Look at me, Mother, won't you let me in?* And when the young men have dug the first trench for the foundations of a new village, the old man jumps in, scattering the bones so that the living village will rise up out of the dead, and lies down among them, hands folded, *flesh, and blood, and skin,* and prays aloud for death.

Grigori bought it in Greek and I got the Faber translation, I remember, *Christ Recrucified*, and worked through them both page after page in my room after work, teaching myself Greek. When in tears I read this part aloud to Grigori, we looked it up in the Greek.

Is true. He shook his head. My mother and my father same, he said, Refugee from Turks.

But not the same time!

Same time, yes.

This century?

I tell you, catastrophe of Mikra Asia was. 1922 — Smyrni, Ayvali.

It was a shock, when the whole feeling of the book was so old, or rather, comfortably timeless and remote, a parable, a classic. *Flesh, and blood, and skin. Mother, let me in!* That rhymes. *Lo, how I vanish, flesh, and blood, and skin.* How come? And scans, in English, it's in verse. I must be confusing it with something else, then. *Alas! Alas!* Yes! *Allas! whan shul my bones been at reste?* Chaucer, it was Chaucer all the time, not Kazantzaki, one of the pilgrims' tales it must be. Or was it in the Kazantzaki too? No, it's just that they dovetail. Pilgrims' dovetails.

Chaucer! Was Greece even there in his day, as a part of the known world? Depends when it was. The fourteenth century? I forget. Maybe earlier: no later, anyway. *I knokke with my staf, bothe erly and late.* And three young men take him for Death: they want to kill him. *An old man, hoor upon his heed.* And he lives up to it. No, he is not Death, he says, but he can tell them where to look: under that oak. The men are sworn blood-brothers and they will murder each other for the gold they find buried under the oak. It was the time of the crusades because one of the pilgrims was a knight who had been in the Holy Land. As for

Greece, though? Troilus and Criseyde, at least, courtly lovers in Troy, and Eros was behind all their woe, the same Eros, Erota! And as a customs man, wouldn't he have seen any number of crusaders and the treasure they brought back? — whole shiploads of loot from the Greek lands among others, the jewelled crosses, gold, an enamelling of blood. Greece in his day must have been Byzantium, the gold skin on the rim of the known world, the holy city, the Rome of the East, although on the wane, already sacked by the crusaders and ripe, over-ripe for the Turks. Mikra Asia is Little, Minor Asia. Smyrna, and Ayvali, and Troy, close to Gallipoli. Both my grandfathers died at Gallipoli, one on land and one drowned in the landing. Family history. These are long threads to be spinning out. Old men who pray to the one earth, the all-holy, the earth. Which is my mother's gate. Thin threads. Loose threads.

May the earth not eat you, say the Greeks, and this is the worst curse they know. Worse in its way, far worse in Greek than: I fuck your mother's bum, and: I fuck your Panagia, and all the rest of the litany of insult. What would become of you if the earth refused to eat you? A vampire, I suppose, with a red mouth and a smile, glowing in the coffin. Or something frozen in time, like the fallen gods and the goddesses they find, naked or robed, with the wings of angels, sunk in the earth and in tombs and dry watercourses and cisterns and on the seabed, whole or scattered, here a marble head, there a bronze arm. The people of the north lay in their oaken hulls awash in the fens for hundreds of years until the peat-cutters dug them out. One of the labours of Psychi was to ride on Charo's boat into the underworld, the *káto kósmo*. She came back up out of the earth's mouth through a cave that has been flooded for a long time, or for ever, a sea cave in the Mani, half underwater.

Someone has taken a photograph down and left it lying on the tablecloth in the *sála*. Kyria Sofia peers close and jumps: him, in the cane chair in a brown light barred with shadow, still in his dusty work clothes ready for the milking and in his pride of possession. His gaze and the tilt of his head are full of a strong pride. And the glint in his eyes through the cross of shadows, as if he knows, as if he has caught her looking. The past is closed. The past is a dark doorway and he stands guard. He was all eyes. They followed every move I made. In the hospital he arched and fought for breath and his eyes started out of his head, and when he fell back I closed my hand over them. But they rolled open and his mouth hung crooked. Holes of darkness filled his face. He that I once loved has been fifty years in the earth. He that I never loved has joined him there, while I grow old alone. Age is another death. The past, death, and the future. Or there is no past, no future, and only the doorway.

Like a woman with child, that draweth near the time of her delivery, is in pain, and crieth out in her pangs; so have we been in thy sight, O Lord. We have been with child, we have been in pain, we have as it were brought forth wind. She closes her eyes with the strain of remembering, one hand on the skin of her throat where earlier in the day the baby's head rubbed, furry, a soft bulk, her fingers wandering on the black dress — poor little one, she has no mother to suckle her — until the nipples under it ached with need. The dead men shall live, the Lord said, together with my dead body shall they arise. Awake and sing, ye that dwell in dust: for thy dew is as the dew of herbs, and the earth shall cast out the dead. Come, my people, enter then into thy chambers, and shut the doors about thee. For, behold, the Lord cometh out of his place to punish the inhabitants of the earth for their iniquity: the earth also shall disclose her blood, and shall no more cover her slain.

In that day the Lord with his sure and great and strong sword shall punish leviathan the piercing serpent, even leviathan that crooked serpent; and he shall slay the dragon that is in the sea. In that day, sing ye unto her, a vineyard of red wine. The Lord will come with fire, and with his chariots like a whirlwind, to render his anger with fury, and his rebuke with flames of fire.

Body and soul, she thinks. Yes, go on, look all you like. She puts the photo back on the wall. I want you body and soul, you said, and I will have you. Only a fool could talk like that, and I told you so. Body and soul! I tell you to know, you will never come near my soul.

I told you so. I said you would never come near. And when I give my word you should know I keep it.

After lunch, having stoked the *sómba*, she lies down and falls asleep in one breath. Andrea and the baby are already asleep inside. Bell and Vaïa leave two billies at the house with the goats and walk on through the graveyard in the green light that has followed the drizzle. "Theia Magdalini," Bell says.

"Yes, poor thing. She suffered. And here is our grandmother." Vaïa stops short. "Grigori must have shown you."

"No, never! Nor did Mamma. I wonder why. - *at - ina* — *Katerina*. They didn't name you after her?" It has never struck Bell before.

"Baba refused."

"Is this where Rina got her name?"

"No, Andrea's mother is another Katerina. It feels right for our grandmother's sake, though, that we have a Katerina."

The grave is spattered with lichens, overgrown and in shadow. They walk out into the sun. "Baba refused?" Bell says.

"Yes, since she pushed him into the marriage. And our uncles were on his side, Mamma's brothers. It was they who chose him. And he never forgave her for it. Yiayia Katerina, that is."

"Oh, but Vaïa! He *loved* Mamma, he was mad about her, it was so obvious!"

"I know he did. And Mamma?" She tips her head back in denial.

Bell is open-mouthed. "I know she was always scolding him."

"She never wanted him. She had someone else she was in love with. They ran away together and my uncles brought her back at gunpoint to marry Baba. You mean you didn't know all this?"

"No!"

"And she never forgave him. Or them. I was sure you knew."

Bell shakes her head, amazed. "Imagine it! Imagine Mamma in love," she says and Vaïa flicks her a look. They are close enough to the grave to hear how the water is dripping off the black oaks. A handful of hyacinths, blue and pink and white, is on the marble among Bell's dry wildflowers. Her brothers, Bell thinks: the one with bare gums and a blind eye in frills of red flesh, dead now in another village; and one a walking skeleton, Aunt Magdalini's widower, a benign old man who has forgotten who his sister is. And the young man Mamma loved? Vaïa, rummaging, has filled the lantern with oil which rolls and glows, flecked like amber, as she lights it. Bell lights the candles. The incense in the burner smoulders and goes out. "Not again," Vaïa sighs.

"I wish," Bell says to her back, "I could have seen him again before —"

"It happened so fast."

"But he was all right after the operation, Grigori rang us."

"For a day or two he was and then the shock killed him."

"We could hardly believe it. Especially Yanni."

"If he had refused the operation" — Vaïa strikes another match, blows on the incense and sits back on her heels in the wet grass — "he might still be alive now."

"Oh, but think, stomach cancer! The blockage was almost total. What sort of life would that be? What sort of death?"

"I still say Grigori has too much faith in doctors."

"Does Mamma blame Grigori?" Bell is quick to say.

"Not as far as I know."

"He died fighting."

"When he came round he wanted to talk. It was the first time ever. 'The one great grief of my life,' he said, and I thought he was going to say the marriage, but no. Or if he was, could he have said that aloud, and to me?"

"Was it so bad? Since he loved her."

"*Because* he loved her. I think so. Is there anything worse? To live side by side and not be loved!"

"Would he care, after sixty years?"

"He never gave up hope."

"That might be a reason for its not having been the great grief," Bell says and Vaïa glances up. "So — what did he say?"

"He said: 'My boys have had to make their lives in Nexoria.' This incense" — she blows and the ash lifts — "why won't it light?"

Bell shakes her head, lost. Nexoria has the sound of a name she ought to know. A familiar name.

" 'They had to go out to live.' And then he cried."

"What did he mean?"

"Out of the fatherland. One was in Australia and one at sea."

"Ah, *exoría*!"

Exoría is exile. More than familiar.

"He cried and wrung his hands."

"But how was it his fault? And they were with him at the end, the boys, weren't they? And he planted the olive trees. I love it, Vaïa, that the house has olive trees."

"You know what the saying is: when you plant an olive, you plant it for your children to eat of."

Bell shakes her head, smiling, and it's true, she does know, or she used to. The reason being that they are slow trees, olives, long-lived. She turns around in a full circle to look at the pear, the oaks, the vines in the fields, in case this is the last time she comes here.

"Lefteri was not, though," Vaïa is saying now.

"Not —?"

"Not with him. Lefteri — they never come here."

"No?" Bell is floundering again. Does Vaïa realise she hardly knows Lefteri? "Mamma said they buried the boy in Thessaloniki," she says at last.

"Naturally they did. They would have the child buried where they lived." Bell, having baulked at the name, sees that Vaïa does too. "It upset the old ones. They wanted him to be here."

"So is that why?"

"No. Lefteri has turned away from God and his mother since he lost the boy."

"God and the Panagia?"

"What Panagia, *kalé*, Bella? God and his own mother, Mamma, *our* mother. They had a quarrel, Lefteri and Mamma, at the grave. She said it was God's will and he cursed God to the face of the *papás*. She was struck down with grief — she lay in bed for weeks. Never say his name in front of her. And then he was at sea when Baba went into the hospital in Kilkis. They had words again here at the grave. He felt guilty that he was not at the deathbed so he lashed out at Mamma. Grigori never said?"

"He bottles things up."

"He does. He takes after Baba. That was how I saw it, and Andrea — who knows, though? Lefteri is more of a stranger now than Grigori who lives so far away."

Bell picks up the hyacinths and sniffs. "No. Look, she must have been here." The sweetness has gone out of them already. They could be paper flowers, left too close to a fire and singed at the tips.

"Of course she has. Let's go? They will have done the milking by now."

Grigori?
 Hullo? Hullo?
 Grigori! What is it?
 He die, Bella, my father die.
 No. Oh.
 He ask me hwat to do? I say, have operation —
 He wanted your advice.
 — and they saying is my fault!
 But how could it be anybody's fault?
 I pain, you know?
 I'm sorry! Grigori, wait on — here's Yanni.
 No, I carn talk more. I pain.

"She has aged so terribly. She is withering away. I would never have known her."

"Yes, ever since the boy died. And she has had Baba to nurse."

"Look, I know she hates doctors —"

"No, no, we make her go. All they ever find, they say, is old age. And she will insist on fasting, and they throw up their hands."

"She lives for the Church now."

"She fears death," Vaïa says.

"Who doesn't?"

"No, *she* lives her days in fear of death, I mean, the angel of death."

"What?"

"He brushed by her, didn't he, when he came for the boy and then for Baba."

"Charo?"

"Charo, Satan, the angel with the sword of fire." Vaïa spreads her hands. "The lightning, the worm, how do I know, Bella? God?"

"Exile, all right," Bell says on the way out, "but Grigori comes back every year. He spends a quarter of his life here, when you think about it."

"His roots are in Australia now, though. His livelihood, his child. Every year when Grigori left, Baba used to cry."

"In a way, though, the fatherland is the world for the Greeks. How does the saying go? Wherever there is earth there is fatherland."

"The ones who leave might say that. Never the parents."

The girl is standing with their billies in the shade.

The gods are invisible among us, a presence, a stirring of the air. Only in death do they take on their body of stone.

The Buddha strove to douse the flame of the self and be lost in the void. If, as I believe, this is what death is, then there is no need to strive.

See how I wither. *In no part of me am I like her yet except for my hands, the backs of my hands, these reddish yellow sheets of silk smocked over the veins and bones. The hands are the first to age, then the neck, then the upper arms.*

Is it true what Vaïa said, that she lives in fear of death? What are the signs?

Vaïa: palm tree, palm branch, as in Palm Sunday. Is it her full name? Κουκκουβάγια = κουκκου cuckoo + βάγια = owl.

Η γη να μη σε φαει, May the earth not eat you.

When you plant an olive you plant it for your children to eat of. Only half the saying. Which tree do you plant to eat of yourself?

Wherever there is earth there is fatherland. Οπου γης και πατρίs. Fatherland, but the word, like earth, is feminine. Πατρίs, πατρίδα. Vaterland, patria, patrie, enfants

Sonya holds her breath, but the shape hovering in the depths of the *sála* is only Theia Bella. With a finger to her lips, Sonya sidles up behind her and hisses: "Where has she put the *tsourékia*? Show me?" Bella jumps and gapes, but she recovers her poise fast enough, beckoning Sonya into the storeroom and unveiling the tawny braids. A sweet and spicy smell comes up. "Please, Theia Bella," Sonya whines, "give me some, I'm so hungry." And it works: her aunt breaks off a fat chunk. With a grin of thanks, Sonya grabs it in both hands and shoots over the road to Lyka's. The poor old thing, it's not fair. She munches, brushing away crumbs. Good *tsouréki*. But did she have to wring out that grey mop of hair on the porch like that for the world to see? Hanging it out to dry like a dishcloth. Sonya winces: and I hate the way she stalks around jingling and gaping at everything with that long face of hers and her long hands, all spotty. What did she come for, anyway? It's not as if she belonged. Acting the poor widow, all so sad and humble, when she only got divorced. They are both alive. Why not make the most of it? My uncle does. I am never getting married. I will have lovers and lead a free life. No one even likes her. Lyka might think she's nice, but Lyka doesn't have to put up with her. What right has she to have a room all to herself, I'd like to know, when she's not even a relative? She's not my real aunt any more, I only call her that. *I* am a real aunt! I may look like a child to her but I am a woman *and* an aunt.

Bell has been thinking about what Vaïa said. She sees with new eyes now the family photos kept in place, all the old ones of Lefteri and his family, and of her and Grigori alongside those with his new wife, not pregnant here, or not showing; groups on the porch under grapes and leaves that hold the light, with the old man proudly at the centre and the three little boys, all called Yanni, one blond and two dark, one in each arm and one, hers, on his lap; and a late photo that Grigori took, which Yanni loves, and has stuck on the wall over his desk at home, of the old man sitting back in the cane chair, the whitewash behind him turned orange in a late summer glaze of light; a coffee cup on a tray at his elbow, pots of herbs in the yard, a gold hen, a tuft of grape leaves. A strut of shadow has fallen between his eyes, slitted as they are against the evening sun, and fixed with calm pride on the camera and on his son holding it.

Peering close, she gets a whiff of chocolate. It comes from the bowl of chocolate olives kept for offering to the mourners on his memorial days. Her mouth waters. Her hand has just closed over one when a voice hisses at her back. She jumps and reddens, her hand thrust in her pocket. Sonya! But the child is only after *tsouréki*. Alone, Bell sucks the chocolate; she licks her brown palm. We are two of a kind, she is thinking. Sneakthieves both. Sonya couldn't have seen, though, could she? Surely not! How can I have sunk so low?

Kyria Sofia grumbles her way through the chore of making the *magierítsa*, rinsing and chopping up the rinsed liver and spleen and pancreas and gut of the kid, and the heart with its cavities strung with cords, all veils of skin and white fat and so small it can fit into one hand. As soon as the meat goes on to boil, the wet weeds from the garden have to be sorted and washed and the snails and slugs pulled off before some of the leaves are added to the saucepan and others put aside for tomorrow's salad; and she has to do everything, considering that Bella has never known one weed from another and Vaïa has her hands full with the baby. Why do they have to have *magierítsa*, anyway, she wants to know — is there a word in the Holy Scripture, one word anywhere, about *magierítsa*?

Wiping her hands, she corners Bell in the *sála*. "Have you confessed yet?"

"Confessed what?" Rubbing her hand over her mouth.

"You can hardly go up in front of the world tomorrow, can you," Kyria Sofia says, "and take Communion?"

"Don't worry. I won't."

"When was the last time?"

"A while ago. I remember I got the flu."

"At church? At Communion?"

Andrea looks up from the newspaper. "How have you sinned, my child?" he drones and Bell makes a quick face.

"What would you know? Shame on your mocking!" Kyria Sofia shrills. "And what about Sonya?"

"Sonya is a mere child."

"The seeds of sin are inborn. Ach, why do I waste my breath? I was talking to Bella."

"I baptised her, let's not forget. I was her godfather."

"So you were!" Bell laughs. How could it have slipped her mind? "That hot day, remember?" she says. "Mamma, do you remember the children all had ice-creams —"

"Her godfather! *Your* only god is Lenin. You would do well to burn all that Communist filth of yours and read the Holy Scripture —"

"I *have* read —"

"— where it says that all but those who die in Christ will sink into hell under the burden of their sins."

"*Málista. Málista.*"

"— and the ice-creams were melting down their fronts because it was so hot, Andrea, remember?" Bell says hastily, to head them off. "And the cicadas were ringing in our ears."

She rounds on Bell. "And that goes for you as well, my lady. I tell you to know. Whoso eateth my flesh, and drinketh my blood, hath eternal life; and I will raise him up at the last day. For the trumpet shall sound, and the dead shall be raised incorruptible, and we shall be changed. At the last trumpet in the wink of an eye we will all come to life, dry flesh and dry bone, like the monk's fish in the City that you know about."

"*Sout*, Mamma," Andrea says. "Speak softly. The baby."

"And don't you tell me you got the flu from the wine of God or the bread. O fools, and slow of heart to believe. That is a lie and a blasphemy of Satan. The Jehovah's Witnesses say that you can but they are black liars! As if God would let us come to any harm in church!"

Sonya sidles into the kitchen where Andrea, humming, is warming the bottle, the baby asleep on his shoulder, while Vaïa and Yiayia boil the milk and stir the *magierítsa*.

"Baba?"

"Mmm?"

She runs a finger over the pattern in the plastic cloth. "Is it true that vampires hate bread?"

"That can't be right," her mother says.

And Baba: "Don't you mean garlic?"

Her grandmother just tightens her mouth and glares.

"And not bread?" Sonya says.

"Not that I know of." He knits his brows. "No. What gave you that idea?"

And Sonya, off-hand: "Oh, I just read it somewhere."

She watches as her grandmother unwraps a loaf from its towel and hugs it to her breast to saw it into fat slices. When Sonya tears a slice and eats it, so does Yiayia. Bella comes in and, having browned as many as will fit on the *sómba*, sits down munching, and Andrea absently helps himself. So does her mother, flourishing a spoon and peering around.

"What are you looking for, Vaïa?"

"It wards off the Evil Eye — garlic, that is. Just saying the word: May you have garlic. Have we honey, Mamma?" she asks.

"Bella, you bought honey."

"Here."

"Thanks."

"And garlic, did you want?"

"No, no, no!" Laughing, she twists the spoon in the honey and then in the milk, and licks it while Andrea fills the bottle. "Ach, what a lucky Beba," she croons. "Who is going to have milk and honey now?"

"The mercy of God is the milk," Yiayia says suddenly, "and His wisdom the honey," and behind her back Sonya sees her mother and Bella roll their eyes at each other and pull wry faces.

The τσουρέκια failed to rise but her bread is the poetry of earth. If she gets her own way and goes into a convent and they find out, she'll end up back in the kitchen anyway. No, Sister Sofia, dear, you are our golden-handed one. Now you just leave the praying and preaching to us and you get on with baking the bread for the greater glory of God. Salvation through bread. Yes, and why not? Her own bread becomes His body in the mystery and who can do more? The παπάς? Hardly. This is my body which is broken for you. Who but the Panagia herself, his own mother?

Milk and honey are wealth. Το έλεος του Θεού είναι το γάλα, she said, και η σοφία του είναι το μέλι.

"Who is coming to the *anástasi*?" she says, pulling her coat on, and none of them will meet her eyes.

"We all are, Mamma, later."

"At the last minute? You, Bella?"

After all, she said she went to church on the Fridays of Lent. That is something. One of the thieves crucified with Jesus repented with his last breath and was saved, as it is written in the Gospel. Who is to say that Bella is beyond hope?

"In a little while."

"Well, the door is open."

"Yes."

He is the door, and a light into the world, and he is the good shepherd.

All the *kafeneía* and the new discos are full, flashing with red light, a roar of smoky music held in behind glass doors. Vaïa has gone to fish Sonya out. At eleven, at the peal of the bells, the latecomers walk to the church in a slow drizzle. The bier still stands dripping out in the yard among the pines. All the village is here, the women and children packed into the church, most of the men outside smoking. Everyone has a candle with a white wick. Cousins in the dark call out "Bella" and appear in the light to shake her hand in welcome. A hand grasps her sleeve and this time it is Vaïa, in a raincoat and jeans, the same as Bell. "What's this I see! Blue jeans?" Bell demands and they burst out in naughty giggles. Before midnight all the lights go out, only to flash on again as the priest and congregation surge out, exchanging kisses and lighting their candles at each other's, so that soon the dripping pines are lit from underneath with a green fire; first fruits of the cross, the light of the world. The *papás*, hoarse with chanting, reassembles them by the bier. At the words *Christós anésti ek nekrón*, Christ rose from the dead, they all chorus *Christós anésti! Alithós!* Truly! The great hymn swells, *zoï*, life, *zoï*, and her eyes are swimming with tears. More handshakes then, and smiles, kisses, eggs are cracked, a few fireworks fizzle and bang. Sonya turns up at last. They all walk home together, shading the candles in their free hands to keep them from the windy rain: the swoop and sway of candlelight, as always, flattening into petals and spiralling up, a procession of fiery hands. Bell's candle keeps going out and being touched alight again. The porch is wet under the vine and full of shadows that rock and crawl as first Vaïa wipes her feet, then Sonya, and each of them in turn — but not Bell, whose candle has a wet wick now and refuses to burn — reaches her candle flame up to draw a cross in soot on the lintel.

The baby is asleep, the *magierítsa* bubbling in the saucepan, and Andrea has made a start on the wine. They pick a red egg each, checking for cracks, and aim it at the point of the egg the challenger is holding. Bell's egg cracks straight away; she peels and eats it while the game goes on until Sonya, who could not have cared less, she says, has the only intact egg. Kyria Sofia will be in church for some time yet and has told Vaïa not to wait, so they sit down to the green soup and the wine. "Our first Easter without Baba," Vaïa says, "but he is always with us in spirit," and Sonya shudders and pushes her bowl away.

"Sonya!"

"I hate *magierítsa*!"

"You should have something." Her mother frowns. "A cup of milk, then?"

"It's got skin on it."

"Not if I strain it."

"It has, the bits get through."

"Do you always have to complain?"

"Leave me alone. I'm not hungry."

"Too full of Coca Cola," Andrea mutters.

"I'm going to bed."

"Clean your teeth."

"Can I watch television?"

"No television," Andrea says. "The baby's asleep."

"Oh, why!"

"Do as you're told."

"But I'll turn it down low!"

"I said no."

Music videos are supposed to be on and she has fixed the wire so that the sound works, even though the screen is still a whirl of silvery forms. What was the point, if she is not allowed to watch? She hovers in the doorway, mutinous, but he only stares with raised eyebrows until she trails off. She would slam the door if she dared: she jams it shut.

They are stacking the dishes when a shriek comes from the bedroom, and a clamour, the baby. They rush in to find the room awash with the grey glow of the television screen and the baby underneath veiled head to foot in the sheet, hands clenched on the edge of her cot, wrenching at it and roaring. Sonya is rolling on the bed. "Ach," she gasps, "make me stop! I'll piss myself! I can't stop!" Vaïa grabs the baby and jiggles her up and down, breaking her sobs.

"Well?" Andrea says.

"I got such a fright! Suddenly this thing came swelling up in a white sheet! I thought it was a ghost!"

"O-o-o-oh!" Vaïa croons to the baby on to her lap. "My soul, my little one, my golden child, don't cry, no! No, no."

"And it was Beba, but I realised too late to stop the scream coming out! And then *she* got such a fright —"

"And the television?"

"Ach, *psychí mou esí*." Already the baby is goggling up, wet-eyed and heaving gulps of relief. "*Chrysó mou,* ach, *chrysó mou paidí*!"

"Well, I just put it on for a moment" — Sonya twists herself in her arms, her mouth frozen in a grin — "with the sound on very low, and I suddenly saw —"

Andrea is staring coldly. She closes her mouth.

"Go on," he says. "You were saying? Very low, *málista*."

"Well! I'm sorry."

He turns the television off and then the light. "Now do as you're told for once. Goodnight."

"Goodnight."

"Sleep well."

He has left the door open a crack on the darkness of the *sála*. "Baba?"

"What now?"

"Shut the door, please."

Pushed too far at last, he slams it. In the kitchen the baby smiles blankly, falling asleep on Vaïa's shoulder while they whisper and laugh and finish off with hot milk — it has threads of skin that snag in their mouths — mixed with honey. When Kyria Sofia trudges in at last hoary with rain, a red egg in each hand, they greet her with kisses and a chorus of *Christós anésti*. They want to heat up her share of the soup, but *magierítsa* is a sin, she says, nothing to do with the holy mystery. *Ade*, Mamma! When this is the best *magierítsa* you ever made! No, she means what she says. No *magierítsa*. A red egg? She ate one on the way home. Wine? One sip then.

She has her dead candle to prop up with the rest in the jar: one for Vaïa, one for Sonya, and yes, a third one, so Bella did go, though there are only two black crosses on the lintel; four candles with her own. Now she can slump down on the divan. They try to tell her the story of Sonya and the ghost and she does her best to listen, her eyes closed and her lips stretched in a tired smile, falling asleep.

EASTER SUNDAY

Bell wakes more than once to a fall of quiet rain in the early morning like a cat lapping milk. By the time she is up and dressed, however, the yard has dried and the sunlight is breaking through. Andrea has already spitted and trussed the kid, wrapping it first in sheets of brown paper in which the pools of oil shine like lantern glass. She finds him slinging it between two forked sticks over a sheet of corrugated iron weighed down with hot coals in front of the old barn. When the handle is turned the head spins, a red beak with tinfoil eyes, its teeth clamped. The forelegs are tied up with string, the back legs staked apart under a bare pink tail like a boy's cock, and the iron turd of the spit. Chain-smoking and yawning, Andrea hunches on a log and turns the handle. In a sprinkling of rain and thin sunlight all morning Bell and Vaïa and Andrea will take shifts on the log and turn the spit over the litter of grey coals, sipping coffee and sharing out hunks of *tsouréki*, their faces singed in a shimmer of heat. There are bees around, and a cat Bell has never seen before goes to sleep on its back by the barn with its paws over its eyes as if it belongs here. From time to time Andrea inspects the kid in its lace singlet of browning fat, and tilts or flattens the sheet of iron.

"Amazing, the heat from so small a fire," she says, squatting beside him one time, ready to take over, and he smiles up through drops of sweat, silent.

After a while she tries again. "The last time you did this, our father-in-law was here."

"Too sick to eat, though."

"No roast kid."

"He just sat where you are and talked about the war. The Albanian front and so on."

"Against the Italians?"

"His finest hour. The battles in the mountains blow for blow. Write it, he said. Who for, I wonder? A lot has happened in fifty years."

"And did you?"

"No, his mind wandered. He was too far gone."

"My turn?" she prompts him, and he changes places with her, stretching with a loud yawn. The heavy spit is warm from his hand.

"Have you been in the mountains? No? You should go. Do what Yanni did and climb Olympus. We could all go. See the gorges, the lakes."

"The wolves, the bears."

"The ghosts."

She laughs, remembering Sonya. "Why do you say that?"

"About as likely as wolves or bears these days."

"Are they hunted out? Really. Oh. I have a fear of heights, though. Of falling off rocks and mountains especially, and no wonder, I'm so clumsy." She lets go of the spit to spread her palms and show the red spots. "Grigori hated the mountains. He had to sleep in the snow for two whole winters when he did his national service."

"So did we all. Everyone goes through it. The mountains are the backbone of our defence."

"So you know your way around them."

"We were sent up there to teach when we got married. Our first jobs."

"I remember! Rina was born there."

"Conceived here, born there. Conceived at Easter, in fact. And born at Christmas."

"Isn't it strange how this house —"

"Yes, it's at the marrow of our lives."

"Mine too."

"I meant yours and ours."

"Grigori has had a weak chest ever since the army. He nearly died in the snow in Australia. He had double pneumonia and pleurisy and there was no doctor on the mountain. I had to put *vendoúzes* on his back."

He shifts on his haunches, grinning up at her, his face red from the fire.

"Of the mountains," she says, persevering, "all I know is that they are a wilderness of bare rock. And a charnel house, as I have read, in the War and Civil War."

"So were the plains. So is the whole earth if it comes to that."

"Anyway, as if I will ever dare to come another time!"

"Oh yes you will."

"About Baba — how did you mean, too far gone?"

"What can I say? The old woman gave him a sponge bath so he would be decent for Easter. He propped himself up on his elbows and I shaved him. Poor devil, he was as light as a child. He was a dwarf in his pyjamas."

"He told Vaïa that the great grief of his life —"

"The sons in exile. I know."

A silence falls while he lights a cigarette. Any talk with Andrea is pitfalled with silences. She has never known him to go on for as long as this.

"He always seemed calm to me," she says at last. "A stoïc. A fatalist."

"I think so, yes. In his old age he was."

"We never talked, he and I. Shyness, I think."

"He was no talker. Only in the *kafeneíon*. And since we were opposed, politically ... I think we understood one another. He *was* a fatalist. He believed in God, however."

"Even after Lefteri's Yanni?"

"More than ever after that."

"Like Mamma."

"Ah, she abased herself. His position was rather that we can never make sense of our fate any more than a dog can fathom the mind of its master since it lacks language, that whole dimension of the word. We are like the dog, only more so. Puppets in the master's hands."

"God's Karagiozides."

"*Málista.*"

The danger sign, a *málista* for yes. Bell has always subsided in the past. Now she shakes her head and smiles up. What is there to lose?

"I will never forget your Karagiozi," she says, "and the Accursed Snake."

"In another life."

"Before Communism."

"Ah! Among other things." He reaches under the kid to change the angle of the corrugated iron, and the heat flays Bell like a wind. "The play ends and the sheet drops, the lantern flares and lights up all the little struggling souls dangling on the strings. Then it goes out and they fall, just so much waste paper. That was the general idea, I gather: no players, no audience, no story, in the blink of an eye."

"Is that a Christian philosophy?"

He sits back on his heels to look at her. "There's room for it, I'd say, in Christianity. Wouldn't you?"

"I don't know. Would Mamma?"

"*Anáthema!*"

He stubs out his cigarette and stands up to go. "Tell me," Bell said hurriedly, and he waits, yawning, stretching above her. "How did they live here after the Civil War? The feuds, the hatred — the house in ashes?"

"All Greece was in ashes."

"Grigori would never speak about it. It was the same with Gendi Kule." She sees the skin go tight on his face. "Whatever I asked I met a wall of silence."

"Vaïa is the same. I think after a war the instinct must be to go to earth. It might be wiser when all is said and done."

"What might be?"

"To meet a wall of silence with silence."

Then he is gone and she is on her own at the fire, cranking the roll of meat, until Vaïa comes out to relieve her.

With a clamour of the bell, church is over. Vaïa has dressed the baby in new clothes and has her out on the porch to be admired by the time Kyria Sofia gets home. She arrives flanked with relatives in their best clothes, men who peer and poke at the spitted kid and advise Andrea that at this rate he will be lucky to sit down to it before sunset. They all ask Bell when she is leaving and when she says Tuesday some of them make sympathetic faces.

"Touch wood, Tuesday is unlucky," a boy chirps.

"So what?"

"No, he says well, *jánoum*," his mother puts in. "Tuesday is an evil-rooted day."

"The fall of Konstandinoupoli."

"Not only that, Bella!"

"With any luck the evil will be all worn out," she says.

They ask her when her son will come to Greece again. When he can, she answers, when his studies allow. When Lyka and Theia Kalliroï come with orange-scented biscuits in a ribboned basket, Bell tells them about the ghost in the cot while Sonya squirms and giggles, interrupting. Zoumboulitsa arrives, kisses everyone and sits down with a smile.

"Ah, Bella," she says, "*Christós anésti!* How good to see some sun! That hand you have, may I see it for a moment?"

Bell fumbles in her pocket, but the keys are in her other jeans. "*Alithós anésti*. It's in my room, Theia. Why?"

"I think it might be a holy hand."

"How do you know?"

"Christ has his hand like this in the ikon, his right hand, and the Bible is in his left hand. Christ Pandokratora."

Kyria Sofia is listening: "He has! You are right, he has, I have seen it too."

"I'll go and get it."

"No, sit down, *jánoum*. Some other time."

At about two o'clock Andrea peels the oily paper off to reveal the meat, satiny brown and pink, all but the head, which is still red-streaked like a pomegranate. In triumph he carries it to the kitchen. The head is set aside for the baby. Ach Beba, look what we've got for you, Vaïa croons, but when she hacks it off and splits it open it is half-raw, two red shells cupping a porridge with a crinkled skin and a ravel of red threads all over it. She puts it in a pot of water to finish cooking.

The plates are ready. Andrea carves and shares out the meat. Pink drops spring to the knife blade and Bell pops open a wine of the same pink. There are potatoes baked in the *sómba*, platters of dandelion salad and feta, home-baked bread, retsina and rosé, olives, apples and oranges. Bell has a film to finish off, and the old woman laughs into the lens, a scoop of blood under each eye as she squinnies in the weak sun by the window. The baby treads in Andrea's lap, eager for the flash. *Ná!* And she clasps her hands. Everyone laughs. The old woman crows aloud with wind, startling the baby, and everyone laughs again. *Sorry, sorry!* And now she burrows her head in the baby's lap like a white cat and makes her squeal and slap. The gloom has lifted. Since she came home from church Kyria Sofia has been light-hearted, almost her old self. So much so that, giddy with wine and relief, Bell wonders if she was mistaken all along about the ill-will in the house. Maybe it was all brought on by hunger, tiredness, anger, a storm easy to calm. All it takes is a red egg laid on Holy Thursday. The next time the village has a storm, will there be a hail of red eggs out of the doorways into the mud and rain, out into the real hail? A spill of sun through the clouds and there they are, the red and the white, lying in an unearthly peace where they fell, rinsed, luminous. Bell takes a long gulp of the straw-coloured wine. This time tomorrow she will be packed and ready. On Wednesday morning, noon at the latest, she will walk in the door of her own house.

"Oh, I wish Yanni were here," she says aloud, "he would have loved all this." The old woman gapes for a moment, misunderstanding perhaps, so Bell says quickly, "*My* Yanni."

"Yes, he should ring me now and then. Why does he never ring me?"

"You know what children are like. But I will tell him. He has never had a Greek Easter."

She is braced, flinching, for a retort.

"Send him over any time" — the old woman is grinning up — "and I will take care of him."

Towards the end of the meal Andrea pours the red wine he has had uncorked and breathing, and they move out on to the porch in the sun to finish it off. The mist has already begun to mass low over the garden again. When no one is looking Bell lets a thread of her wine spill on the ground between the grey vine root and the wall. To the goddess and her daughter, she thinks. Good red wine of Agia Vrissi. Holy Spring, it means. Like Holywell. Also fountain. Also tap.

When they are clearing up, just the two of them, Kyria Sofia goes and fiddles in the bowls of red eggs, peering and tapping and lifting them to the light. "*Ná*," she says at last, "take these home."

"What!"

"Wrap them up carefully. The two are to crack with Yanni and the three are for the other household."

She means Grigori's.

"How can I? It's against the law, Mamma."

"What law?"

"Well, you know, quarantine."

The old woman scowls. Is she about to say that these are holy eggs and how could God let them spread germs? Bell's skin prickles with sweat at the thought, and her heart quails.

"I know that! They are hard-boiled, sterilised, what danger can there be in a hard-boiled egg?"

Bell shrugs in her relief. "Well, they confiscate any food at all at Customs."

"You can always hide them."

"Five eggs!"

"All right. Just the two, then. Take the two."

The red eyes, the pleading hands, an egg in each. With a sigh Bell opens her own hands.

When Yanni rings, he has news: his stepmother has gone into labour in the hospital. Sonya is outside under the plum tree rehearsing, quietly though, with Lyka. Bell calls her in and watches as she preens on the phone talking to her Australian cousin. He wants a photo, she says, and luckily Bell has a shot or two left on her last film. She poses Sonya with an arm over Lyka's shoulder, the sun in a drift of white on the tree, a gold hen at their feet.

The show begins. Sonya has written and cut out tickets, just as Rina used to do, but has sold only one, to a stolid fat boy in shorts who comes and sits on the edge of a cane chair next to Vaïa, Andrea and Bell. Lyka and Sonya, laughing helplessly, race through a dialogue and smile, and bow. The boy gets up without joining in the applause. I've seen it, he says to the air around, it's a show on television. Shrugging it off, the girls begin a new item. But as he stalks away they falter, their wings droop. The show is over.

The cross is the Tree of Life and its fruit is the Light of the World. (The Cross, the Bodhi Tree.) How we are drawn to it, all flocking like moths into the branches.

I said I wished we had Yanni here, that he would have loved this. Confusion then. Did she think I meant Vaïa's Yanni, or Pappou, or the dead Yanni? **My** *Yanni, I said, he's never had a Greek Easter. Whose fault is that? I expected her to say, but she grinned. "Send him over any time," she said, "and I will take care of him."*

I spilled the wine on the shrouded earth into the open mouths of the dead.

She fears God/death (Vaïa said). Yes, God **is** *death (and not love). Death, God, Nirvana, the clear light.*

The need to sit; the equal need not to be seen — caught! — sitting (she never knocks). (But if I were kneeling instead, would the fear be less, or different, of invasion?)

To meet a wall of silence with silence, Andrea said. (The old are as silent as the dead.) To trust time and silence to wash the past clean.

She sighs. What to do with these eggs now? Take them and declare them and hope for the best? How likely are they to get through? Or try smuggling them in, as Mamma said? Either way they could end up in a bin at Customs. Which is unthinkable, to let good food get thrown away, the real sin against the Holy Ghost, to her mind. And to Mamma's, in this case. Holy eggs. Take the easy way out, then, eat them at the airport, or on the plane? What Bell would really like to do is take them and leave them on the old man's grave, if she could without being seen, with so little time left now and so many people around. Not that there is any harm in it. Red eggs are left on graves in Greece, they have turned up in tombs that go back to the age of the goddess. As long as Mamma never suspected that they were *these* eggs. She would do, of course. She would know straight away. Bury them at the foot, then. But going home without them would mean having to coach Yanni in a lie, since his grandmother would be sure to mention them on the phone. Which might be a worse crime, if anything — offence, violation. Worse than smuggling.

Bell must have dropped off. When she goes out to make a coffee it is late afternoon, and Kyria Sofia is reading in the *sála* with the lamp on. She follows Bell into the kitchen but she will not have coffee, since the doctor objects. She peers up over the white lenses of her glasses: she will have tea.

"Have you slept at all, Mamma?"

"I was not tired."

"All will be well, no need to worry."

"May the Panagia grant us a good delivery for her."

"Yes." *Kali eleftheriá* is said to all pregnant women. Good freedom, good delivery.

"Her first child."

"So it will take time. It's bound to."

"Yes. Well, we must have patience. I have found this for you to read."

"What?"

Trapped. Bell rolls her eyes at the stooped back, the white topknot fraying down it in wisps. From behind, her face hidden, she has dwindled to a doll, a rag doll in black. Have patience. Make patience. Just as you make a child, and make Easter, here in Greece you must make patience. Smiling, the old woman turns. "Some stories of Agia Sofia. Only if you want, that is to say."

"Well, yes. Thank you." She eyes the booklet.

"How the holy temple came into being and was lost to the Turks."

"My eyes are swollen and sore, that's the trouble. From the sleep. Since I never sleep in the afternoon as a rule."

"To take with you, I mean. Grigori can bring it back."

"But it belongs here."

"All right, then, I will just tell them, if you want, some of them."

"Do you know, by the way, Mamma, that my grandfathers both died fighting against the Turks in the War?"

"Don't tell me!"

"Yes, at Gallipoli in 1915. One has his grave there. The idea was to take the City and Gallipoli was on the coast near there."

"I know, I know — Kallipoli! That was the Great Idea."

"They were both in the landing but I don't know whether they knew each other. My mother's father's ship was lost when his ship sank in the bay. My father's father got ashore though. He was killed later."

"*Má!*"

"It's a small world, we say."

"So do we. All the more reason, then, Bella, to know the stories, then, yes?"

"You say well."

"Well, like certain holy ikons, the Temple of the Holy Wisdom came from God although, unlike some, it was the work of hands. For the King had it in mind to build a temple to the glory of God greater and more beautiful even than Solomon's temple in Jerusalem which was lost, but no one in the City could come up with a plan great and beautiful enough. One day in church, however, just as the Patriarch was giving the King the holy bread, the Lord's body, it fell to the floor. The King scrabbled for it on hands and knees but it was nowhere to be seen. In despair he looked heavenward and beheld a bee flying out the window with it in her mouth. The order went out to all the beekeepers in the kingdom to watch for the bee and at long last the chief carpenter himself came on a hive with no honeycombs. Imagine his joy and amazement when he saw inside it a church of wax, no larger than a human heart and perfect in every detail, which the bee had made by grace of the holy bread."

"And they built the temple to match?"

"It matched exactly."

"Now I really must see it. The Perfection of Wisdom!"

"Yes, go and see it. And go to the grave of your grandfather, Bella. It is not important that you never knew him. These are bonds that matter, the bonds of blood. Anyway, as I was saying, that was only the first of the many miracles of the Temple of the Holy Wisdom. How could there fail to be miracles in a temple that had the robe of the Panagia herself and drops of her own milk? And the true cross of Christ and the nails, and the crown of thorns, and the sponge, the reed, even drops of the Lord's blood. They had the slab of stone from the tomb. They had the skeleton of the hand of Ioanni the Forerunner with which he once poured the river water over the head of the son of God."

"They have all that?"

"Not now. They *had*, I said, *kalé*. Not that the Turks are to blame for that. The Franks got in first. The Venetians ... They sacked the City, the so-called Crusaders, in a river of Christian blood."

"How do you know that?"

"It is in the history books for all the world to know if it wants."

"We were always saying we would take you back there one day. Grigori and I? And the day never came."

Kyria Sofia shrugs. "As for what the world *says*, and what it *does* ..." She leaves unspoken what else they used to be always saying, and the enormity of Bell's defection. After all, didn't they always say they would live in the village for ever and take care of his parents in their old age?

"I —" Bell falters. What is there to say?

"If I stay well, who knows, one day? — God willing, I might still go. And when I do, who knows? — the City might be in our hands again."

"*Ela*, Mamma. After all this time?"

"If the King is restored to the throne."

"Is that likely?"

"If such is his fate. He was given the name Konstandino."

"*Sigá!*"

"What do you know, Bella? You know what they used to call Greece? Psorokostaina. And why? She was scrofulous because she was so poor, our Greece — a poor mother who can't feed her children and so they are driven into exile. And she was Kostaina, the wife of Kosta. Of Konstandino."

"That is to say?"

"That her fate is bound up with the name Konstandino. It was the name of the first king who founded the City and the last king who sleeps in a cave. They have always said that one day a new Konstandino would be born to take his City back and that he would be a six-fingered man. Our King in exile was born with six fingers on his hands and feet, I tell you, Bella, to know."

"But the Turks have been there for over five hundred years!"

"They occupied all of Greece for hundreds of years or have you forgotten? They had the Middle East, the Turks. They had Egypt, Palestine. How long were the Jews in exile from Jerusalem? But they are back there now. Is it not so? Do you know when we got Thessaloniki back by the grace of God? Not until 1912."

"That was in a time of war."

"One of many times of war."

"Don't forget there are a lot of Greeks in Turkey."

"And Turks in Greece. We have God's promise that the City will be ours again one day. Let me tell you to know, Bella. On Holy Saturday night in the City many people — not only Christians, but Moslems, dervishes! — have heard the plainchant in the Agia Sofia and seen lights spring up in the windows, the light of candles, more and more candles gathering in the dark, and nothing was there when they forced the doors. This is a sign."

"What if everything that happens in the world is a sign?"

"It is! *I* believe that. Yes! If only we knew how to read them."

"Does anyone?"

"Not in our day. Listen, Bella. These things are common knowledge. Just this morning didn't you hear them say that when the City fell to the Sultan — are you listening? — it was a Tuesday and ever since then Tuesday has been a day of ill omen?"

"And the monk's fish jumped out of the pan into the water of life."

"So you have ears and you listen. The Agia Sofia ran with blood that day. On the night of the last day of the siege the people crowded in and received the sacrament. In the middle of the night the walls of the City fell under the cannon fire. The liturgy was still going on when the great doors fell open and all but the young women were slaughtered, and they were bound with their own scarves and dragged away into slavery. The priest, however, was in the middle of the liturgy: his blood was not spilt, I tell you to know. He vanished into the walls with the holy chalice. And he is there today waiting to finish the liturgy in peace. And the altar was saved. There is no altar now. It was smuggled out on a ship which sank in the Sea of Marmara and since then, no matter what the weather, the sea is always as still as oil over that place. It has been granted to many Christians to see the altar in the depths, which one day will be back where it belongs."

Bell shakes her head. "Mamma —"

"And still the slaughter went on. The Turks clambered over the dead to strike the living, until the nave and the aisles brimmed with corpses, and those who have been there say you can still see the red handprint of a Turk high up on a marble column. But like the priest, the King was never found, Bella. In the thick of the battle an angel seized him and turned him to marble and, as I say, he lies in a cave by the Golden Gate against the day when God sends the angel with his sword to raise him in the flesh. And again the stones will run with blood."

"Like in 1922?"

"Only then, you think? She is soaked in the blood of war."

"As is Makedonia."

"As is Makedonia and everywhere on the earth where men have lived. If I know anything, Bella, I know what war is about."

"I never want to."

"God forbid. Who does?"

"The Greeks invaded and the Turks came up behind them and wiped them out. And then they turned on you who were innocent and scourged you with fire and sword, children! They sent you into exile."

"They died for the Great Idea. As your grandfathers did."

Exoría, exoría. Bell bites her lip.

"For justice, Bella. To die a good death. A martyr's death."

"To live by the sword."

She shakes her head. "In a great cause. And since whatever lives must die."

"Must die in war? Since you know what war is about."

"That is in God's hands."

"Not ours?"

"Look at your hands, Bella, look at mine. Do you see them stopping a war?"

In the half dark of her room Bell rewinds the film, snaps the camera open and drops this last roll into its plastic case. There they all are at long last, all in the bag, spool on spool. The film will be more static than most, but all films are alike, she should have said to Vaïa: all more or less static, fragments that melt before our eyes into a stream of light and dark, a black river overlaid with glimmers, reflections, rainbows. It is a matter of degree, that's all. Let me just get this right, she vows, and then I'll make a real film.

She flicks back to her notes on the plainchant. *This is a music fused with the word and made flesh in the voices of men.* The Church is feminine, *i ekklesía*, and she only speaks in a man's voice. She scribbles in the margin: *In the ikon the same fusion occurs on the visual plane. Words in oil or chips of stone appear among the bodily forms, Jesus, the apostles, the saints, the mother, the words of God and men. (The skeleton of the hand of Ioanni the Forerunner pouring the river water.)*

(If only I could paint!) she adds. Or better still, do mosaïcs, real ones, not only of photos. If only she could make an ikon in gold and lapis lazuli of what Mamma said just now: a Baptism in the desert, sand and stone, the stone of God — the *son* of God — standing in the river naked while a skeleton hand pours water.

Kyria Sofia pulls the blanket around her and stretches out on the kitchen divan, the house asleep all around her. What a strange thing, she thinks, that Bella's grandfathers should have died for Greece. Has she ever mentioned it before? I would have remembered if she had. They fought at Kallipoli in 1915 to save our City and one has his grave there. Where is the other grave? Perhaps the ship where it sank. How strange, to know where to find a grandfather's grave. In death he is one of us. That being so, maybe she was meant to meet our Grigori in Australia, after all, and marry him. Everything is meant that happens in the small world.

Mustafa Kemal had a Greek mother, he who grew up to be the Ataturk and the scourge of Greece and the victor at Kallipoli.

They lived in Thessaloniki. Their old house is still standing and I know it well. How he came to massacre us, his mother's people, is a mystery to me. Then, it is a great mystery anyway — the mother, the son.

Desperate for rest though she is, sleep refuses to take her. So, she thinks, does death, Charo, who has taken so many. Since Yannaki died and more still since Yanni died, may God forgive them their sins, the things I have lived through, known and half-known and only imagined, or feared, suspected, have all joined hands and I no longer know which is which any more. Not all of a sudden, but slowly over these last months more and more I have become aware, looking back, of how thin my life has worn, going into holes gently with every wash like an old sheet until it is more creases and shadows than substance. Only my body has substance now. Pain is my substance. I swell, aching, filled to bursting with pain. How much longer must I stand here on the threshold of death, on the wrong side of the door? I sleep and I wake. Nevertheless not as I will. Even if it be only to go on feeding the hens and baking the bread of God.

When Bell wakes she is shivering on the bed, fully dressed, having dozed off. There is no sound in the house, in the village. Where is everyone? Asleep, they must be. She pulls the bedcover up around her shoulders. The notebook has fallen on the floor, open, and the pen, and ink has soaked into the *kilími*. A black drop of ink like a knot in the black stripe, so small, luckily, that even with good eyes you would only see it if you knew it was there. *She* won't see it.

Soundlessly she opens her door, crosses the *sála* and puts her head around the kitchen door: an empty blanket lying on the divan. So it is all right if she goes in and makes more coffee. She puts the *bríki* on to boil, shaking it because a spoon stirring might wake them in the next room. More than once she swings round having felt eyes on her back. The black shape of the old woman fills her mind, sitting up, boring into her with crimson eyes. No one is here — Bell even pats the blanket gently and shakes it —

and yet the feeling persists. She sips the warm sweet mud of her coffee in a chair facing the divan, on guard. And to think that this wraith, this old rag doll, this bloodthirsty old hag, was wild with love once, even ran away for love, in those days, imagine! And they married her off at gunpoint. Is that why young girls are anathema to her? And Eros too, the beautiful young man, the beloved, Erota. She is a Psychi who has lost Erota and lost hope and grown old at her tasks. No wonder she hated the story! Erota is a demon. No, only the end, not the story, it was the end she hated. All the more so because she was carried away, wasn't she? — she listened, she drank in every word. To say he was a demon is all very well, but Erota was not the villain in the story. He was not the force of evil. Is love ever? Hate was. Hate and anger, and envy.

No larger than a human heart.

It must have been a common enough story in her day. They still arrange marriages now. How many thousands got married by proxy to come out to Australia? I know some who did. *We* married for love. So did Vaïa. The brothers always knew they were not going to have a say. Grigori said in Australia what a wilful girl Vaïa was, clever but wild, with her heart set on finding her own man. She didn't waste any time either. Andrea was a fellow student and there was no one else in the world once she set eyes on him. She was giving birth to Rina almost as soon as they were married, and proud of it. No apologies, and no scandal. And already Rina is married with a *béba* of her own, unto the fourth generation, a line of beautiful wilful girls. Because look at Sonya now! The ruddy limbs and flaming hair. A black fire.

And doubt was an evil. I was forgetting that: doubt and self-doubt on the part of Psychi, embodied in a drop of hot oil. And of course, so was the ill luck of being found out.

She was married off at gunpoint and she never forgave him for it. She was relentless, pouring out all her thwarted love on her sons, who left. And *his* love? Because he was no less thwarted, it seems. Didn't his own mother live and die in his house hated for all those years and even beyond the grave? What was that line in the ballad? *Sic counseils ye gave to me, O. The curse of hell frae me sall ye beir* ... Yes, but his curse was not for her, only for them if they dared to bury him by her. Even so. The curse of hell. Did his mother know? How terrible if she did. How did she bear it?

"You're awake, Bella? Where's Mamma?"

"I don't know. At the henhouse?"

The dish of scraps is missing.

"I'm going for the milk. Are you coming?"

Bell gets to her feet. "I'll just put on some wood first."

Vaïa lifts the lid: "No, it has wood. She will yell if we let it go out."

"The woodpile is getting low," Bell says.

"Well, it will do. This is April. Come on, then, Bella."

"She won't chop it, will she?"

"She could never lift the axe these days. A boy comes. You know I keep telling her she should come down to us now, at least in the winter. Why stay here alone in the cold, in the snow? She says she will, but not yet."

"Grigori will want her in Australia."

"Out of the question," snaps Vaïa, and an awkward silence falls. Too late to turn back now, they are out in the street with the billies, greeting, being greeted. Bell, who has been thinking of bringing up her talk with Mamma about the monastery, holds her tongue. How would Kyria Sofia get on in Australia, anyway, she wonders. Would she be happy? But if Vaïa won't hear of that either ... And now she has taken offence.

But no, Vaïa is looking ahead with a rueful smile. "Mind you, she was handy with an axe when she was young," she says in the tone of someone settling down to a long yarn.

"I know! In the Civil War. The beekeeper's mother."

"He told you, did he? Grigori?"

"No, Zoumboulitsa. She thinks the world of Mamma."

"She has reason to. Do you remember the beekeeper, how we always bought our honey from him? Poor Pandeli. He died."

"I know. So many of the ones I remember are dead."

"But the young ones are coming on."

"Vaïa, that saying you mentioned, what was it again? About olive trees, yesterday?" Bell says. "When it's for your children, you plant an olive. And when it's for yourself you plant a what?"

"A fig tree."

"A fig tree! That's it."

"I mean to plant more."

"Figs?"

Bell looks surprised. Vaïa is surprised, hearing herself. When did she decide this? "We have enough figs: no," she says, "olives."

"Oh, olives! Yes!"

Vaïa spins around, clanking the billies, suddenly delighted with herself. "Two is not enough."

Gathering all her things on the bed under the lightbulb to start packing, Bell discovers that the silver hand is not in the pocket of her other jeans, or in any of her pockets, or her case or her bed. How long has it been missing? The smell of it is still strong in the palm of her hand, but the metal loop that held it on the keyring is wide open and the hand could be anywhere. But again she searches the room, the floor, the piles of clothes, and it isn't.

She asks the old woman, in the kitchen with Vaïa boiling the milk, if she has seen it.

"Your silver hand?"

"With my keys? The holy —"

"Oh, that."

"I've lost it. It's fallen off. You haven't seen it at all?"

"No. *Sorry*."

Bell smiles. "I've looked everywhere."

"We must ask the world."

"No, never mind."

"A silver hand?" asks Vaïa.

"Yes, have you seen it?"

"A trinket of Bella's, Vaïa. A lucky charm."

"How big, Bella?"

Bell makes a ring of her thumb and forefinger. "No, look, it's not important."

Vaïa frowns. "Someone must have seen it. Is it valuable?"

"No, not at all."

"We will look," says the old woman.

"Best to forget it."

"No, well, no harm in looking." Vaïa is stiff with affront.

With every corner of the other rooms crammed with belongings, what hope is there of finding it? Bell smiles and retreats, shaking her head, angry with herself for making a fuss. Kyria Sofia and Vaïa are both suddenly grim, withdrawn against her. She can feel through two doors how they have closed ranks against her, and she has no one to blame but herself. Did they really think she was accusing anyone? That was the last thing in her mind.

She can't help moping after it, all the same. Is it so unlikely, if it comes to that, for someone to have taken it? Who? Not Andrea. Mamma, then? Vaïa? Sonya? What about Zoumbou who admired it loudly, who asked to see it this morning? That could have been a ploy. Any one of them could have stolen it. The faces rise one after the other, all hateful, secretive, alien. Let this be a lesson to me in detachment, she tells herself, God knows I need it. What about me, if it comes to that? Haven't I reached out my hand and stolen a chocolate olive? And now in revenge the house has swallowed up my hand and it serves me right! *If thy right hand offend thee* . . . Oh, the sanctimony of it! And I am sick, she thinks, in a sharp pang of disgust, *sick* to death of that above all, the odour of sanctimony. The house is slick all over with it, dank and greasy, oozing out of these very walls, the whitewash, a whited sepulchre.

It could have happened any time in the week, before I took the chocolate olive, even, because it knew, the house already knew I would. Is there anything it doesn't know? It lies awake at night listening to the ticking of our hearts. *Ade!* I don't care any more. I don't give a shit. Only let me get out of here in peace, that's all, in one piece, no more rows, no showdowns, and never set foot in it again, and it can do what it likes with the hand.

When Bell comes out again she finds the light on and only Andrea there, hunched over a pile of newspapers, underlining and taking notes, an open sandwich in his free hand. He glances up, and she gives a nervous smile.

"Have some. Eat." He waves a vague hand over the table.

"Too full."

"This is dinner. The others are out visiting."

"What about the baby?"

"They took her with them so I could work. There's bread. Roast meat, this weed salad —"

"I may never eat again. I only want a coffee. Will you have one?"

"Not for me. And there's the wine."

"Oh, so there is, yes." She pours a glass of the rosé, clinks it against his and takes a deep gulp, her eyes closing. "Ah!"

He laughs. "Who needs coffee?"

"Oh, me, I need a coffee too. Just a Nescafé."

"You may never sleep again."

"I will. Don't say that. This is my last night."

"Is it really? So it is."

He lights a cigarette and lapses back into his reading while she waits by the stove for her water to boil, watching him under her lashes. The photos after all have told less than they might have of the truth. Andrea may have aged and grown thin, half-bald, his scalp gilded under the lamp, a tired man. All the same, in the flesh he still has his old — his young — brusque tenderness, and the eyes of the young man he was, red and lined though they are. Far from mellowing, he is more intense than ever. The wildness is in harness now — his life is in harness — but the impassivity is all the more ominous. His shadow has grown heavier. As have his burdens. As for Vaïa, she is growing so like her mother that Bell shakes her head in disbelief. She is the Kyria Sofia of thirty years ago in everything but the hair: Mamma's was pure white even at that age. Does Andrea mind that his wife is turning into a mirror of her mother? Unless living side by side blinds you to change. You simply fail to notice what a stranger can see at first glance. Maybe Andrea is turning into his father. Grigori has been turning into his for years, but would I have noticed if we were husband and wife now? Husband and wife. The Greek words are the plain everyday man and woman, *ándras*, *gynaíka*, and this to Bell's ear has always given them overtones lacking in the English, a forthrightness, an archaic simplicity and nobility, a breath of the Garden of Eden. Do you not have a man? the Greeks say, anywhere, on a train, a ferry, strangers. And where is your man? Andrea is Vaïa's man. Vaïa is his woman. They are probably too busy to notice. Life is hard with a small child, however well broken in you are. To live side by side, Vaïa said, and not be loved.

When she makes her coffee there is enough water left for another cup, so Bell repeats her offer in a murmur. No, thanks, no coffee. He pours them both more wine, and sits staring into his glass, rocking it under the lightbulb.

"Bad news?"

"Ah. The usual." He closes his eyes and drinks it down with a flourish. "Good news is no news."

He turns one of the newspapers around to show her the headline: BLOODSHED TO COME IN THE BALKANS.

"Is that right, do you think?"

"The omens are not good, I must say."

"Greece?"

"Well, obviously, I hope not. I'm inclined to see Greece as having war in her bones by now, mind you, like earthquakes. You know how it is. We can bet we're in for an earthquake sooner or later, when we live in an earthquake zone. If you see what I mean."

"Maybe you should all come out to Australia!"

"Do you think so?" Her doubt must be showing on her face.

His head tips back. "The time for that was under the Junta. Twenty years ago when we were young we might have. Not now."

When they come in, mother and daughter, they knock on her door to say goodnight, and stand there chatting for a moment. Vaïa turns on the threshold, her look of concern barbed with a smile, to ask if the hand has turned up. No, no, really, Bell has forgotten all about it by now. When the door closes the thought crosses her mind to call out that it has, yes, on the floor in the *méros*, say, having rolled into a dark corner. But what if it turns up later? Or they ask to see what all the fuss was about? No. She sighs. She has had a narrow escape. Whatever put that thought into her mind? — it was a trap.

The house is dark and quiet again, Bell switches her own light off and waits for long minutes, half an hour. Silence. Then with the nail scissors in her hand she creeps through the *sála* and out the creaking iron door to the familiar yard; a dampness and the glow of moonlight on the roofs and trees and in the puddles by the fence where she reaches and snips a sprig off each of the olive trees. Stealing again. Only for a keepsake, and no harm done. All the same she could have asked, she could even have said they were for Yanni — one is for Yanni — and Kyria Sofia would have said yes, of course. Only she would have told everyone, even in front of Bell perhaps, and the mere thought makes her press the olive leaves to her hot cheeks, the thought of all their kind smiles fixed on her. There is a twitching in the trees all around, a breath of wind, faint and unsteady, and stars are showing.

She has the door open now, and so far no one has woken up. If she is ever to take the eggs to the grave, now is the time. It has to be in secret, it would look so ostentatious, so sanctimonious, done in full view. It has to be at night. But the air is cold, and there could still be someone in the street to challenge her, very likely, and ask what she is doing creeping in the dark and the cold alone to the cemetery where no one goes at night. What if they saw her from one of the houses? A black shape stumbling in the mud, furtive under the streetlamp, a blood red egg held in each hand! She has scandalised the world enough. For that matter, the old man would rather Yanni had his egg. Shivering, she wipes her feet and closes the iron door soundlessly, groping her way, and then her own door. The bed clasps her. Cowled in the bedclothes, she pulls out her diary, which falls open at a bay leaf she picked from the *epitáfio*.

Nothing flows, nothing but piss and mucus — no blood, no tears, no dreams, no action. I came to — behold? A condition of stasis.

Απόγνωση: από + γνῶσις, knowledge. A state of desperation, bewilderment, at the wits' end.
Απελπισία: από + ελπίς, ελπίδα, hope. Away from hope.
Απορία: α + πορία (πόρος). Absence of a way, tracklessness, wonder(ment). Απορῶ is I wonder. Απορῶ γιατί ἦρθες.

When did she write this? Rereading the page she has to laugh. *Stásis* is on signposts all over Greece, it means bus stop. She closes the olive springs inside and slips the diary under the pillow. Her hand encounters something hard and cold — the hand! — and she throws the pillow aside. Not the hand. Snake-enfolded on the sheet, the Buddha.

The right hand bent, thumb pressed to the first two fingers, right nipple to left nipple, forehead to navel, the dance of the right hand over breast, head and belly, in the **mudra** *of making the cross. What could be simpler? I was put on the spot. I was in the grip of my old self-consciousness — paralysed, tongue-tied — yes, it* **was** *my egoism. Egoism on her part as well, to step in and take me over — not that that lets me off. To have come all the way here and then withhold the one gift of love that she expected — needed — of me! And in the name of my* **freedom!** *(****Hier stehe ich.****) But to her no one is free who is the servant of God.*

No larger than a human heart, she said. And the Zen poet in the

Scriptures: "In the cooking-pot of the world, cook well and not badly; the human heart is the free-moving ladle."

Some can no more believe in death than I can believe in the afterlife, the Resurrection, Rebirth in the six realms, Heaven and Hell, Nirvana. Sit where the heart of the light is this Buddha on the sill in the morning with the mist at his back and again at night. The begging bowl is a dark lake and his robe is light.

*I am one of **those born within the realms of desire and form** but I can only believe in death.*

If only as a sop to her feelings! But it was more than egoism. What she said today, the stones running with blood, the hands. And irremediable, because the truth is, yes, that the cross is a horror to me. I didn't know — I didn't want to — how strong it was, my horror of that corpse twisted in agony and spread-eagled on the hill of skulls. The horror must be dulled by a long familiarity or how could we hang that around our necks? We are so used to it that we have never even see it. If there was a crucifix in the church here I failed to see it. I failed to make the sign. It horrifies me not only because he is dead, the man of sorrows — not at all because he is dead — but because he was put to death. Innocent himself, he is riddled with murder. He carries the germ of murder in the name of God. Wherever that cross has taken root in the world it has served to spread hatred, torture, murder, a black plague.

The living world as a shadow play like the one on the white sheet, Karagiozi, the shadows, the voices, the creases that hold the yellow light like water.

Sonya, restless in the heavy heat and breathing of the room, sees a vampire creep into the graveyard whispering to itself, a moonlit face as white as pearl, starlit, with black pits where the eyes should be, and blood-filled clenching hands.

Bell is in a field with the sun across it, late in the day when all the heat goes out of it: bare but for the grasses with bent heads that look like flowers but are pink shells of seed like peppercorns, red drops with the sun in them so that the hot ground has a shimmer like a swarm of red flies. Birds with red breasts circle, squealing, high and sunlit and following them with her eyes she sees the moon, full, faint. Further on there are tall stones and fences of rusty wire, a flagon of brown glass alight like a campfire, black logs of shadow and strings of dry vine with yellow fruits the size of tennis balls, cool and sour green inside or dry, spilling out flat little seeds, lentils.

She walks past grass in tufts and ant mounds, and immortelles under thick domes of dust, and sea shells, and brown glass that holds a gold light as the sun moves. Her legs are burning. She sees that she has leggings of blond fur, a coating of little burrs so sharp that they draw blood as she picks them one by one off her jeans and socks. Red studs shine in the blond hairs. The sun is flat to the earth now, and barred by the fence. Beside it, away from the other graves and turned at a slant to face Mecca, are three rusty cots full of the feathery grass, two unmarked and one with a headstone, a lobed arch, a spear blade, engraved with the threads of some lacy script, Urdu, or Arabic. Exiles. A horse beyond the fence shifts and snorts as she approaches, a shadow fringed white with dust in the last of the light.

EASTER MONDAY

Since this has been the last night, and she will spend tonight trying to sleep sprawled across three chairs at Athens airport, Bell has hoped for a good sleep. Instead she has slept lightly, waking at daybreak with the feeling, an illusion, it must be, of not having been asleep at all, except that she also has a strong memory, at last, of a dream. She was in a desert, in the one place where there were trees standing, a ring of dry banana trees around a greenish pond with a bridge, green rushes, hollow green and tough, and rocks. A brittle scraping and clacking of yellow slats, although the land dipped there and hardly a breath of the hot wind reached into them. The pond was mud around an eye of water in the shadow of the banana fronds, water as dark as mud where a web of fins, a mouth, a gullet, shivered, lifting into the light.

No one is moving in the house. She can switch on the light. No one is likely to come barging in now. She is safe if she wants to meditate. This is like being a child again, sent to her room in disgrace until she is ready to be a good girl. The shut door and the stillness of the house beyond, charged with angry presences; the casement window tugging its iron arm, the draped leaves dark and a fretting and whining in the branches. Only now I have a Buddha for company, she thinks, a still point, an eye in the storm. Thank God for the Buddha!

She is smiling — what would Mamma say? *Anáthema!* — with the Buddha already in her hand, when the impossibility of it strikes her, the fact that today more than ever there is no substance in her tight-knit enough to mirror the Buddha in his sitting, no strength by which to gather herself and sink into the shape of repose. Man and snake they rear up, gazing with brass eyes into her disorder. Her legs are already aching. Restless, she folds and unfolds them, gets up and switches on the light, folds them again. The nun on Paros, tucking her red robes in, sat on the cushions on the floor among the niches and alcoves of the white room, folded her legs and chanted the mantras, telling them on a rosary. *Om mani padme hum.* The red beads slithered through her fingers. Bell has a sudden urge to cry. She closes her eyes, but no tears come.

Giving up in the end, she hides the Buddha and, still restless, fills her pen, opens the shutters and flattens their leaves back against the white wall, a slabby roughness as cold as snow to hands that are still full of the warmth of sleep. A grey light glimmers in, enough to turn the electric light sallow, mustardy, so she switches it off, throws her clothes off the cane chair under the window, and sits there with the daylight on the page.

Here we are in another season, or no season, a blank, another world. The whole of the north is sunk in fog. The house is a morgue, and the church out of bounds now, to me. A wasted week, seven whole days of this inaction and ill-will, huddled over the fire in the stove.

*I take the Buddha out of hiding and sit for the sense of calm, the span of it, detachment, equanimity. The breath. But I can never bring myself truly to **want** the breath without the body, the flesh, the whole stinking bag of bones, of entrails, the black earth. As far as I can see we live once, body and soul, once and for all. Why practise to attain Nirvana and be at one with the void — oblivion, the abyss — when we have it coming in any case (its true name is death)? If there is a cycle of rebirth, though, and I am one of those lost souls who are doomed to it because in ignorance we grasp at life — amen to that. I am come that they might have life, and that they might have it more abundantly, Jesus said. And they came flocking. The one commandment, live, and let live.*

They are having a heat wave at home, Yanni said. A heat wave,

I love those words. I love a heat wave in mid-April, and the sea flat under the north wind.

The tune of the hymn of the *anástasi* keeps coming back, sung not as she heard it on Saturday night but in the children's voices to which she awoke at this time every school morning in the weeks after Easter those twenty-odd years ago, high-pitched and frail, off-key, blown in ragged on the wind, the children singing before they marched in. Grigori was still asleep at her side or already up and out in the sun. *Christós anésti ek nekrón*, they sang, Christ is risen from the dead, *thanáto thánaton*, and then the phrase she loved best, the slow wail of *zo-o-ï, zo-o-ï-ï*, life, life: word for word, barely intelligible — *thánatos* was death, so was it death put to death? — and yet the whole so impressing itself on her that she was never afterwards to hear it sung without an upwelling of tears.

The phone rings when no one else is awake yet except Vaïa, who is bustling about in the *sála* with the baby slung on her hip. "Hullo, yes?" she shouts, "Yes, yes! What are you saying, brother? Bella! She has given birth," she calls with her hand over the mouthpiece, because Bell is suddenly standing there, half in the light at her door.

"A boy or a girl?"

"A boy or a girl? A girl! Mamma? No, she must be still asleep (Bella, call Mamma). Yes, Grigoraki *mou*, she is tired out — of course I will! And may she live long for us. What good news! (Bella? You speak, go on!) Bravo, tell her, bravo! (*Ade*, Bella!)"

"Grigori! Wonderful news! I don't know where Mamma is. She's not in the kitchen. Are they all right? Both of them?"

"They fine, fine."

"Have you seen them?"

"They both fine."

"Who does she look like?"

"Like my mother. Is look like my mother!"

"Well! Congratulations. May she live for us."

Sonya, slipping past into the storeroom for *tsouréki*, has found her grandmother asleep on the mattress on the concrete floor, wrapped in a creamy fleece. "Here she is," she calls. "Yiayia? She's in here," and they crowd into the doorway.

"Mamma, Grigori was on the phone. And she has given birth!"

"What did you say, Vaïa? When was this?"

"Just now!"

"You should have called me!"

"We looked and we couldn't find you," Bell puts in.

"Quick, ring him back!"

"We can't, he was at the hospital."

"Amán!" — and is she all right?"

"An easy birth, he said, and the baby is four kilos."

"Four kilos!" Bell gasps.

"Tell me," Kyria Sofia says, "she has made a girl?"

"How did you know!"

"The photos, *kalé* — I could tell."

"Ade!"

"Well, since I was right? It was obvious. So, we have another girl. Good, and may she live for us. We must give thanks to God."

Andrea wakes and is told the good news. They laugh and talk over a breakfast of toasted *tsouréki* and jam and milky Nescafé. The visits of yesterday go on into today, in the sun of the porch and in the yard. Andrea minds the baby and reads while Bell and Vaïa trail from house to house gossiping. The photo albums come out and, narrowly watching Bell, everyone hears the good news. Some cousins ask her if she is scared of the flight home. No, they double-check for bombs and weapons at the airport, she explains, and they keep clear of the Gulf and the fires of Kuwait: the flightpath goes due south over the Aegean and up the Nile, turning east at Luxor to cross Saudi Arabia. They tell her how daring she was to come with the war on, while she smiles, denying it. If I had waited for peace, she says, and they throw their hands open: of course, you could wait forever. She can think of nothing but the flight now, promising herself a window seat and seeing how the Nile will uncoil in a hank of blue and green over the desert, the Sahara, all its yellow folded sheets and feathers of sand, so unlike the carved sea floor of the desert of her dream. Because yes, she had a dream in the night, after all this time, a dream she is beginning to remember, about the desert, an eye of water, a good dream, silent, soaked in a warm, deep light. There was a graveyard. It might have gone on to a fire in the dark, all sparks and stars, and a glaze of morning frost, but this is all too far out of reach for her to place the graveyard or know what brought it to mind, so clear, every seed and shell and flare of glass. It was in Australia, somewhere far inland, and this is all she can be sure of here and now: there were galahs, and grass with seeds like pomegranate seeds on the dry sand of some place in the far north and she has been there or she will go there, one or the other. If she believed in omens, it might have been her own grave. The heat of the day in the dust and shards of honey-brown glass and the long shadows of headstones.

They find Andrea on the porch scowling over a newspaper with the baby asleep in his arms. Vaïa lifts her away carefully, and he looks up, red-eyed.

"You are tired," she says.

"I'll survive."

"This was supposed to be a rest. A break from the struggle."

"No time."

Vaïa shakes her head in despairing resignation at Bell and goes in, but Bell hangs back to look at a sketch on the table, a poster with a hammer and sickle, a fist, a slogan, a lost cause; and he raises his eyebrows in what might be offence at the smile on her face.

"I can see the need," she says in answer. "But for the struggle, I think there would be no hope of a just world."

"I think I might settle for a better one."

"Is there any hope?"

"Any amount of hope. Don't go thinking I'm the only one. Hope!" He sighs. "Why we go on flogging ourselves."

Γέννησε. Κορίτσι έκανε. Grigori has a daughter. Sofia it is, then, or Sophie. May she live for us, all the family is saying. May she live for you, the outsiders say, even to me. Να μας ζήσει, να σας ζήσει. A new child of the house. The place of birth doesn't matter, only the bond, the blood tie. Να μας ζήσει, I said to Grigori myself without even thinking but I stand by that. May she live for us, I said. So, my son has a half-sister. Buy her a blue bead if the airport shop is open. Solace, security in a blue bead, a new child, a honeycomb of living flesh, a Sofia.

Out of the desert as you fly over, eyes open, a pool, an oasis. The eye of Matisse out of a world of smoke, fire, blood, last Tuesday. So these eyes open in a face of sand — luminous blue green silver — and close.

Q: I wonder what you came for.
A: I need a new life.

Bell's plane will leave Thessaloniki around midnight. She will be spared the bus this time, since Vaïa has found some cousins leaving after lunch today who can give her a lift as far as the railway station; from there she can catch the airport bus. If nothing goes wrong, she will soon be off over the bridge, leaving behind the plane trees and the river, the evergreen, evergrey olives, the sown fields with a fine stubble of green on their redness. She will swoop back across the Vardari, the Axios, broad and swollen, bruise-dark under the mist of the late afternoon, with barely a glance. There will be conversation to be made and her mind will be kept busy. In no time they will be plunged into the city traffic. Then the wait at the station, the wheezing bus. The airport with its lines of light by the sea.

Here behind her back, all this will already be starting to shrink. Before she knows it the house will be back to its proper size in her life. She will call it up only to find it no more than a slide, an enamelling on black plastic, a rainbow slick on a puddle, a lantern slide in a box with all the others: there to be thrown up in light on a screen for a few seconds, or not, just as she chooses; and either way, no threat.

So far so good. Lunch is a hasty affair of sandwiches and apples peeled, quartered and offered on the point of the knife, the radio blaring out the news though she catches none of it. Surrounded by family and wellwishers the car slips in through the gate and brakes at the porch. Everyone is here already, Chrysoula, Zoumboulitsa; Vaïa, of course, Andrea holding the baby, more people than she can put names to in her confusion. Kalliroï arrives out of breath and Bell presses into her hands the copy of *Tracks*, to give to Lyka. The world crowds around to wring Bell's hands and kiss her. *You see, I told you, didn't I? She wears mourning*, a woman proclaims. All jingling and tangling in the chains around her neck, catching their hair in the silver snake and the moon and the blue opal, laughing, they clasp her and wish her a good journey and a good meeting with Yanni. While room is being made for her case in the boot she begs for a last moment inside. Take your time, they say. Now that the house is clear of any trace of her presence she can take a last look in the *méros*, the kitchen and the warm room, where she rolls up her last few Greek banknotes and tucks them in under the baby's bedding. She notices in passing that the chocolate olives are all gone. She stops short: yes, nothing but a brown smudge in the bowl, and now she can wonder idly who — not that it matters. Let them think that she took them. They can think what they like. She is free, or very nearly, out of danger, anyway, unscathed! No loose ends, a clean break, a good exit, no hard feelings, with even her books intact, and her Buddha. At last she is on the move again, at the threshold of the way home, having done what she came for, more or less, and giddy with disbelief at having got to the bitter end unscathed. She can say goodbye once and for all. There will be nothing to ever bring her back, not in this life. She will not be making this mistake another time. After all, once the old woman is gone — and where *is* she? — the house will be nothing more than a house, a shell, a shed skin on the other side of the world; stone and earth, lime, wood, fire and air.

A lantern slide. So be honest for once. Why not?

I need a new life. She takes a moment more to stand in the old bedroom with the shutters zigzagging out, half in the dark, half light, for old times' sake and just in case the house should relent — who knows? — and disgorge the lost hand. The car horn gives a beep. It is all happening too fast. She is nowhere near ready. She might have known! I need a new life, what was that supposed to mean? You have a new life every day that you wake up, and how would coming here make any difference? Liar! A new life! You came for absolution.

No. That's nonsense.

Liar.

Absolution? That's impossible. How could she give me absolution! She wouldn't if she could. Rightly so.

So you were after the impossible.

All right, then, for argument's sake, absolution. But there's more to it.

The car is hooting again and she calls out in reply. Absolution or whatever — reconciliation, release? — she has to leave it at that. There is no more time for anything. How could she have spent the whole week in chatter about the past, in mooning about hour after hour and in idle, futile reminiscence, in bickering and sulking, waiting the time out while hate and self-hate hissed at each other in the attic of her mind? And all the while what she had come for, if only she had known at the time, stayed unsaid, unthought even, and unthinkable: the last words, the deathbed ones, when there are never words. Or there are three, saying nothing, or everything, whose time has passed, only in Greek it's two, isn't it, *s'agapáo* . One and a half, really, *s'agapáo*. And it's too late anyway, the car is packed and waiting and the house empty. "Mamma?" she calls. She can hear choruses of goodbyes outside, and calls for her to get in. No time for anything now but one last sight of the house which she never expects or hopes to see again, before she runs out into flares of wind, darkness, light, dazed in all the sudden turbulence. The porch is alight under the grey twists of the grapevine, the whole façade, slab on slab of silvery light and shade, and the blind glass of the window panes reflects only the shutters and the sky, a fringed cloud, vacancy.

And where is the old woman? Not inside and not outside either. Where is she? As if the moment has been sprung on her, at a loss, wringing her hands, Bell cries out — "Mamma!" — stopping short, and is caught up in a strong hug. Black woollen arms strain around her. White hair blocks her mouth.

"Good journey!" she hears. "Good journey and good meeting with our Yanni."

"Mamma!" She stoops and returns the hug. "I looked and I couldn't find you anywhere!"

"Here I am."

"Thank you for everything!"

"Nothing! You did well to come, Bella. Do you hear?" And in an undertone: "The eggs? You have them?"

Shaking her head, Bell pats the cloth bag of films. The eggs are rolled inside two pairs of clean socks; she still hasn't worked out what to do with them.

"Be sure not to let them fall."

"They are well wrapped."

"Come again." This, in a normal voice. "Whenever you can."

The flayed eyes and bent claws.

"Do you hear that, Bella?" cries a voice. Vaïa.

No. Never.

"Of course she will come. *E*, Bella? She will come," chants the chorus.

"I — of course," Bell utters.

"Only don't make the same mistake again" — seeing Bell's face writhe, she falters — "and come too late. That's all. Come in time. And may we hold strong in God's name."

"Still she doesn't speak, why?"

"*Ade*, Bella, speak up!"

But you know I will —

"I hope —"

"Sofia, you know she will!"

— never. I will never —

"And bring Yanni with you!" cries Kalliroï.

"Yes, and let us find him a bride!" That was Chrysoula.

"All right, I'll tell him."

"And Bella" — Kyria Sofia can't reach Bell's ear and the words break damp against her neck in a bubble, a laugh or sob — "I have a sharp tongue. If I said anything to upset you —"

"No!" She gasps. Everyone is here. The world is gathered all around and looking on, hushed.

"— do you hear —"

"You have been — so —"

"— you know I am old now, forgive me."

"No, no, it's *you* — who —"

In her shame and sorrow the words stick in her throat. She can't seem to see properly. She can't loosen her grip somehow either, and the other will not let go. "*E,* Bella? *Sorry,*" the bundle in her arms is murmuring, and the eyes gazing straight up into hers now in their pouches of blood are the eyes of a hurt child. Everyone has stopped breathing.

OTHER BOOKS BY BEVERLEY FARMER

A Body of Water

Like a body of water fed by many sources yet remaining whole and self-contained, this imaginative new work draws on journal, notebook, story, poem, tribute and criticism to produce an astonishingly powerful, many-layered montage. It lays bare the creative process, the connection between text and context, experience and art. As well as presenting five beautifully developed and complete stories in the inimitable style of *Milk* and *Home Time*, Beverley Farmer also incorporates the day-by-day ideas and influences that sustain and nourish her creative output.

> "Beverley Farmer is a Recording Angel of the intensities of the emotional life ... she shows how to look at the physical world with fresh eyes, and how things thus seen are refracted by the mind."
>
> Don Anderson

> "I know of no other Australian who has even tried to do what Farmer has given us, let alone succeeded in all the ways she has in *A Body of Water*."
>
> David English, *Australian*

> "... richly rewarding in its complex counterpoint of themes and voices, its marriage of mind and experience, text and context, its serene and literate prose."
>
> Katharine England, *Advertiser*

> "*A Body of Water* resonates with those essential qualities for which the work is to be treasured: depth, humility, sustenance."
>
> Kate Veitch, *Sydney Morning Herald*

ISBN 0 7022 2283 6

The Seal Woman

In mourning for her husband lost at sea, Dagmar leaves the wintry landscapes of the north for the tranquility of Swanhaven and a healing Australian summer. In the house where she spent her honeymoon twenty years before, she begins another journey, from grief to serenity and unexpected harvest.

Suffused with exquisite aquatic imagery that reflects the currents in Dagmar's own moods, *The Seal Woman* charts the interplay of myth and language between the hemispheres.

> "*The Seal Woman* moves and challenges, informs, amuses and stimulates. Above all, it is rich in its imagining and in its human tenderness."
>
> John Hanrahan

> "Farmer's prose (plangently beautiful and vivid with seashore and season), like poetry, invites dipping into and savoring again and again."
>
> Katharine England, *Adelaide Advertiser*

> "An intense and hauntingly atmospheric novel."
>
> Karen Lamb, *Age*

ISBN 0 7022 2522 3